Queen Heir

NYC Mecca Series Book 1

By: Leia Stone and Jaymin Eve

*To the king or queen in all of us. May you leave behind
a legacy that others will remember.*

NYC
Mecca
Manhattan
Bronx
Queens
Staten
Island
Brooklyn
The Island

Chapter One

The tolling of the bells, long live the Queen.

THE FIRST THING my subconscious registered was the tolling of the bells, a distinct plucking twang which surged through my alpha bond. I'd heard it only a few times in my life, mostly during times of unease within the boroughs. It was a special form of communication the queen of the wolf shifters could use with her heirs and alphas. But this twang was different. Weaker almost.

Shaking off the last of my sleepiness, I finally registered the true nature of the call and surged upright, eyes wide and heart hammering in my chest. The mental bells finished their tolling then, dying off with one last clank, like that of a final nail into a coffin. My wolf rose up within me and both of us let out a long howl, echoing across the room. Pain strummed inside me, sharp and metallic. Every part of me felt it, the loss of power, the emptiness where there used to be a tie to my queen.

"Arianna!"

Calista's voice cut through my howls as she burst into my room. I had to take many deep breaths to push my wolf down. Acting on autopilot, I swung my legs over the side of the bed and rose, hurriedly crossing the room and meeting my advisor halfway.

"Arianna," Calista said again, softer this time, more unsure.

"The queen has fallen," I said. The words singed my tongue as they crossed it; everything would change now. The world as we knew it would descend into chaos if a new queen wasn't crowned quickly.

Calista's head fell to her chest then and I could feel her surge of emotion through our pack ties. "I can feel the emptiness ... but are you sure? How has this happened?"

As an advisor to multiple heirs throughout her long life, Calista had been through a lot and had seen it all. She was one of the strongest women I knew and her voice still wavered.

Closing my eyes, I reached out through my alpha bond to my pack, the thousand-plus shifters of the Bronx borough in New York City who were at my command. It took mere seconds to double-check what I already knew. The bond that bound me to my queen was severed and the mecca power that had once coursed from her to me was leaking everywhere. The chimes ... they must have been her last attempt to reach out to us. She had literally just taken her last breath.

Tears pricked the back of my eyelids, and yet I knew I would never let them fall. There was no room for my weakness today. I could already feel the dissidence within the packs. The power grid, which balanced our world, the mecca, was weakened.

Opening my eyes, my wolf rose again, this time in response to the unease of my people.

"How did this happen?" I said, unable to stop the low growl from leaking out. "Find out how this happened!"

Calista was used to me when I got like this, and barely blinked as she whipped out her huge tablet device and started scrolling.

"I have no details yet, Your Majesty. There's literally nothing in the alerts." She paused for a moment. "Wait ... a summons has just come through. We have to leave immediately. Looks like you're going to find out what happened from the council."

My steps faltered at her use of *Your Majesty*. I had known Calista my entire life, she always referred to me as "Alpha," Arianna, or "pain in the neck," never "Your Majesty." Yes, I was an heir, but the queen could theoretically live forever and there were only a few years I was even eligible for the crown, so we never took my lineage too seriously, never thought I would be queen. Now I was one of four in the running to be the next ruler of the entire wolf-shifter race and the three boroughs we controlled, and protocol dictated everyone refer to me as royalty. I wasn't sure how I felt about that, but there was no time to ponder it.

My eyes shot to her tablet again. I hated that she had no details. The other three heirs would already be preparing themselves to take the crown, but my main concern was on what had happened to the queen. She was powerful, one of the strongest leaders we'd ever had. They said her lineage could be traced directly back to the time of the Tuatha de Danann, the fae who'd initially built the mecca millennia ago, before they all disappeared and were rumored dead. And now she had fallen. Could the bears have done this? Did they kill my queen?

Was war now coming for us all?

Calista hurried off, ducking into my huge walk-in closet and emerging moments later with a pile of pressed and folded clothes in her hands. Official dress code was apparently required for this summons. She handed them to me, and wasting no time I dashed into the bathroom and struggled into the black leather pants, knee-high leather boots, and red silk shirt with crossed swords and star-shaped insignia denoting me as an heir to the throne of the red house – the same house of the fallen queen. The moment the true queen fell, the Summit began, and I needed to play my part or my entire race would weaken. After tucking the shirt in and brushing my teeth, I strode from the room to find Calista looking at me with pride.

"I've waited twenty years to see you wear that."

I gave her a tight smile and turned my back to her so she could braid my long white-blond hair.

To be honest, I was hoping this day would never come. I liked my life. Being the Bronx alpha and heir to the queen afforded me all the power and luxuries I could ever need. I had no real desire to go after the throne and be thrust into the political arena, not to mention carry the burden of ruling tens of thousands of our kind. But if the queen had been killed, it was only a matter of time before the bears stepped in and tried to wrest our territory from us. The loss of power would be devastating to my people.

New York City, and the five boroughs inside of it, was a magical hotspot of power. Early shifter leaders had learned that whomever was strong enough to rule was strong enough to join with the mecca. They could then share this energy with their entire race and strengthen the shifters' naturally occurring gifts of speed, healing, and strength.

My people ruled Manhattan, the Bronx, and Queens. The bear shifters ruled Staten Island and Brooklyn. Being at the seat of power in one of the five boroughs trickled out into the entire race around the world, and since we ruled three of the five we were the strongest. Although, even with two seats, the bears were a close second on the power grid. Over the years the bears had been our allies and our enemies. Depending on their king at the time. But right now they'd surely be gearing up to attack.

Without the bonds of a queen, we were vulnerable for the first time in a hundred years. The bears would be ready to claim another borough for themselves and tip the power scales in their favor. The only hope of stopping them was for one of us four females, all alpha heirs, to win the Summit, take the crown, and become the next queen.

"Where's Finn?" I said, suddenly missing the presence of my white wolf familiar.

Calista didn't reply. She knew Finn and I were bound and that I simply needed to calm my erratic energy and focus on our link.

The queen has fallen, I told him, and tried to sense where he was.

I know. I'm coming, he sent back, and I was filled with his warmth, power, and steadfastness. He was in Central Park, hunting. He liked to chase the birds and squirrels there in the summertime, while I slept. Finn had no need for sleep; he was a magical creature that none of our history books could explain. When a young shifter is born, their heir status and royal lineage is confirmed by the presence of a familiar. If they have the power to take the throne, a few days or weeks after that infant's birth, an animal appears. For me it was Finn, the white menacing wolf who stood over four and a half feet tall and resembled a small horse in stature. In my age group, the other three heirs had a snowy white owl, a huge, thick and insidious snake, and a hawk.

Royal heir familiars stay in service until death. I rubbed the teeth mark scar on my right wrist, seeking comfort from the familiar shape and texture. That's where Finn had bit me on my fifth birthday, the day we were bound. Ever since then we could share words and thoughts into each other's minds.

If I died, so too would my familiar. It doesn't work back the opposite way, but that didn't really matter. His soul was bound to mine and if he died I would go crazy, unable to function. I would not be dead, but neither would I desire to live.

Thankfully, familiars were nearly impossible to kill.

"Ready?" Calista asked me when she was done braiding my white-blond hair into an intricate braid crown. Shaking off my thoughts of Finn, I nodded, facing her fully. For once she looked vulnerable, my fiercest advisor who had one time encouraged me to rip off a rogue wolf's manhood for raping one of my females. Now she looked … scared. The emotion made me uncomfortable.

"There is no place for fear in the Summit," I said, my voice low.

Her chin jutted up, jaw clenched, as she nodded. When I turned my back to leave, I allowed myself my own moment of vulnerability. I knew why Calista was afraid. She feared I would die. I'd trained my entire life for this series of tasks, battles, and tests of strategy, but the danger of death during the Summit of the four heirs was very real.

I never seriously thought I would get to this moment.

I left through the double doors of my master bedroom, striding across the hall and out into the main area of my top-floor penthouse. My dominants were waiting, all six of them already suited for battle, two females and four males. It pained me not to have Violet here, my best friend and the Bronx pack's rare and only magic born. The Red Queen had sent Violet to London on official business and she would not be back for a few more days. There were only four magic-born wolf shifters in all the world, so Violet was often called on for help in other countries.

My dominants closed in around me. They were on high alert.

"You think we'll have trouble on the way?" I inquired of Blaine, standing at the fore.

The husky alpha wolf with deep auburn hair was one of my oldest friends and the commander of my dominants. Squaring his shoulders, he said: "You have just become one of the most valuable women in the shifter world. We're not taking any chances."

My heart stilled. That really put it into perspective for me. The entire shifter world would be watching, waiting on this outcome. If one of the four heirs didn't rise to power, then the wolves around the world would weaken and the bear king would certainly leave Staten Island and invade our territory, stealing our power. I wouldn't let that happen. No, the Red Queen's legacy would live on.

Some of the panic must have crossed my face because Blaine reached out then, before catching himself. Touching me as an heir had never been a problem, but protocol dictated that no one touch the queen. She could touch them but not the other way around. I fell under this royal banner now, so I closed the distance, squeezing his hand.

"You were born to be queen," Blaine said as he leaned in closer to me. "None of the other heirs even have a chance. Just think back to all the times you kicked my ass in combat, and in mecca chess. You got this."

I smiled and, with a nod, pulled my hand back, feeling more grounded. He'd reminded me that I was still the same shifter I had been twenty minutes ago, before the entire world changed. I had trained for this and I was ready.

Calista was at my side, so I quickly asked: "Is Winnie accounted for?" My little sister was only five, and since the death of our mother I'd taken over the role of her protector.

"Still asleep," Calista said. "I have given instructions for her to be locked in with her advisor and royal guard until further notice."

I nodded. Winnie would hate the house arrest, but it was for the best; she was a vulnerability for me now. I let my eyes linger on her closed door before shutting a steel trap over my emotions. I couldn't think of anything else except the Summit.

"Let's get moving," I barked. I knew Finn would meet up with me no matter where I was. Nothing kept him from me when he wanted to be at my side. As we passed through the door and into my personal elevator, I caught my reflection in the mirrored doors.

I look like a queen.

The red silk collar of my shirt was so prominent against the white-blond of my hair, done up in Calista's braid crown. The bright shirt also contrasting against my alabaster skin, inherited from my Danish and Norwegian mother. I never knew my father, but I was told his heritage was Polynesian islander. Which explained my dark lashes and brows, and what some have called disconcerting turquoise eyes. Right now those turquoise eyes were pinched in anxiety and my alabaster skin was washed out. I might have been dressed like a queen, but I didn't feel like one.

Calista followed me closely as we took the elevator down to the ground floor. My home was in the penthouse of an eight-story high-rise with over 160 units that housed my most dominant wolves and their families. Although it was built in the early 1900s, it was completely modernized. It was one of the first things I'd insisted on when I inherited it at my rightful age of sixteen.

"Talk to me, Calista." My voice was brisk as I strode from the elevator and out into the underground car park. "What should I expect? Have you been briefed at all?"

An heir's advisor lived for this moment, to coach an heir through the Summit. They trained their entire life for it. I glanced down at her. I was five foot ten and she was at least five inches shorter, petite and pretty, with short, pixie-styled brunette hair, and large dark brown eyes. She held nothing in her hands, and was dressed simply in jeans and a tank, but underneath the cute packaging my advisor had ninja skills and a brain like a supercomputer. Her photographic memory stored information in perfect and precise order, so I knew any data would be relayed to me succinctly and with a hundred percent accuracy. Which was important in this situation. The slightest slip-up would be viewed as weakness and used against me. I needed a sharp advisor who could make life or death decisions in a second. Calista was the best in the five boroughs. Over a century old, though she looked barely twenty-five, she had advised many past heirs, and out of the four heirs of this age she had chosen me. She came from a long line of royal advisors and I was grateful to have her in my camp now.

"The alert just said that the queen has fallen and all alpha heirs are called to the Summit. Time is of haste."

No doubt the old farts on the queen's council were being deliberately obtuse. They were powerful but at the constant whim of a queen who would always be stronger. They had to take their little shows of dominance where they could.

"Well then," I said to my people, who were all standing at attention, waiting for me to enter the sleek vehicle first. "Let's not keep them waiting."

As we traveled the three miles to the closest magical teleportation area, the vortex, I tried to focus my thoughts. I had been trained for pretty much anything I could encounter in the Summit. Combat. Magical studies. Etiquette. I even knew which damn spoon and fork to use in a setting of fifty. If I was the victor and took the crown, it would be my duty to rule all wolf shifters and to mate with a strong alpha.

Heirs were only eligible for the crown between the ages of sixteen and thirty. If you were over thirty and the queen fell, you were exempt from the Summit and you would never rule. This order was put in place hundreds of years ago by the council as it was thought to be the prime age for breeding and best age of cognitive function. After thirty, the wolf-shifter miscarriage rate tripled. Personally I felt like it was just the council's way of controlling the heirs, to get them young and manipulate them to their way of thinking. There were more than a few heirs in the Bronx right now who would be disappointed that they were either too young or had passed the age of thirty.

Of course, once you started to think about the Summit itself, they might actually be the lucky ones. At least they'd always be heirs, afforded plenty of rights and luxuries as their royal blood dictated. The heirs who went into the Summit ended up as queen, dead, or a failed heir.

I would not be a failed heir. Whomever became queen would have the most powerful energy at her disposal, and I wasn't sure I trusted any of the other heirs to wield it. Breanna, Selene, Devina, they weren't good enough. I needed to make sure the house of red ruled again.

I couldn't believe the queen was gone. She was ... a true leader.

The cars were slowing now. We passed through the private gates and stopped outside the small industrial building that housed the vortex, the teleportation grid in the heart of the mecca. My guards stood twenty-four-hour watch on the perimeter to make sure no humans accidently wandered in and found themselves in the middle of a vortex that would shred their weaker human DNA to pieces. Only shifters could use the vortex, and nowhere else in the world did vortexes like these exist. That's why New York City was special, a city I loved dearly, and would hopefully rule very soon.

Some of my determination must have shown in my gaze. Calista nodded, a smile tugging at the corner of her lips. She knew I was ready.

My dominants exited the vehicle first, looking left and right before indicating it was safe for me to leave the car. I took a deep breath, preparing for what was to come. The moment I entered that vortex there was no going back. I would be in the Summit, and there was a very real chance I could die. The first few rounds tested intelligence and power, but the final round was a fight to the death. I needed to be focused, no distractions.

The eight of us wasted no time crossing the concrete parking lot of the warehouse which hid the vortex. It seemed unusually quiet out, and I sent my alpha senses across the area, trying to find the guards.

I reached out and halted Monica, the most dominant of my female guards. "Were there shifters on the front gate when we crossed into this property?" I hadn't been paying attention when we drove in.

She nodded. "Yes, all the security was accounted for on the borderline."

That was good, but I still could not sense the guards who should have been in this inner courtyard area. As an heir I was stronger and faster than even my most powerful dominants, and my nose was better than anyone's, second only to our late queen and Finn. And I could scent no patrol nearby.

"Be on high alert," I warned my people as we slowed our movements, creeping along and making our way to the double doors that housed the vortex.

A bird chirped nearby, and even though it was pitch black the sound of a distant garbage truck echoed through the city street. No one worked harder than New York City waste management—twelve-hour shifts, seven days a week. I wasn't human, and didn't have any real control over them, but I still thought of them as part of my people. I kept my Bronx pack in line and the humans who resided here safe.

Speaking of safe ... there should definitely be guards on the main doors, but even in the dark I knew there were none. Maybe grief over the queen's death had driven them from their post.

My wolves closed in around me, and as we stepped into the dark opening, magic surrounded us with a huge rush, like it had been hidden until we crossed the threshold of the room. We were now awash in the scent of spilled blood and death.

"It's a trap!" I shouted. I knew, without having to see inside, that most of my guards who'd been protecting the vortex were dead.

Before we could retreat and gather more dominants, two women dropped from the second floor right above me. They looked and smelled human, but I could tell immediately from the way they moved that this was a disguise. Only in death would their true form show—bear, I assumed—my own people would never turn against me. Violet would have been able to see past this ruse. *Dammit!* I was missing my magic-born best friend even more now. Finn was closing in, but I sensed he wouldn't make it in time.

One of the "humans" lunged at me then, and without thought I landed a solid punch on her throat. She folded forward, gasping. I could see Blaine out of the corner of my eye, pounding the other female with heavy blows. In my world it was all about equality, so if a woman tried to hit a man, the man hit her right back. Women weren't delicate little flowers here. I didn't know about the bears, but only females were true alphas of our packs. So ... I guess it wasn't really equal. Women would always lead. Males could be dominant, but they never ruled.

Half a dozen more attackers dropped to the ground around us, and as much as I wanted to stay and see how this played out, the tug on my arm from Calista got me moving. I had faith in my six dominants, they could handle most situations. But there was a real worry that since these bears were magically disguised as humans, there was a magic-born shifter in the vicinity, and like Violet, they were powerful and unpredictable. Most shifters had very little defense against magic. It was actually a good thing that there were minimal magic-born shifters. If they ever teamed up, they could dominate us.

Calista was shouting and pulling me along. "Come on, Arianna, they'll be fine. You have to reach the Summit."

Sucking in a deep breath, I shoved fear for my people down and started sprinting toward the vortex. Duty called.

Deeper into the building I stumbled through the entryway of the vortex chamber, tripping over something. Glancing down, I saw that it was two fallen guards. Tears sprang to my eyes – Damian and Marco, slashes bright across their throats, their blood spilling everywhere, sightless eyes staring up at me. A screaming howl built in my chest. While these dominants were not in my innermost circle, they had been protecting me for years. They were my friends. Family even. And they had been needlessly cut down. I knew this was to be my life now, one of death and loss. A queen learned to deal with that as part of her duty to her people. I had to become accustomed to the fact that others would die for me so that I could have a chance to rule.

I already hated it, and despite knowing my responsibilities, I decided right then that responsibility should never trump honor in death.

I stooped and dipped my finger in the blood on both of my guards' chests. I dabbed their foreheads and then my own, leaving a dot right between my eyes.

"I will avenge thee," I said, my voice thrumming with conviction. Those four words had been drilled into me since birth. A death must never go unpunished. I now carried these two shifters' blood on my hands, and I would make it right.

Calista looked harried but proud as she again ushered me toward the ornate disc that harnessed the Bronx power of the mecca. As I stepped on top, one of the female attackers broke free of my dominants and rushed toward us. Ignoring her, I focused my thoughts. The vortexes were one of my favorite parts of the mecca. I had no idea where the large bronze discs – engraved with a slew of unreadable script – had come from, but they were definitely not Earth-made. Shifters long ago had discovered that they were all connected, and by placing one in each territory we were able to use the energy of the mecca as a form of instant transmission.

The teleportation process was not easy, learned through years of practice. I meditated regularly to keep my mind attuned to the energy. Harnessing the biting spike of mecca power and focused my breathing, I sent forth power to the Manhattan vortex, which was close to the royal house.

Once my mind was calm, I took Calista's hand. My advisor was fierce and loyal, but her wolf was not dominant enough to be able to mentally travel the vortex pathways. She needed my help to get through. The female attacker, who had finally reached us, circled around unsure of the visible power of the vortex. Ignoring her, I sucked in a deep breath and allowed the slightest pull on that connection to Manhattan; like reaching out and grabbing a cord floating in the ocean. And all of a sudden we were snatched from Bronx, flung along the magical ley line, and deposited in Manhattan.

I don't think I could ever describe the traveling process to a human. It was magical and if you had never felt magic, well ... I guess the sensations were a lot like those really intense rollercoasters with the huge drops. During the entire thing, your stomach feels like it's in your throat. Your equilibrium is gone, and so is all control. You are at the mercy of a force much bigger and more powerful than you, and you know it could destroy you in an instant. Both scary as heck and absolutely exhilarating.

As my feet slammed down, I released Calista's hand. I was already scanning around the space, assessing the threats which were surely near. Ten of the Red Queen's royal guard were waiting for me.

They all bowed to one knee before me. "Your Majesty."

Standing just behind them was Selene, five of her personal guards surrounding her. She looked her normal overly made-up self. Her dark Mediterranean skin tone and red hair, a mass of curls falling just below her shoulders, gave her an exotic look. Her large dark brown eyes looked black right now.

To give her credit, she did look a bit bent out of shape, possibly even upset that our queen had just died. I didn't see any tears, but she wasn't quite as composed as normal. She wore the deep purple of her house and nodded curtly to me. Her large, venomous snake familiar, Larak, curled snuggly around her shoulders.

I focused on the red guards. "There was an attack at the Bronx vortex, half a dozen or so magically cloaked individuals. The other heirs may be in danger."

I knew Calista was already on her tablet warning my Bronx wolves to be on alert, and to expect attacks.

Five of the guards nodded, and as Calista and I stepped further away from the disc, they ran behind me and into the vortex. Selene merely stood there glaring at the blood on my forehead.

"What happened to the queen?" I asked, not caring which of the shifters before me answered.

One of the remaining members of the royal guard replied: "She was attacked in her library, murdered. There are signs of a struggle and the entire place smells of blood, but we couldn't find any but the queen's." He paused uncomfortably. "We have no real leads." There was true pain on the shifter's face, but I hardened my heart. I could trust no one now except for those few who had proven their loyalty to me. Everyone else was a suspect in the queen's death, even the royal guards.

"Take me to where she was killed."

Without another word they turned, and I was surprised at their ready obedience of me.

Selene strode through her dominants then and blocked my way.

"You aren't queen yet, Arianna. You don't get to come into my territory and give orders." She crossed her arms and I knew she would fight me all the way. Adrenalin and anger coursed through me. I'd lost the queen and some of my guards in one night. Maybe all of them, I had no idea what was happening back in Bronx. Selene had chosen the wrong time to throw her weight around. I was just figuring out the best way to get around protocol and knock her teeth down her throat when Calista stepped forward.

"Statute fifty-six of the bylaws: If a monarch dies, the Summit begins, during which time the previous ruling monarch's heir holds a slightly more dominant position." Calista smiled sweetly at Selene, and even though I'd have preferred to release my anger on her perfect face, I took a small victory at the rules being used against the purple heir for once.

Selene was alpha of the Manhattan borough. I had received multiple reports that she was a strict leader with no tolerance for wolves who slipped outside of her firm set of rules. Being strict was fine – I was strict – but I also loved my wolves. I would die for them, and Selene had shown not one ounce of compassion for her people. The few times we had met there was nothing but cunning in her actions. She was a power hungry, evil snob.

She'd fought for the Manhattan borough when we both came of age around the same time. It was my birthright to rule in the same home of the Red Queen, but Selene pulled her usual crap and threw our laws in my face. She was two months older than me, so she got first choice. The queen had allowed it, then to punish Selene secretly, made Devina and Breanna co-alphas of Queens, giving me my own territory to reside over, all of the Bronx.

For all intents and purposes I was the Red Queen's niece. She was my mom's sister, although I never thought of her as family. I'd never so much as hugged the woman. It was against the rules, and she sure as hell never made any move to touch me. To a certain extent I understood. The queen had no room for weakness or public affections. But still, it kind of hurt every time she brushed me aside.

Though there was one time, on my sixteenth birthday – the first year I was of age – that she told me I was her favorite heir. Which had meant a lot to me.

The guards began to lead the way, and I stepped in right behind them as Selene kept pace with me.

"You just had to show up for the Summit with honor marks, didn't you?" she whispered. "Think that will gain favor with the council?"

Snide wench was probably wishing she'd thought of doing the same thing. Didn't she realize for that to happen her guard would have to die? How dare she insinuate that I had done it on purpose. Damn protocol again. This chick was just screaming for me to punch her right in her fake nose. It was far too upturned to be real. I guess that's what happens when you spend too long in Manhattan. But unfortunately there was to be no combat between the heirs outside of the Summit, so I bit my tongue, knowing one day soon, in one of the Summit tasks, I'd get a chance to officially kick her butt.

It took us no time to traverse the distance to the royal estate. It was a fifty-story, sprawling mansion skyscraper, housing hundreds if not thousands of guards, staff, and advisors. I had been here on a few occasions, but this time felt so different. This time the royal estate was my next possible home.

The lead guard held the opulent double doors for me.

"Welcome to the palace. I'll take you straight to the library of the late queen now. Please note that you're not to touch anything, and will only have moments at the scene. The council is waiting, and the Summit must be initiated with the blood of the four."

I heard the underlying words he wasn't saying. He should be taking us straight to the council, but he was hoping I would find a clue to help catch the queen's killer. Which moved him a little further down my list of suspects. Just then I felt a gust of energy, and the scent of old magic. I smiled. Finn was finally here.

Turning, I locked eyes with my familiar as he bound over to me. His eyes were both fierce and kind, glowing with a yellow hue. The guards stood a bit straighter and even Selene held her breath. Finn was a force of nature. Never had I seen or read about a bigger, more imposing familiar. Even the Red Queen's white lynx was smaller than my wolf. His blue dog collar jingled as he jogged to my side. I made him wear that while he was running around town so as not to scare the locals. The collar also stated that he was a Great Pyrenees mountain dog. Finn was born of magic and could slightly alter his appearance if needed. When humans were around he shifted to look more doglike. Even so, he was a massive sight to behold.

As I sank my fingers into the fur on his back, I felt completely at peace. Though some of the peace faded as I noticed the speckling of blood across his white fur and muzzle.

What happened?

Ran into some trouble on the way. Sorry I was delayed. I reached the Bronx vortex just as you left. The rest of your guards are okay.

I hugged him closer to me, thankful I hadn't lost him or any more of my people. I couldn't think about that though. One didn't anticipate death, they fought against it with every step they had. I had to fight for what I wanted, and I wanted to be queen.

I never in a hundred years thought those words would form in my mind.

You will be queen, Finn assured me. His confidence fueled my own, but my familiar's magic didn't actually include future sight. Unfortunately.

We silently followed the royal guard as they weaved through the massive bottom floor of this building, which housed a dining area, huge kitchens, and lots of areas for entertainment and group meetings. Bypassing the opulent double staircase, we strode to the elevators and were taken up to level five, which I was told was the queen's personal floor. As we exited and crossed the plushly carpeted space, I counted off the doors that spanned the hall. Twenty or more lined each side. The size of this place was unprecedented. Finally, at the very end was a huge double set of doors. The queen's library.

A somber mood fell over our large group, even Selene for once didn't have anything to say. When we paused at the end, I could already scent the death that waited for us beyond those doors. New death. Lighter than I expected, which told me they had already removed the body. At least I wouldn't have to stare at the broken body of my beloved queen.

The same guard stepped forward and unlocked the doors. "What's your name, soldier?" I asked him.

His eyes dropped to Finn, who'd just pressed into my side. My familiar often got that reaction, even if people had seen him before. His massive size and fierce face was enough to stop most in their tracks. The guard recovered quickly.

"Cruz, originally of the Queens borough pack, now fifty years in the Red Queen's service."

I reached out and dropped my hand onto his shoulder. "Don't worry, Cruz, we'll find out who did this and they will pay. Tenfold."

His blond good looks and blue eyes would have made him a favorite of the queen; she liked them sleek and pretty, I had heard. I preferred my boys to be a little manlier, rougher, but I could see that Cruz was going to miss his queen.

As I stepped over the threshold, the scent of death hit me strongly. The scent I'd already been picking up was much stronger on this side of the room. Mixed with the blood was the energy of my queen. Distinct.

Knowing my time was limited, I stepped away from the guards and into the former queen's personal space. Selene and Calista were right behind me, with Finn at my side.

You can do this, Arianna. I had to give myself this pep talk more than once as I crossed the massive marble floors. I didn't need directions toward the place of her death. The scent of blood was strong and coppery, the red pool contrasting the white marble, mixed with the burnt aftereffects of old magic. All of it left a bad taste in my mouth.

The blood was light in the outer corners of the room. But as we moved closer to the comfortable couches and table, which held the queen's tea set, the spatters grew large and thick. My stomach churned. Wolf senses were already strong, but add in my heir abilities, and Selene and I were scenting twice as much as those around us. Finn gave a low growl that made the hairs on my arms stand up.

"Have you already been here?" I asked the other heir. She didn't live in the royal home, but this was her territory and she would have gotten here a lot faster than me.

"No, they prevented any from entering while they removed the body and did the initial investigation." It was hard to tell, she was an expert at hiding her emotions, but I sensed she was upset they had barred her entry but allowed me.

Her words drifted away as both of us took in the scene. Blood had washed the center of the room in swirls and arcs, pooling on the floor and splashing across the floor-to-ceiling bookshelves, which were well over fifteen feet high. There were clear signs of a battle; I wanted to move closer. But first I needed to find a path through which wouldn't result in me tracking the queen's blood everywhere. Selene stayed back; Calista and the guards too. Only Finn followed me as I gingerly stepped nearer.

When I was right in the center of the main kill zone, I cataloged everything I was seeing, examining the walls, the floor, and the space where she had fallen. Closing my eyes, in my mind I had a very clear picture of what had happened. The two tea cups sitting on the table told me everything I needed to know.

Whomever killed the queen had been someone she trusted.

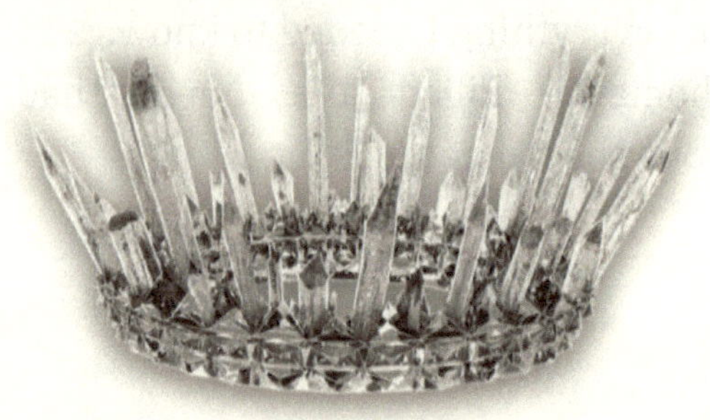

Chapter Two

Do or die. That's the Summit's motto.

CALISTA BROKE THROUGH the surge of emotions which kept me glued to the floor. "Arianna, we really need to leave."

Ignoring my advisor I addressed Cruz. The guards were outside of the library, but would easily be able to hear me. "How did the queen die? What injuries did she sustain?"

He hesitated briefly; his face was pale, despite the deep brown of its normal color. "Her throat, thighs, and both wrists were cut ... to the bone. She bled out in seconds."

A thickness filled my throat, a sense of unease, fear and pain. She'd been slaughtered like a freakin' animal on the floor of her library. I forced myself to focus, to push down the images assaulting my mind. I needed to be strong so I could avenge my queen.

"Who dined with the queen this morning?" I asked, my voice hard, both hands gesturing toward the shattered teapot on the floor. "Who was the last to see her alive?"

He shook his head. "As far as we know she was alone all morning. No one entered or left her building. I was on duty at the front door and can attest to the security of the grounds. Her other guards were stationed outside the library, as they are every morning when she takes tea and surrounds herself with the calming of her books."

The Red Queen, or Rosalina Devlin, as she had been known when she was an heir, had loved to read. A trait we had in common.

I pressed the guard further. "There are two cups here and clear evidence of a second inhabitant."

Not to mention the queen didn't murder herself.

He had nothing more to say, but someone had let my queen down here today, and until we figured out who that betrayer was, all of us were in danger.

"Ragnar?" I didn't see the body of her lynx. Maybe they'd removed the familiar with her body.

The guard cleared his throat, looking uncomfortable. "Missing."

I inhaled rapidly. Missing? Okay ... maybe he had been out hunting like Finn and was dead somewhere. The council would hopefully have word through their contacts in the human authorities.

Finn interrupted my thoughts: *I didn't sense any of the other familiars while I was out this morning.* I couldn't even process that so I just nodded. My eyes fell to Selene.

"It wasn't me," she said, reading my expression. "I have plenty of witnesses who can attest to my whereabouts all night and this morning."

I'm sure she did. Selene had a veritable male harem stashed away in her home.

"But we should investigate the other heirs," she finished. "If anyone has motive to kill the queen, it is us."

"There's no time," I said. "The Summit is starting. We're going to be too busy trying to destroy each other."

I didn't believe any of the heirs had the skills to kill the Red Queen, not alone. But with help...

"I really need to sniff out this area," I said, turning back to examine the blood again. My human nose was picking up a few variations of scent, but my wolf would be so much better.

Another guard answered this time, a female. "I'm sorry, Your Majesty, but there really is no time right now for you to shift. If it helps at all, we have had our best trackers in here already. They detected nothing but the queen and some flowers from the garden."

Calista backed her up. "The council summons just came through again. We must move."

I fought for composure, knowing my wolf wanted to be free, and I needed her; my body was already prepared to shift. But unfortunately they were both right. There was no time. The council would not even remotely deal with the queen's death until a new queen was crowned. The vulnerability to our boroughs was too great right now.

I carefully stepped back through the blood, doing my best to catalog the various scents. I was picking up on lots of familiar smells, the guards, the queen, even Selene, but there were also a few things that were odd. Energy was filtered around the room, and it didn't feel like that from wolfborn, or bearborn. And what was with the flowery smell?

Were there even any plants in the room? Had the queen been in her garden this morning before having her tea? She'd been killed very early, long before the sun came up. It didn't make sense that she would have been walking in her garden at that time. But then again, what did I know of the queen's habits. I needed answers. Everyone in the castle needed to be questioned.

When I reached the doorway, I turned to Cruz. "Seal this room. No one else goes in and out until a new queen is appointed. Then it will be her duty to investigate fully."

He nodded. "As you wish."

Selene rolled her eyes, but before he could shut the door my hand snaked out and touched one droplet of blood, touching it to my forehead. I whispered, "I will avenge thee," and tried to ignore the wetness that had gathered in my eyes.

"Showoff," Selene murmured as we walked away to the council hall.

My teeth clamped down in anger at her coldness. "I hope the final round is you and me," I told her.

She grinned. "I've been hoping that since the day I met you."

Bitch.

Her creepy snake slithered down her arm to come face to face with Finn. Finn confided in me once that familiars could talk to each other; I wondered what they were saying now. Whatever it was, my wolf wasn't sharing.

The scent of the queen's death lingered as we took the elevators back to the ground floor. From there we were led into the grand hall. The moment our group stepped through the door, I was under the scrutiny of the legendary wolf council. I took a moment to scan my surroundings. I would not be trusting anyone until I had the queen's murderer's head on a stick.

Once I had the room mapped out, I focused on the eleven council members who were all sitting with their backs very erect against their high, ornately carved chairs. Each had a codex of honor on their laps. This book brought me back to my school days with Calista. I threw my copy of the codex in the fire when I was twelve.

Firstly, I hated that outdated book.

Secondly, I had memorized the entire thing.

Being queen meant you ruled all, yes, but the damn council was intertwined in everything you did. So I had to play nice here.

Bowing my head only a few inches as protocol demanded, "Council," I said in a strong but respectful voice.

Selene bowed deeply, gave a low curtsy, and a few council members frowned. The low curtsy was appropriate when we were just heirs, but now that the Summit had started we were in line to the throne and above our previous place. I tried not to grin. When I was queen they would give me a head bow and I would never bow to anyone again. It sounded cold but it was our way.

"We heard you had trouble getting here?" Councilmember Jeran asked me. His eyes lingered on my honor marks before falling to observe Finn.

"Yes, we were attacked. Two of my guards were murdered."

A few council members frowned, a few looked angry, and the others simply nodded as if it was an acceptable part of the lives we lived.

Suddenly, the doors flew open and Breanna walked in. Her yellow shirt was covered in blood, brown hair a matted mess, and she wore one honor mark on her forehead. Her large brown and black hawk was perched fiercely on her shoulder.

The council looked disturbed.

"Where is Devina?" one of them asked.

Breanna pointed to the honor mark on her forehead, her hand shaking slightly. "Gone."

Now *that* caused an outrage. The entire council stood and began shouting, gesturing wildly.

"Lock down the building! Close the hall. No one leaves this house until a new queen is chosen."

I picked this completely inappropriate time to think about why the hell I hadn't eaten breakfast. The Summit until coronation could last anywhere from three days to two weeks. Looked like I was living here until I either died or took over. Already it was down to three of us.

May the best heir win.

I stood upon a dais, Breanna on one side of me and Selene on the other. We wore fresh sets of our royal colors – red, purple, and yellow for the line we descended from. There was no longer a green representative. That still hadn't settled with me. Too much death, too quickly.

Below us, gathered together in the large space, were some of our people. I still had all six of my trusted dominants, Blaine, Jen, Derek, Ben, Victor and Monica, bloodied but alive. They had arrived not long ago from the vortex battle. They'd heal soon and be back to fighting fit. Well, the physical stuff would heal. All of us mourned our friends who were lost guarding the vortex.

My dominants were joined by another fourteen of the strongest members from my Bronx wolves. The council ordered that each heir have twenty of their pack members to join with the royal guards who would be split between the three of us. Since this Summit had begun in bloodshed, we would be on high alert for the full duration.

Finn sat beside me. All the heirs had their familiars close by, and I took comfort from his presence. His energy was not unlike the mecca itself, on a smaller scale, and I was used to the strength and warmth of it.

We got this, I said to him. He winked one of his large, yellow eyes, and I couldn't stop my grin.

"We need to secure the next queen immediately," Torine said, drawing our attention. With his tufts of white and black hair, small stature, and large dark eyes, Torine was one of the oldest still walking this earth and his council was respected above all others. That being said, he was approaching his three-hundredth year, and at around that age a wolf began to go rabid, losing all humanity, all reason. The alpha of that wolf then had the duty to carry out the Act of Honor, ending the life of their ailing charge. I couldn't really imagine Torine going rabid one day.

I shook my head to clear those thoughts and focused on what he was saying.

"The queen and one heir already murdered this morning. If we don't fill the void in our pack powers, we'll no doubt find ourselves in the midst of another wolf-bear-shifter war. They'll come in force. They've already sent assassins to try and stop this Summit, and rumor is they are amassing an army."

The council was assuming, as I had done, that the attacks on us heirs had been from the bear shifters. Despite their human appearance and scent, there was no way they were humans, and that really limited the options.

Bears made sense. Throughout history, we had been more enemies than allies, and mostly only ever crossed paths during peace negotiations – which were almost always failures. Still, I'd heard news that their new king did things a little differently. I seriously doubted it. Brutal by nature, the bears were interested in power and nothing more. They had short tempers and were quick to anger, unlike wolves who respected strategy before striking. That's why we were in the place of highest power. We thought before acting, unlike the big brutes who went screaming into battle and died for their hasty decisions. We also bested them through numbers. But Torine made a very good point. Without the energy of the queen tying all of us together, we were in a vulnerable position, and the bears were already taking advantage of that.

"Either one of you ladies want to concede to me?" Selene murmured, her voice confident. "It's not worth your life, and we need to get this sorted straight away."

Breanna and I exchanged a glance, and it was clear both of us had the same thought. *No way in hell.* We might as well spit on the queen's grave. With a shake of our heads, we both turned back to the front. There was no point even replying. Selene had no honor and would never avenge the fallen. Over my dead body would she be queen.

And even if I had thought she would make a decent queen, the Summit didn't work like that, you had no option to forfeit. We had been trained from birth for this. All of us would fight for our place, for our chance to rule. I would never let Selene just take the role. The queen's energy filtered to every single pack member, and Selene's cold heart would influence the wolves in the worst way.

With my hand resting against the thick fur of my familiar, I focused closely on Torine. He was now kicking off the initial Summit events. Once everything was officiated, the first challenge would begin. All of the council and pack members were turned to face us now. My Bronx pack, wearing red armbands, were close to the front, none of them willing to be far from me. My heart ached to not see all of my most trusted dominants there. But there was nothing I could do now but take down those responsible for killing my two guards at the vortex.

"We have three heirs who will compete for the honor of being queen: Arianna, from our beloved Red Queen's lineage. Selene, from the Purple Hearts pack. And finally Breanna, from the ancient Yellow Wood pack."

Another of the council stepped forward. He held a large flag in his hand that was a checkered four-way pattern, each section a color of the royal houses. "Let the Summit begin," he shouted, and the crowd followed with shouts and howls. Even Finn beside me seemed to burst with newfound energy.

The three of us held our right hand out as Torine stepped out from his council area and crossed the dais. From a sheath at his side he took an ornate blade, one infused just slightly with a mix of silver and iron so our wounds would not heal quickly, and slashed across each of our palms.

I clenched my fist, ignoring the biting sting, and let my blood drip into the large ceremonial cup below us. From here it would overflow and run down and into the center of the mecca. The royal home was built above one of the largest reservoirs of mecca magic.

Our blood sacrifice was used to set the magic into motion. Once it started, there was no stopping the Summit until the coronation. The second the final heir's blood filled the cup, it drained mysteriously, flowing into the mecca. Howls were still ringing out around us, and I could feel the tingles of magic on my skin as the energy beneath us responded to the stream of blood we were feeding into it.

My eyes fluttered as the power washed over and through me. I had always had a particularly close affinity to the magical mecca, which was odd since it was not shifter in origin. We were only its guardians, and had the responsibility to not let it fall into the control of those who would either abuse the power or destroy themselves – humans especially.

As the cut on my palm finally sealed itself, the blood sacrifice was complete. I stood taller, my body ready for whatever was going to be thrown at us. We had no idea of the events, they were randomly selected from thousands of options by the council. Which meant we could only hope it was a task we had an affinity for or had studied at some point in our life. Although we were all genetically ready to be queen, only the strongest, most cunning, and level headed would rule. This was how it had been done for hundreds of years. Of course, I'd never expected to be called. Queens generally lived a hundred or more years. But here I was.

Selene was the last heir in the purple line, so she had a lot of pressure on her. Their line had not been queen for a very long time. Devina had a three-year-old heir sister, and five retired heir cousins who were hard at work trying to produce more green heirs. So even though she was cut down before the Summit started, the royal green line would live on. It was drilled into us since birth that our duty was to be a strong alpha heir, to select an exceptional breeding partner, and try and produce more heirs. Just because we were heirs, though, did not mean we would automatically have children who would receive familiars. But we had the best chance.

Of course, to be an heir-brood mare was not exactly a joyous destiny.

My mother died giving birth to Winnie. Wolf births were very dangerous, the fetus constantly shifting form – blood loss was common. On top of that, for some reason unknown to us, heirs had an awful time getting and remaining pregnant. My mother had six miscarriages before she had Winnie. She never talked much about getting pregnant with me, so I went with the assumption I'd been easier. Winnie, on the other hand, she'd talked about constantly. Before there had even been a belly to show her miracle pregnancy. I'd sit at her feet and listen with total focus. I loved my mother, but just like my aunt, she'd always held me at a bit of a distance.

My attention snapped back to the council as silence descended and all eleven of them rose. I could feel magic sizzling in the air. The Summit had officially begun. The far door to the grand room opened and in walked Sabina, the Manhattan pack's magic born, powerful and ancient. But she was still no match for Violet. No one was.

Even though I had gazed upon the magic born my entire life, their unique looks and energy still held me mesmerized – me and everyone else. The magnetism of them drew your gaze, held it, and kept you in their thrall. Sabina's white skin was void of any pigment, along with her white hair, lashes, and brows. All magic born were extremely pale in coloring, which made them even more beautiful and fascinating. Their wolves were truly a sight to behold, a beauty that could not be replicated by any other. Their fur shimmered iridescently, almost like fur made of mother of pearl.

Sabina made her way across the room and met my eyes briefly. I liked the queen's magic born. She was mature and level headed. I'd never had a single reason to fear her, or worry for my queen. But now that the Red Queen had fallen, was there more to the magic born that I'd never seen? Did I miss something there – more importantly, did the Red Queen? Did the magic born have a desire to rule? Could they?

Sabina stood with the council and closed her eyes, breathing deeply. No words were exchanged, she knew what needed to be done. When she opened them again they were a glowing ice blue, and as she raised her arms up to the ceiling, she pushed lightly with her hands and a burst of energy shot out. Within moments, a thousand aged scrolls were dancing across the upper eaves of the high ceiling, many feet above us. The sight filled me with both fear and excitement, the wash of emotions trickling across my skin and mingling with the magic in the air. Maybe it was that we'd just been connected to the mecca through our blood, but I would swear the energy was so much stronger than usual. Or maybe this is what it felt like to be almost queen.

Torine stood straighter, his dark eyes locked onto the scrolls whooshing above. He had the honor of selecting the first task, the first step to one of us earning the right to govern the mecca and all wolf clans.

The ancient wolf crooked his finger at a scroll, and somehow the scroll knew it was the one wanted, because with one flick of his wrist it descended into his hand. I could barely contain myself, my emotions inside were a mess. I wasn't sure I'd ever been such a mix of scared, excited, nervous, and exhilarated – compounded by the constant sorrow permanently etched into my heart. Three deaths I must avenge. One could never forget.

Torine took an unnaturally long time to unroll the aged parchment.

"The first task," he said, his voice booming across the silent packs, "is war strategy. This is a game of cunning and intellect. Brute strength will serve no course here."

My lips quirked into a smile and I saw Calista give a slight grin. Breanna gave me a side look and there was nothing but fear in her large hazel eyes. It was common knowledge that I was best with strategy among us, besting all of the other heirs in the few tournaments where we'd played mecca chess. I'd been playing the popular shifter game with Calista since before I could talk, and for the most part liked logic and reasoning. Selene might survive this round; she wasn't completely useless, but Breanna was screwed. I had no doubt in my mind that I stood a good chance of winning.

There wasn't much to say about Breanna. She was pretty unremarkable. She was the smallest of us all at five feet three, with plain brown hair. She was one of those no personality or true power wolves. She did the bare minimum at all times. Lazy, really. Oh, she had some skills, especially in one-on-one fights, but nothing compared to most heirs. I really wasn't sure what it was that triggered someone like her to be born with heir status and receive her familiar, but I think a mistake was made.

There was shuffling around on the floor below us and the guards began backing up and lining the walls, making room for the council to prepare the test. Greggor, a council member and old wolf from the Purple Hearts pack, had disappeared, but was already returning with a giant rolling mecca chess board. Now I was really smiling. I hadn't been totally sure that war strategy would be played out on the mecca chess board, but thankfully it was. Selene was also grinning. Breanna let a curse word fly but stood tall.

Torine's voice bellowed and carried throughout the great hall: "This test has two parts. Part one is worth fifty points to the winner. Part two is worth twenty. These first few rounds are very important in building points. Whichever two heirs have the highest points before the final round will be the ones in the final battle. The winners of each round will also be awarded with gold, and special spell books for their pack's magic born." The mention of spell books got me excited. A long, long time ago, when witches still existed, some of them inter-mated with our wolves and the result was the magic-born wolves. Over time, the witches began to die off, and their knowledge was lost. All that was left were these highly coveted and guarded magical spell books. It was a prize far more valuable than gold.

Despite the tremor of my muscles, and the churning deep in my gut, I held on to the confidence that I could do this. For my pack and late queen.

There was nothing worse than losing and going back to your pack as a failure and living the rest of your life as a failed heir. The only honorable thing an heir kicked out of a Summit could do was produce more heirs. And who would want that as a destiny? Not this shifter, that was for sure.

My pack didn't need the gold from winning. We were one of the richer boroughs, but I had to get some of those spell books. Violet would be so overjoyed. It always annoyed me that the council was so reluctant to share with the packs, but I also understood their reasoning. This magic was far beyond our knowledge and abilities. We didn't want our magic born killing themselves or anyone else in failed spells. So they exercised caution in allowing this information out into the packs. Clearly the Summit was the one place they thought worthy to give the extra awesome prizes.

Greggor gestured that we should approach the board. I unbuttoned my sleeves and rolled them up and a few of my wolves started chanting my name softly. One look from Torine shut them up. I took a second to give them a wink and small grin as I passed close to them. They wanted reassurance from me, to see my confidence. I couldn't give them much, but I could give that small gesture before again focusing on the task.

The mecca chess board was nothing like real chess. It was similar in that you had two players and the ultimate goal was to guard your queen, but this was a specially designed board that represented the five boroughs of New York. There were vortexes that would transport your character just like ours in real life, and even a small, grotesque-looking bear king holding dominion over their two boroughs. The point was to protect the territory of the three boroughs at all cost while also protecting the queen.

A council member, Lucille of the yellow clan, took a seat then at the head of the bear king's boroughs. *Crap!* That meant I would be playing against an extremely wise council member and not one of the other heirs like I thought.

Torine locked eyes with me and said: "You'll each get a chance to play, but Arianna, since you're the Red Queen's descendent I'll allow you to choose if you want to go first or last."

This was a test. I knew it. I felt it in the way he asked the question like he was shrewdly choosing each word. These bastards would be adding up points throughout this entire thing and weighing how we did, deciding where we stood. If I said last it might make me seem weak, but I would also be able to see how the other council members played, get clues on their faults and weaknesses. If I said first, was I being too cocky or hasty?

I met Finn's gaze, and he gave me a nod, but there was no voice from him. He was letting me make this decision with no influence.

The answer came from my wolf inside ... her instinct. "First," I said clearly, and was rewarded with a head nod from Calista. Two councilwomen came across then and escorted Selene and Breanna from the room. Ah, excellent, they would not allow us to watch each heir. I had made the right choice then. Torine gestured for me to sit and I took a steadying breath and joined Lucille at the board.

Finn settled his huge weight close to my feet, on constant alert to the shifters around me. He was in guard mode. Like the rest of us he was unhappy with all the attacks. He wanted justice for our fallen.

It will be done, my friend, I assured him.

I know. Now win us this Summit.

Ah, my old friend, always big with the pep talks.

As I focused on the board, my fingers itched to touch the pieces. This game calmed my mind for some reason. Even sitting here, I felt slivers of tranquility washing over me. This was my usual spot when I played, that of the queen, and Calista usually played the bear king. Unable to hold back any longer, I ran my finger along the Red Queen figurine.

The board was about three feet by four, in the exact shape of the five boroughs. The Hudson River ran right along Manhattan and was represented with tiny bits of blue shimmering glass beads. There was a whole network of dials and compartments underneath the game that would take your pieces and move them or keep them if your character died. Each side had a control panel so we could type in our instructions. The small replica buildings stood tall, and I recognized my own apartment building as I gazed at the Bronx.

"Ten minutes on the clock," Torine said as he tapped into his keyboard; the clock immediately began to count down. The person in the strongest position at the end would win.

"Your Majesty, Queen Heir, has first move," Torine added, before taking his seat on the side. He held the position of official overseer of this trial. Without hesitation, I placed ten of my fifty fighters in kayaks along the waterway separating Manhattan and Brooklyn. They spanned out to also protect parts of the water from Staten Island. These waterways were a large vulnerability for the queen and by placing warriors there, it would hopefully force the bears to stick to the vortexes for travel.

Lucille's turn. She sent ten bear warriors to her vortex point on Staten Island. It was a good strategic move because all the vortexes were connected and from there they could travel to any of my boroughs. If I wasted men at each vortex point and she had a larger attack in mind, I would leave the queen vulnerable. I had to protect Manhattan at all costs. The queen was the most important person and her borough must be an iron shield for our people. I decided to send ten guards to the Manhattan vortex, leaving my remaining thirty in the royal house. If the bear king sent his men there, I would strike them down.

My stomach turned as Lucille sent thirty bear warriors on foot to the Brooklyn Bridge, giving the bears a direct connection to our Manhattan territory. That was more than half of her warriors, and I only had ten in the water to fend them off. Was this her attack, or a distraction? Should I go after the bears at my border or the bear king? I had my warriors at the vortex; I could send them through, but then there'd still be thirty of the bears at the queen's feet waiting to pounce on Manhattan.

Don't panic. I had thirty warriors left in the castle and the Manhattan vortex was safe – the queen was safe. Then I got an idea. Schooling my expression, I sent instruction for the remaining thirty of my warriors to go on foot to the border of Manhattan and face off with the thirty Brooklyn bear warriors. Now each of our warriors were facing one another. In order to make them engage in a fight, it would take another turn.

Just as I expected, Lucille used her turn to engage war. The game would simulate fighting for the duration and predict losses based on statistics. Thirty against thirty was even. Both sides would suffer heavy bloodshed.

My turn. I took my Red Queen from her safe castle and placed her on the Manhattan vortex. Lucille was trying to hide her look of pride, but I saw it. Sometimes if you wanted a task done right, you had to do it yourself. The game knew the strength of each player. One warrior would kill one warrior, but it would take thirty warriors to stop the powerful Red Queen. With only ten bears at the Staten Island vortex, I could easily send my queen through and kill them. Any time you moved your queen, you got two turns. I used one to move her to the vortex and my next to send her through to the Staten Island vortex right in front of the bear king's palace.

Lucille could send her remaining ten warriors from inside the palace to the vortex to fight my queen, or use her turn to engage the fight with the guards who were already there. She surprised me by doing neither. She instead pulled her king from the castle and placed him at the vortex facing my queen. Smart. He would be better protected with his measly ten guards there. I knew that if my queen could kill the bear king, the war would be over, because the bear king's power would begin to drain just as ours had the moment the queen fell.

Because Lucille moved her king, she got two moves, and she used her next one to engage war. I sat back calmly, watching it play out as my Red Queen began to pulverize the ten warriors protecting the bear king. The mecca board knew that the Red Queen was more powerful than the bear king because she had three boroughs in her power – more power running through her veins.

It was my turn but I had no more moves to play out. This would end soon; I had faith in my queen's power. Just as I thought it, the game opened a panel at the Staten Island vortex and ten dead bear warriors fell down. I smiled. Now the bear king and my Red Queen were locked in a vicious battle. My queen did have some depleted energy from killing the ten warriors, but nothing that would compromise this battle.

A player could sit idle for two minutes before being forced to choose their next move. I had one minute left. I wanted to give my queen all of that time, because if Lucille was allowed to play again she would bring her final ten warriors out of the castle to protect the king, and then I might really be in trouble, forced to retreat back to Manhattan – a coward. With ten seconds left, I held my breath as my queen raised her mighty arms and took off the king's head with her sword. This weakened the remaining bears on the board, and the battle at the bridge began to turn in the wolves' favor. I smiled. The game board opened up and swallowed the bear king and that was it.

I had won.

The two councilmen stood and bowed to me. "Well played. Not many people move their queen from the safety of her castle."

I returned the bow. "Sometimes you have to make a bold but calculated move for the bigger picture."

I'd never lost faith in the strength of my queen.

The council exchanged glances, and while it was hard to read anything on their faces, I could sense approval. I was then dismissed, but not before passing my Bronx warriors and getting a cheer. I gave them a half smile and left the room feeling a lot better than when I walked in.

Chapter Three

Never trust a bear.

OVER THE NEXT twenty-five minutes we waited outside the large great hall doors. At the moment I was standing with Calista, Finn, and Selene. The overconfident purple heir had already had her turn at the challenge and said she did brilliantly – her words, not the council's. Now we were awaiting Breanna's results. Calista stood erect as an alert pinged on her tablet.

Her head tilted to the side as she read through the notice. I could see the slight surprise on her face.

"What is it?" I asked, wondering if something else had happened. Was there another attack?

She lifted her face, and thankfully there was no anger or stress upon it. "Normally one of the heirs would be sent home after the first trial, but it seems they are letting all of you stay because the Summit trials are designed for four heirs." Her fingers flew across her tablet and I knew she was calculating odds and inputting information for me to read over later. "There will be at least two more trials, and then the final battle."

Selene shrugged like she couldn't care less. Her advisor, a non-descript male whose name I couldn't recall, stepped in and whispered to her. Still the heir's expression was unchanging. I don't think she thought for one second she wouldn't be in the final battle. Just then the doors opened. I could already tell from the red-ringed eyes and the way her head hung in misery that Breanna had not done very well at the war strategy. I didn't want Breanna to be queen, but I understood her agony. Going back to your pack as a failed heir was the worst thing any of us could do. And if she'd just come last in the first trial, she was already way behind and would have to work extra hard to even have a hope of making it into the final battle. If she failed out of the Summit, when she went back to Queens she would no doubt be challenged for her alpha status from another dominant female. Once she was stripped of her borough and heir title, there'd be nothing worthy about her except her blood.

"There are hundreds of trials which could have been chosen, but no, it had to be the stupid mecca game!" she said, her advisor right behind her. Her hawk familiar, Kanu, sat upon her shoulder, and even he seemed to have his head hung low.

The "stupid" mecca game was the most important war strategy tool we had. My opinion of her had just lowered; her statement did nothing but show her immaturity.

"I'm sorry, Breanna," I offered diplomatically.

Selene wrinkled her face, bestowing Breanna with a look like she was a piece of dirt that was ruining her favorite shirt. "Better start making babies. That's all you're good for now."

Breanna's hand snaked out with the speed and force of a bullet and popped Selene in her perfect nose. Selene managed to jerk her head back in the last second, but there was still a distinct crunch of cartilage.

"No one likes you," Breanna spat out, and she stalked off, her advisor at her heels.

I didn't say anything, forcing my expression to remain in a neutral pose, but I was enjoying the sight of the blood trickling from Selene's upper lip and nose, not to mention her two black eyes. Of course, my enjoyment was short lived, because within moments the black faded and the swelling around her nose disappeared. Shifter healing in an heir was twice as fast as a non-heir.

Everyone knew physical combat between heirs was forbidden, Breanna had just broken a major rule, but somehow I didn't think she cared. From the little I knew of her life, it had been common knowledge that she had been best friends with Devina. The heir's death would be hitting her hard, causing reckless behavior.

As different as they were, they had happily co-ruled the Queens borough together. Devina, I had never had any real quarrel with, except for the fact that she was reckless, and at times an idiot. She had been the most beautiful of us, with long golden curls and huge blue eyes, and she'd often used her body to gain whatever favor she could. I'd almost never seen any male – or female for that matter – turn her down. Just recently there had been a scandal with her and a bear shifter. We did not cross the line with bears, it was forbidden, and Devina didn't just hook up with any bear, she'd had sex with an advisor to the bear king. She could have leaked important information about our people – not to mention that having sex with a bear shifter as an heir could potentially produce a hybrid. A hybrid heir was a definite no. I knew of no living hybrids, or if they were even possible. We kept the races separate for good reason, but Devina had been careless and promiscuous. If she wasn't an heir, she would have been beheaded.

There was no way she should have been queen, but that didn't mean she deserved to die as she had.

Selene wiped away the last of the blood, and with a scowl was turning to follow Breanna when the council called us back in. She froze for a second, seemingly undecided whether she wanted to go after Breanna or heed the council's call. With a final hiss from Larak, the snake curled back around his heir and the pair followed me inside the great hall.

I was the first through the door, Selene close behind, and Breanna slipped in at the last minute from the side entrance. Selene's eyes tracked her like a lion stalking its prey. The council had changed into more formal robes now, and Torine was still holding the scroll.

"The first task is now complete. We have assigned points based on speed, accuracy, cunning, skill, and success in the war games. Arianna showed remarkable leadership skills. She set the board up to keep her territory safe, and when needed sent her queen into the battle. All great leaders are on the front line. They do not hide in the shadows. It shows a love of her people, a strength and bravery which will be an asset for our future leaders. She has earned the top fifty points."

I gave a small smile, trying to hide my exhilaration.

He continued, and the shouts that had risen up died off just as quickly. "Selene relied heavily on brute force and speed, taking out the largest group and scattering the enemy's forces. She did not kill the bear king, but did keep her queen safe. She was in second place and will receive twenty points. Breanna lost her queen. She over-capitalized in her initial force, and did not watch for the lone soldiers sneaking in the darkness. She receives no points."

I could see the yellow-shirted wolf hang her head, and judging by the disgruntled noises in the crowd she wasn't the only one disappointed in her skills today.

I honestly couldn't believe Breanna could be so stupid as to let a group of lone bears sneak up on her queen. In a one-on-one situation on the mecca board, if it's not the queen's turn and you managed to make it into her quarters, and she has no guards, then she's dead. They count it as an assassination in the night. Breanna should know better than to remove all guards, unless there was no other option. Hadn't her mentors taught her anything? I knew she was good in physical battle. Maybe they had spent all their time with the swords and no time in the books. Breanna was more of a warrior than a strategist or leader.

Torine continued. "Tomorrow we reconvene here for trial two. Tonight you will be graded on the second part of the first trial. You all will practice diplomacy and entertain a guest for dinner. It's your job to be as political as possible so as not to anger, offend, or incite a war."

I felt a chill down my spine.

"Who is the guest?" Selene asked before I could.

"A councilman of the bear king," was his reply.

Both of our jaws dropped in unison.

The bear king could have been responsible for murdering our queen for all we knew. Now his councilman was allowed at our dinner table? This was one of the few things I absolutely hated about politics, and possibly being queen. Still, I had to accept it as part of my role. Unfortunately.

I remained behind for a few moments so the council could speak to me about my prize for winning the first trial. I was able to glimpse the small pile of gold, and the very valuable leather-bound magical tome before it was returned to the vault. The gold and spell book would remain in the royal safe until the end of the Summit. If I died, the gold would be handed over to the next alpha of the Bronx. The spell book would be given to Violet. I couldn't wait to tell her. She'd be thrilled to get her hands on some new material.

I gave a nod, and Calista bowed deeply, before we were whisked off to our sleeping quarters. I knew Selene and Breanna were on the same floor as me, but the guards informed me I had been given the grandest of the three suites since I was the direct heir of the late Red Queen.

As we traversed the halls, I whispered under my breath to Calista: "What have you heard from Violet? I need her back here immediately."

I wanted to get her in that library before those scents were gone, finding out who killed my queen was high on my list of priorities. Calista typed away on her tablet and pulled up an email. It was from Violet, addressed to me.

Oh my God, I felt her death all the way across the world. You will be called to Summit soon, I need to deal with a serious matter here and then I'm on the first flight home. I love you. Stay strong and kick Selene's ass. We will avenge our beloved Red Queen. –V

I couldn't help the grin that lit up my face. Even though I had never expected to be called to the Summit in my lifetime, Violet and I used to play Summit games as kids. Even then we'd hated Selene.

Calista saw my smile and gave me an eye roll. "Violet has never been politically correct."

No she wasn't, which was why I loved her. She gave it to you like it was and had the power to back up anything she said. No sugarcoating and no bull.

We reached the large double doors to my quarters. Half of my dominants went in first to make sure it was secure before I was allowed to step into what was basically a three-bedroom apartment. The royal home was even more massive than I'd expected.

As my eyes alighted on what would be my quarters for the next little while, I had to admit that despite my own lovely apartment building in the Bronx, there was absolutely no expense spared within the royal building. Glistening travertine floors, marble countertops and gold accents, decadent furnishings in shades of cream and bronze and rich reds. Everything was of the highest quality, and spaciously designed.

The residence took up some of the most prime real estate in Manhattan. It was priceless. Humans didn't know about us, we used magic to keep our secrets, but we still ran their cities. We had the best real estate, people in all positions of power, and our fingers on the pulse of our boroughs. Even if humans outnumbered us, we had the magical mecca at our disposal, which more than evened the odds.

As I stepped further inside, a maid scurried along the hall. She wore the red emblem of the queen on her uniform, and her expression was neutral. Respectful. As she closed in on me, she gave a low bow, and when I returned that with a nod she hurried out of the open doorway. The queen staffed over a hundred people to keep her residence going, and as soon as time permitted I intended to interview every single one of them. Someone saw something last night or this morning, and I would find out who killed our queen.

Calista closed the door of my opulent suite then, and I was just about to beeline toward my bedroom when she called out to me.

"What?" I growled, the wolf rising in my voice. Generally I had better control, but I was tired and hungry. "The obligatory dinner isn't for hours and I need sleep and food."

The queen's death had been very early this morning. It was about noon now. I was running on no coffee, no breakfast, and four hours of sleep because Blaine had talked me into playing poker with the guards last night and I had been up past midnight.

My heart clenched then as I realized that Damian and Marco were no longer with us. Their loss would stay with me for a long time, and I was scared that the loss of shifters I cared about was just one of those things I would have to continue to deal with.

Calista put one hand on her hip and stared me down. "I know you, Arianna, better than you know yourself. You think the bear king killed the queen, and the second you sit down to dinner you'll lose your cool, accuse his representative, and lose the points you know they'll be awarding for behavior tonight – and possibly throw the whole city into a war."

I smirked, distracted at least from my grief. Calista was right; she did know me. "I'm not going to be the only one thinking that. Come on, Cal, who else is powerful enough to take down the queen of three boroughs in her own home, where she's closest to the mecca? The only thing that throws me is the scene we witnessed in the library. That seemed like the sort of place she'd take someone she trusted, and no one would ever trust a bear."

Calista stared off into space for a moment, her brilliant mind no doubt calculating. "It's all a bit odd. In general, the Red Queen was not the trusting sort, and she was beyond intelligent and cunning. Somehow she always knew when someone was lying. I just don't think the bears could easily get the drop on her. It didn't even look as if she fought back in that room."

Calista was right. There had been no signs of battle between a bear and wolf. Or even a minor struggle. No books out of place, nor shelves turned over, just massive amounts of blood.

"Maybe they somehow took her by surprise, drugged her or used magic?" I really wanted it to be the bears. I needed a place to release my fury.

Calista continued analyzing, tossing things around in that computer brain of hers. "What if the person who was responsible wanted to make sure we'd blame the bears? They're our natural enemy after all. It makes sense. Maybe they were trying to start a war so they could ... I don't know ... divide us and take control of the magical mecca."

It was a good theory, but honestly what other race was there that would even remotely have a chance of controlling the magical mecca? It destroyed humans' minds in moments; they were not equipped to handle it. Not to mention the fact that the Red Queen was the most powerful of our kind. There was no one person, shifter or even magic born, alive that could take her down so quietly. A troop of fifty guards maybe, but one being ... never.

Right? Was there someone I had missed?

"Is there any whispered words of a rogue shifter with strong enough magical abilities to take on the queen?" I asked. Calista had a database with very detailed records on all of our people. But it wasn't always totally accurate because we relied on input from other alphas and such. As you can imagine, Selene was not very gracious with her time and information.

She shook her head. "No, we haven't had any magical disturbances for a long time. No unauthorized activity on the ley lines. It's been very quiet. Obviously a powerful magic born like Violet might have a chance, but..."

But Violet was in London and would never betray our queen. Would one of the others? If it wasn't the bears who'd attacked her, and us tonight, then who? One of the heirs was dead, and so were our guards. Something bigger was going on here, and I felt like I was missing a piece of the puzzle.

I could not believe any one shifter or person had the power to take on the queen.

The entirety of New York City was a power grid of magic, and it enhanced the person tied to it through the vortexes. The queen was tied to three of them, and the bear king to two. No one else even came close, not even the magic born.

Calista continued to watch me. She would not let me rest until she was assured of my actions tonight. I groaned. "Fine, I will be diplomatic at dinner, but I will make it clear that the queen's killer will be caught and revenge enacted."

Calista didn't seem thrilled with my response, but nodded. She was smart enough to see that was the best she was getting from me.

As I walked to the master bedroom I was trying to weigh up which thing was more important to me right now, food or sleep.

Exhaustion made up my mind for me as I crashed into the pillows and let sleep take me.

A few hours later, the scent of bacon drifted through the room and my eyelids snapped open. Calista knew how to wake me. Coffee or bacon did it every time. Shuffling out of my bedroom and into the open dining area, I saw the table littered with an array of mouthwatering food. Oh my God. I shouldn't be so excited, what with the queen's death and the Summit, but...

I was sort of bouncing on my toes. "Are those mac and cheese balls wrapped in bacon?"

Calista smiled. "Yes, the queen's chef is quite exquisite. Promised that we could have anything the heirs' hearts desired. I told him you ate like a five-year-old and so he came up with this."

I stuck my tongue out at her, although she wasn't wrong. I was a pretty picky eater. Fancy food freaked me out. Slimy oysters? No thanks. Caviar … just keep walking.

But this, this was my kind of food. To go with the mac and cheese balls there were truffle garlic fries, and chocolate lava cake, and mmmm raspberry lemonade.

Dropping into my seat, I took a deep breath as I savored this moment, before diving in. Shifters loved to eat; we had fast metabolisms, especially if we'd recently shifted or used our abilities, so food was a gift from the gods. We also had strong senses, which was why I couldn't stomach seafood. The scent of old fish was not very pleasant.

The moment I popped the first bite into my mouth, I completely lost my mind and started shoving food in with abandon, chewing as fast as I could. Sure, I'd been taught etiquette, decorum, and how to eat with eighteen different forks since I was very young, but sometimes you can't make a wolf shifter eat like a lady.

While I stuffed my face, Calista just rolled her eyes.

"Dinner is in two hours. I'm allowing you to eat because … well, right now you look like a pig in a trough."

I snorted for effect and somehow still managed to shove more bacon mac and cheese balls in my mouth.

Calista turned up her nose. "The more grotesque eating you do here, the more refined eating you can do at dinner."

I didn't care what her strategy was, this food was awesome. As an alpha I expended even more energy than a regular shifter. It was impossible for me to get fat and I needed four thousand calories minimum to keep my brain running. Constantly checking in with my pack and searching through those bonds drained me. I heard a low whine and smiled as Finn trotted up to my side.

I thought you hated human food. Only liked raw meat, I teased him.

He opened his mouth and I saw drool forming. *You know I can't resist bacon.*

I smiled before popping four mac and cheese balls into his mouth and he wolfed them down, his chest rumbling in his happy wolf way.

I'll be outside in the courtyard if you need me, Finn said then, loping off.

Some heirs were attached at the hip to their familiars, like Selene, but Finn and I had a more independent relationship. He was always there when I needed him, but we gave each other our space.

"So ... I have done some research on our bear councilman..." Calista placed a tablet on the table in front of me, close enough so I could see, but still out of touching distance. For its own electronic safety. I stopped eating for a moment, staring at a picture.

Holy heck. This guy was huge.

What did he advise the king on, lifting weights? He was at least 250 pounds of solid muscle, with a full beard and a shaved head. He also had a neck tattoo which I couldn't clearly make out from the photo. It looked like a crossed set of throwing axes in some sort of emblem.

Overall he looked exactly the way you'd expect a bear shifter to look. Huge, thick muscles, broad body, squinty eyes, and roughly hewn features. But I knew from personal experience not all bears were mass and brute strength. The guy I'd kissed on the Island that summer – a memory I did not like to think on, or talk about, it had been a moment of weakness – was kind of scrawny. Granted, who isn't scrawny at fifteen, but I couldn't believe he'd ever turn out to be as huge and imposing as this advisor to the king, even as a grown male.

"His name is Gerald and he's the king's war councilman. When we extended the dinner invite we said any one representative could come. The king has sent a message by sending this man."

My hands stilled over the plate. Yes, he had definitely sent a message. "You know that our queen just died and you send a war council leader. The king intends to declare war."

The waver in my voice startled me a bit. I was an alpha and an heir; fear was foreign to me. With our queen in power and four heirs, we were untouchable. Now we had three heirs and a dead queen and our magic was leaking out all over New York City. Fear was becoming very real to me.

"Maybe not." Calista was trying to be diplomatic again, or at least keep me from losing my mind and trying to kill the muscled mountain of man who was the king's representative.

"Hah! You think he intends to declare peace?"

Calista raised one eyebrow and shrugged.

To be honest, I didn't know much about the bear king or his people. Our studies included them of course, but the truth was, there just wasn't a lot of information out there about them. They kept their people locked down hard, and even though secret dalliances occurred at times between bear and wolf, pillow talk must be minimal, because no new info made its way to the leaders.

If I became queen, I would have to deal with the bear king from time to time. In the past the bear shifters had been a problem for us, but the dark war was over now and we had settled into a tenuous truce, a peace treaty that had held for over a century.

But nothing lasts forever.

I gripped the steak knife in my hand and met my advisor's eyes.

"Mark my words, Calista, if the bear king declares war on our people, I will slit this man's throat in front of the entire council, because he'll be all but admitting to killing my queen."

Calista shook her head, but not before I saw her smirk. She knew me well and she knew I would carry through on my words no matter what her personal advice was. I was honor bound to three of my people now, and I would see justice done.

Two hours later I was ready for the dinner. Dressed in a lace-up corset dress that was the color of blood, I had a knife strapped to my thigh, and another in my ankle boots. My hair had been expertly braided, and Calista had instructed the makeup artist to dramatically enhance my eyes with black smoky shadow. They looked larger, and their aqua color was bright and striking against the kohl. My lips, too, were covered in a bright red gloss. I finished off my outfit by donning golden arm cuffs, designed to protect my wrists in battle. I was mixing dining attire with my standard battle dress to send a message. I could be pretty and proper, but I could also kill.

As an heir, my appearance was examined closely, especially during the Summit. I would have to get used to it. It hadn't been so bad before the Red Queen's death, I could wear whatever I wanted – except on official duty days – but when I was queen I would have attendants waiting on my every need and would be expected to wear the finest clothes and have my makeup and hair ready at all times. It was my least favorite part of the job, but appearances were important when you were under the scrutiny of millions. Our NYC packs were only tens of thousands, but as a queen I would be linked to the entire wolf-shifter community. They no doubt were sitting with rapt attention at their computers now, waiting to hear word of a new queen. The power loss here affected them all too.

Just before we left, Calista pulled me in front of the mirror. "Say the phrases."

I rolled my eyes. Not this crap again.

Her glare cut through me. "I'm serious. It works. Say them."

Calista thought you could affect reality by being overly confident and saying positive statements. It was cute and she was my dearest ally, so I humored her.

"I am going to be the next queen. I will pass the Summit with grace and ease. I will win." The words left my lips and I did feel a bit more in control, a bit surer. Maybe Calista wasn't completely crazy, even if it was a placebo effect.

Calista smiled and we made our way to the dining hall with twenty guards at my back, a mix of royal house guards and my own.

I arrived a little early because I knew that would carry favor with the council; they were sticklers for punctuality. And sure enough, all eleven of them were already seated along the huge banquet table. As I strode across the room toward them, I was pleased to see Finn waiting for me, his huge body seated near my place at the table.

The dining room was huge, the large rectangular table in the center. The heirs would be at the head of the table with the bear councilman. The queen's council and other important dignitaries were already seated along the rest of the length. Stepping further into the room, I sighed at the pure overindulgence here. There were three large chandeliers hanging from the ceiling, each the size of a small car, and must have held a million glittery crystals to be sending off sparkles like that. The walls were lined with priceless pieces of art, and the floor was marble inlaid with gold.

Closing in on the table I could see the settings were ornate, and overdressed as always. We wouldn't want the bears to think we were poor or something. I noticed from the corner of my eye that Breanna had arrived and was crossing the room. Looked like Selene was late, I tried not to smile at that. I stepped across to greet the council, as duty dictated, but I was cut off as the doors to the far end of the room opened.

A massive, bearded man strolled in, Gerald, looking even more mammoth than in his photo. He wasn't wearing formal attire, and instead was outfitted with dark denim jeans, a tight black t-shirt, and leather wrist cuffs, a huge sword hanging from his belt. Sucking in a deep breath, I straightened my shoulders and prepared myself for this test of my queenliness. Turning from the council, I took a few steps toward the male, opening my arms in a welcoming gesture.

"Welcome to Manhattan, Bear Shifter Councilman Gerald. Please take a seat." My voice was even, not overly pleasant but not yet on the verge of killing him.

He surprised me by bowing deeply and unsheathing his sword, laying it on the ground near the edge of the room before he joined us at the table. Torine caught my eye and it was clear that we shared the same thought. He came in peace. No man unsheathed his sword before declaring war.

Because I got here early, I chose the center seat at the head of the table, with Breanna taking the chair to my right after she quietly greeted our guest. Finn settled in at my back, and I knew he'd keep me safe. I gestured for Gerald to sit to my left for many reasons, most of which was to irritate Selene when she arrived and saw the seating arrangement. The queen's council and other honored guests were all seated now. Our guards stood around the perimeter, and staff scurried about the space, making sure everyone had drinks.

The huge, ornate double doors opened again and Selene strode in looking like she was attending the opera. We were all formally dressed, but Selene had clearly taken it too far with her lacy geometrical hairpiece and golden-painted swirls of glittery artwork along her arms. The extra time had made her late, and would cost her valuable points with the council. She spied the seating and scowled at me.

"Thank you for inviting me, Your Highness," Gerald told me as he gripped his water glass with a big meaty paw.

Close enough now to hear his words, Selene groaned. "She's not the queen yet, just an heir."

Those words should not have been the first thing he heard from her, and I could see the disapproval cross the councilors' faces.

I had to bite the inside of my cheek to keep my retort in. "You're welcome, Gerald. We're always welcoming of all visits in the name of peace."

He gave me a nod, those dark glittering eyes assessing me closely. I was usually very good at reading the emotions of others, but he was keeping everything inside. He was very contained for a shifter. His bear scent was earthy and filled with forest tones, foreign but pleasant. Gerald eyed Finn, who remained behind my chair, and was staring at him.

"Is that your familiar?" Gerald asked, the slightest of awe in his tone.

I simply nodded and Gerald smiled. "Bigger than some of our female bears."

I gave him a polite smile, and as the waiters began to serve the first course I focused on the plate in front of me and tried to mask my confusion. The bear war councilman was making light conversation, being polite, smiling, and unsheathing his sword. What the hell was he here for? Didn't he know our queen was murdered?

When everyone was served, we all stared at him, waiting for him to take the first bite. As a guest it was the protocol. Instead he just sighed, hand hovering over the plate before he dropped his fork, looking at me. For some reason he seemed to have chosen me as the one he was going to focus on tonight. Despite the fact that I hoped to be queen very soon, I wasn't queen yet, so his disregard of everyone else was a little unexpected.

His voice went deep, husky with emotion. "I don't want to do the political thing tonight. Can we speak freely?" He was still looking at me, but I knew everyone else was listening in.

Some of the tension eased within me. His attitude was refreshing. And I was very curious about what he was going to say. Still, I wouldn't let my guard down too far. This could be some ploy to gain my trust and then declare war or kill me.

I nodded. "By all means. You may speak as freely as needed."

"We didn't kill your queen." He dropped that bomb and the room fell silent. The only movement was from the guards as they took a minute step forward. Gerald continued: "I know it's the only logical explanation, but we didn't. Someone attacked us too, possibly right at the moment your queen fell, and tried to take out my king. We lost twenty royal guards in the battle."

Holy shifter! Why hadn't I heard of this? Probably because we'd been focused on our queen's death and the Summit. Still, Calista was usually up-to-date on this type of data. I suppose our two sides didn't exactly share information easily.

Gerald regarded me, waiting for my answer. I knew I had to tread carefully. The entire council was watching and I didn't want to seem weak.

"Thank you for your statement and honesty. Our queen was killed alone, without guards, and by my reckoning there is only one person alive that's strong enough to defeat a queen with the power of mecca flowing through her veins."

He exhaled loudly. "My king, yes. We agree this is the logical explanation, but that is why I am here to tell you he didn't do it. If we wanted to overthrow you, we have many plans which could be enacted at any time. Top of that list was one which involved killing all of the heirs and then the queen so there would be no one to take over. This would weaken your boroughs, and we could step right in and claim the power. But our king was not planning on attacking the wolves. He has no plans to ever attack unprovoked. War is not his style."

That was interesting. War had always been the bears' thing. They loved to brawl and battle. They loved power. Seemed the rumors about their new king were right; he was different.

"We have surmised that the simultaneous attacks," continued Gerald, "both aiming for our leaders, by a small group of magically enhanced individuals, was a means to play our packs against each other."

Exactly what Calista had surmised. But again, we were left with the question of what magical individuals could have done this? The witches had died out, and no other enhanced humans had emerged in all the years since.

The silence extended for many moments as I mulled over all of his information. It did sound as if the same sort of magically disguised people who had attacked me at the portal entrance had attacked the bears. There must have been more of them if they almost took out the king and destroyed twenty of his army.

"How many attacked you?" I asked.

"Three separate groups of fifteen. We fought back and managed to kill many of them, and as more of our people arrived they started to retreat, taking their dead with them. We have one body left, which our magic born is examining. So far they have found no evidence of it being anything but human."

His eyes locked with mine and I knew both of us shared the same thought. They had definitely not been humans. I needed to ask Calista if there had been any bodies left from our attack. She had been handling the cleanup and investigation for me. I'd had to focus solely on the Summit.

For some reason I completely believed Gerald. Not only did I sense nothing but truth from him, it also made sense. His admission that should they have wanted to take over our boroughs they would have taken out the heirs first was a good plan. It would have completely destroyed shifter hierarchy and thrown us all into chaos.

Apparently not everyone was of the same thought though. Selene's nasally voice came across the table: "Why should we believe you?"

The council scowled at her and Gerald shrugged. "You don't have to believe me. You can continue on your own and good luck finding out who killed your queen. Or we could share information and try to find out together."

That sounded an awful lot like an alliance. As heirs we could not agree to anything like that yet.

Torine spoke up: "Our investigation is ongoing, and to be honest we don't have anything solid yet to go on. If you have anything more to share, then please do."

The bear shifter's features tightened, and I understood why. Torine was wanting to take without giving, and that was not a great foot to start off on. This was one of the reasons the council annoyed me. They thought they could make these type of decisions, even when the queen had been alive.

I decided to go out on a limb. "Before I arrived to the Summit I was attacked in the Bronx. Just as your attackers were, they were magically disguised to look like humans, but with the strength and ability far beyond any human. At the time I figured your bear magic born were involved."

Gerald nodded. "The people who broke into the palace looked like frail humans but they certainly were not. They ripped through us in seconds, and it was only through sheer numbers and the power of our king that we weren't all destroyed. Just as you did, at first we thought it was wolf shifters, but then..." He trailed off, looking around the table and the room. "Can we speak privately, Your Highness?" he said in a low voice.

Breanna looked affronted, getting in before Selene this time. "She isn't queen yet."

Gerald pinned her with a look. "I know a queen when I see one."

I managed to contain the smile trying to curl my lips.

Torine stood. "Please join us in the drawing room." He gestured to Gerald and me.

Oh my God, he was going to allow it. I stood quickly before Selene or Breanna could say anything to screw this up, and Gerald and I swiftly followed Torine into the drawing room. The ancient wolf shifter closed the door so we would have some privacy. Finn followed and sat on the other side of the door. He would hear everything I heard anyway, and it was sometimes better he wasn't right in the center; his presence unnerved most people.

Gerald gave me a calculating look. He was gauging whether or not he trusted me. Now I was certain of two things. One, he had big news. And two, I was dying to know that news.

I broke protocol and stepped within his personal space. Despite my height I still had to look up to him. "Please, tell me."

Torine scowled but I didn't care. And Gerald nodded. Some of his assessing stare faded away.

"Were any of your magic born present when you were attacked in the Bronx?"

I frowned. "No, we only have one in my borough, and she was out of town."

He nodded. "We also only have one on Staten Island, and luckily he was present during the attack."

Okay...

Gerald leaned forward and whispered: "He said that for the most part there was nothing but human weakness in their scent, but for a split second, when they retreated, he scented an old magic, a magic so powerful that it was reminiscent of fairy tales he was told as a child."

Chills crept up my arms, because I knew then exactly what he was talking about.

"The fae," I breathed.

Gerald nodded. "They've come back. The Tuatha de Danann have returned from the Otherworld."

Torine nearly had a heart attack. I saw his face drain of color, and he actually reached out for my arm to steady himself.

"That's impossible. They were..." I tried to find the right words, "eradicated."

Gerald shook his head. "They vanished. No one eradicated them. Legend says they went to their world, which lies somewhere in a realm parallel to ours. Now it seems they may be trying to come back."

I knew nothing about the fae. They hadn't been seen in over five hundred years, so they were not a part of my studies. I don't think we even had books of them, just tales told from mother to child. I would have to ask Calista.

"Our legends say the Tuatha de Danann used to rule this land. They were revered as gods. They built the mecca here in New York City as a means to control the power, but then, for some reason, moved on to another world, the Otherworld."

Torine's voice startled me. I had forgotten he was here even though he was still holding onto my arm. I gently shook his hand off and tried to get a hold of myself. Despite the fact that we all knew the fae had once existed, it had been so long ago. The possibility never even crossed my mind that they could be behind our attacks.

Gerald then bowed deeply to Torine and me. "I rushed over here to warn you before war was declared by your side. We cannot be divided right now, we must work together to learn everything we can about the Tuatha de Danann. Once you have completed the Summit, my king would like a word with the new queen. Now, if you'll excuse me, I must get back to bury my people."

I could only nod as he walked away, exiting the drawing room. I moved to follow and see him out properly, but Torine grabbed my arm again. In many areas council members were above protocol, but still, he should not be so forward with a queen heir.

"Don't breathe a word of this to anyone else. Focus on the Summit, we will deal with everything once the queen is crowned." Chills danced up my spine again. I met his eyes and was shocked to see a deep and biting fear there. Maybe Torine knew more about the fae than I did. My first duty as queen would be to pull every piece of knowledge of the fae from the council until I had enough to write a book. I would not be ignorant in the face of my enemy any longer.

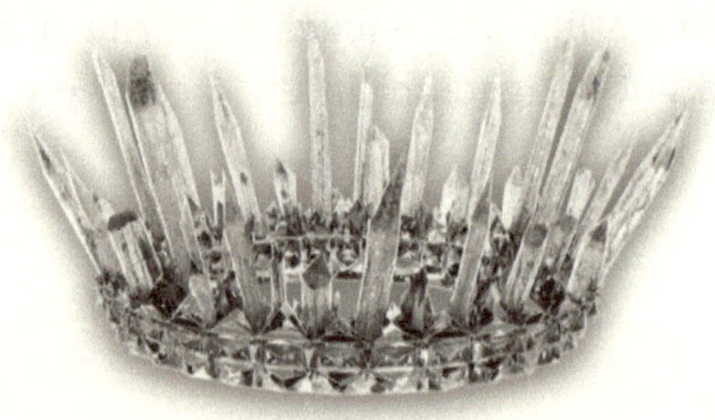

Chapter Four

Power drunk is worth the hangover.

THE NEXT DAY I was awoken early by Calista. I'd barely slept last night, the bear councilman's message continuing to reverberate through my head. Fae. Was it even possible? It would explain so much, and yet we had no idea why they were emerging again. Or why they might have killed our queen. Not to mention simultaneously attacking all of us. Maybe they had been hoping it would create a war between the shifters, and if the new bear king wasn't so reasonable it would have.

With a sigh I rolled over and stretched myself out. I knew there'd be no answers this morning, so I forced myself to focus on what today would bring. The second test was arguably the most important of the Summit. It involved a test of our magical strength. For reasons unknown to us, each heir had the ability to harness the magic of the mecca and funnel it out into the shifters around the world. That ability was in our blood, in our house lines, and was the reason we had familiars. There had been some "heirs" born into the right line and house but who never received a familiar. They were automatically rejected as possible heirs. Their connection to the mecca was too weak.

On top of our familiar, we were also tested at birth to make sure we were in fact heirs. There were a few different tests, one which included holding a cell phone. Heir's magical ties to the mecca should be strong enough to short circuit all cell phones and most laptop and tablet devices when we came in contact with them. Electronics hated us.

Just another part of being a queen heir.

Today would be the biggest test of all, our true magical potency. A leader weak with the mecca could mean a weak race, and the council would not allow that.

I hated this part. My belly was tied up in knots because I had no control. No strategic training, cunning mind, or physical strength would matter here, it was up to fate and your blood. Rumor had it that if you didn't do well in this round you were automatically booted by the council. They would not tolerate a weak heir. I'd seen the vortexes rip a submissive wolf in half. It was nothing to be messed with.

"Arianna?" Calista had been saying something.

I shook my head and traipsed into the bathroom to brush my teeth and get ready.

"Sorry, I'm nervous," I said.

Calista smiled one of her all-knowing smiles. "I was there the day you were born. I saw your heir test. You will be fine."

That was news to me. I knew Calista had known my mother and the Red Queen very well. She'd been friends with the sisters, and since the Red Queen never had any children, she had decided to go with me as her charge. I was the closest related heir to my aunt. But I didn't know she was present at my birth. The mere thought of it brought a pang to my heart. I missed my mother. She died when I was fifteen, just one year before my inheritance. Fifteen is the age when a girl really needs her mother, I'd gone through so much, growing up so fast. Calista basically raised me and my baby sister. As I brushed my teeth, I focused on the mirror before me. Fierce turquoise eyes peered back at me and I saw glimpses of my mother. Despite the fact she'd had brown hair and eyes, some of our features were very similar. She hadn't been perfect, but she'd been mine, and I wished so much she hadn't died.

"You look a lot like Jesinda."

I was convinced Calista could read minds sometimes.

"I miss her," I murmured as I dropped my toothbrush back into its cup before rinsing my mouth out, and then drying off with a hand towel.

"She would be proud," Calista said, and I nodded. My mother told me at a very young age that being a queen was the greatest gift to our people; we were the lifeblood of an entire race. Yes, I would win this. I would be crowned. I would make my mother proud. I might not enjoy the politics of being queen, but competition was in my blood.

Dressed again in the red shirt of my house, I ate breakfast in my suite. I was glad there were no political duties for me this morning, I wanted to be able to focus, and since I'd spent most of the night mulling over the bear councilman's warning, I was nowhere near as rested as I hoped to be before this particular task.

Calista, intuitive as always, did nothing more than sit silently beside me. She'd already done my hair in its intricate crown braiding, so now all that was left was fueling my body and following her to the main Summit room again.

We left the suite and made our way to the wide staircase. Ten guards descended first, leading the way, the other ten coming down behind us.

"How is everything in the Bronx?" I asked Calista as we walked. I was pretty much locked in here, but our advisors were able to stay in touch and make sure everything was okay in our territories.

She quickly filled me in on the news. "There have been four inter-territory disputes, but they were settled amicably. Only one dead, and two arms severed." It was good when they could sort these things out without an alpha involved. Wolves were hot-blooded and we had a lot of disputes. Being territorial was in our nature, and living in a city on top of each other stirred the inner beast.

Sometimes I had dreams of leading a small pack in the countryside away from the lights and taxi cabs, but I knew a huge part of me would miss New York. As much as I complained at times, I loved this city. The wolves would learn to deal. We always did. Living within the mecca was a great honor and we all knew that. Wolves who lived in the boroughs, were five times more powerful than wolves around the rest of the world.

Calista continued: "Investigations have already started into the magical beings who ambushed us at the portal. Your people are examining the body."

That had been my first question to her after finishing the political dinner. Finding out if we had any of the attackers still, and luckily we did. The female who had attacked Blaine had not survived. Her body had apparently been stored in the ice room of my building, locked down until I was able to get back to the Bronx and investigate. But now I was worried there wouldn't be time, so I told Calista to start a thorough investigation.

"Jimmy went in wolf form?" I double checked she'd managed to get the best. Jimmy was our pack's lead investigator and tracker. It also helped that he was a detective with the New York Police Department.

Calista nodded. "Yes, he went early this morning. The body is scenting as human, nothing more. We'll have to wait for Violet to test the remains in more magical ways. She should be back soon."

Human. There was just no way. Magic and human just did not go together. But that didn't necessarily mean the fae were involved. I mostly believed Gerald, but there was always a part of me that wondered if this entire thing wasn't a bear ploy. Only time would tell on that one. It was annoying me that I couldn't talk to Calista about the possibility of this body being fae. But Torine had made it very clear that I was to keep this information to myself for now. And since I wasn't queen yet, I couldn't really disobey his orders.

I would have to wait for my magic born to return.

Violet was extremely powerful. If anyone could ferret out information on the attackers, it would be her. I couldn't recall if I noticed anything unusual about our attackers in my dash to the portal. There had been so much chaos and blood around, not to mention we were right at the portal so my senses had been dulled by the power of the mecca. It drowned out everything else around us.

We were nearing the main floor, so I hurried with my next question. "How's Winnie?"

"She's fine. Skipping lessons, keeping her advisor busy. I called her an hour ago. She said she hates being locked inside. Actually used the word 'torture,' and said if you're in Manhattan she expects you to bring home Lombardi's pizza."

A brief burst of laughter unfurled from me. My firecracker of a sister was filled with sass and life. Winnie was obsessed with pizza. I swear that girl was an even pickier eater than I was. Every time we came to Manhattan she got Lombardi's.

"Have one of the guards hand deliver the pizza to her for dinner tonight," I told Calista, and she nodded, typing into her tablet.

Winnie lacked discipline, which was probably me spoiling her to overcompensate for the loss of our mother. Calista and I were the only parental figures she knew. Mother always said our father was a royal guard, someone chosen for his impeccable family line, strength, and prowess on the battlefield. But she'd never named him, and no man had ever stepped forward to claim us as his. Mother was traditional, only taking a lover for breeding purposes and not a mate.

He was probably here somewhere in the royal home, but I found myself extremely uninterested in knowing who he was now. Sure, I understood that he'd been used just for a strong dominant line, but I still expected his acknowledgement.

Selective breeding was not a life I wanted for myself; I would continue to fight against it no matter how many times I was told that the crown and magical mecca came first – our responsibilities came first. Heirs were required to breed with the strongest of males, and if I became queen, my match would have to be agreed on by the council. There was no such thing as a wolf king; he would only ever be known as my mate.

Stepping from the stairs we crossed the floor to the main hall. My guards closed in around me. We were not the only ones almost at the hall. Breanna was off to my right, and Selene to the left. All of us must have left our suites at the same time. For the most part we avoided elevators and used stairs to get around. Wolves were not that comfortable in small metal boxes, despite their necessity in skyscrapers.

Sucking in deeply, I rubbed my damp palms against my pants. *The next task.* It was time to focus myself.

Magical strength. Why couldn't the scrolls have said anything else – even the dreaded obstacle course – reportedly so difficult to finish that only about five heirs had ever managed it, the Red Queen being the last one. I would have preferred that. Magical strength had too many unknowns.

"We aren't allowed to enter this time," Calista said when we reached the double doors. "No one but the heirs and council, because it's dangerous to tap directly into the mecca like this. They don't want anyone getting hurt."

Swallowing hard, I nodded a few times. Then Breanna, Selene, and I entered, closing the doors behind us, leaving our advisors, familiars, and guards out there. They would stand and wait for us, no matter how long it took to complete this task.

The room was dimly lit, only a single flame flickering in the large hearth behind the council chairs. The council members all stood there, dressed in ceremonial robes, dark, with gold insignia.

Torine stepped forward. "Welcome, queen heirs. Let's make our way to the mecca connection. Please note that this is a secret, sacred space and you are not to tell any of what you have seen. This remains solely for heirs and council knowledge."

Okay, now I was both nervous and very curious. I liked to know about things, and it pleased me that this would be one secret the council no longer knew over us. Selene looked fine but Breanna was sweating. I looked around, unsure of where to go, when one of the council members went to the fireplace and reached for a book on the shelf. Instead of pulling the book out, he merely tipped it back, and with a whoosh of air the wall shifted and swung open to reveal a hidden doorway. Okay, that was so cliché, but still the coolest thing I'd ever seen.

Selene and I met each other's eyes. I wondered if mine held the same wide-eyed look of amazement as hers. Probably. As the council had said, these were the kind of secrets that only a select few knew.

The council made their way through first, one by one, and I wasn't sure what to expect when it was my turn, but there was only a short pathway to step along, and then we ended up in a large circular room.

The second I crossed the threshold a blanket of mecca magic saturated my skin and I had to take a moment to even out my breathing. Trying to adjust to this level of magic was not going to be easy for any of us. Eventually my heart rate slowed to an acceptable level.

Peering around, my hand covered my mouth to hide my gaping jaw. Before us was the most stunning bluish-purple crystal I had ever seen. Over three feet tall, it was pulsing with magic, an energy which I could feel knocking into my chest, making my heart jackknife inside of me. I took a staggered step toward it, wanting to be closer, even though I feared the magic it was emitting might tear me apart.

I saw that even the council was having trouble looking composed. They stuck to the walls, away from the center.

"What is it?" I asked, not even trying to hide my awe.

Torine looked the most calm of the councilman. "A mecca crystal."

Say what? I didn't even know such an object existed. At first I thought that was all the information he was going to impart, but thankfully he continued.

"This is actually a smaller version of the crystals which exist beneath each vortex point. It's here that the mecca concentrates its energy, connecting between the crystals. There are smaller versions scattered around the boroughs, hidden and powerful. This one was found in Central Park by the first wolf queen, Deandra the Splendid. It was hidden in a lake. She was tipped off after some humans fell in the water and were dismembered. The magic tore through their frail bodies within seconds, but the queen was able to deal with the power. She personally transported the crystal here herself, before taking the time to search out the others. Most of them are accounted for now, safely stored away where they cannot hurt others."

So many secrets, so many responsibilities that our leaders undertook and the rest of the packs were none the wiser. Knowledge of these stones was certainly not broadcast in our studies, not even to the heirs.

"What do we do?" Breanna asked breathlessly, swaying a bit on her feet.

Torine attempted to move off the wall, but as strain crossed his already ancient and lined face, he slumped back against it. "All you have to do is touch the crystal. You may go first, Breanna."

Breanna's face drained of color. It looked like she was sorry for asking. We all knew the Summit was dangerous, and heirs died during these trials. Now I understood why. This stone had torn humans to shreds, and merely being in the same room as it had my entire body all out of sorts. Seriously, if I was having trouble breathing ten feet away from this thing, then touching it would likely make me pass out. At least I'd get to see what happened with Breanna. I would be taking as many mental notes as I could.

The yellow heir just stood there stiff as a board, hands trembling. Selene groaned next to her and began walking forward.

"I'll go first. I'm not afraid." Her voice was loud and brassy, but I could hear the lie in the slight shakiness of her tone.

She strode across the hardwood floor easily at first, but when she was five feet from the crystal she began to slow; it looked like she was meeting resistance, almost as if she had to swim through a thick jelly to get there. Finally, when she was inches from the thing, a multitude of emotions crossed her face: fear, wonder, amazement. She took a deep breath and placed her hand on the crystal before recoiling quickly as a pulse of power shot from it and her hair stood on end. Her mouth was opening and closing like a gaping fish out of water as she stared at her hand, which I now saw was glowing purple.

Torine nodded. "You passed. You may step back."

Selene needed no further encouragement. She all but ran back to the safety of the perimeter. My mind was scrambling. What made her pass? The hair standing up? Calista shouldn't have braided mine so tightly! The glowing fingers? I looked at her again and saw the purple hue that tinged her skin had faded.

Breanna looked determined now that Selene had survived. The test seemed short and simple. She stepped forward with a fierce look in her eyes, and despite seeming to struggle even more than Selene to cross the last few feet to the crystal, she made it through. With a triumphant smile she placed her hand on top.

The second her skin touched the crystal she cried out and grabbed her chest, crumbling to her knees. Something was wrong. This wasn't like when Selene recoiled. This was different. I raced forward and was shocked to find that a few feet from the crystal it felt like my feet had been submerged into quicksand. Trudging through the magic took true effort.

I finally made it to Breanna. She was a ball on the floor, crouched in on herself. There was so much magic in the air that I never realized she was mid-change until I flipped her onto her back. She was now a wolf, a very large, sable-colored beast with yellow markings along her nose and flank. The power of the crystal had forced her change, but not in the usual way. Breanna was barely conscious, and her wolf eyes were glassy, almost like nothing was there behind them. She was foaming heavily at the mouth, like a rabid animal.

"She failed," one of the council said from where he was positioned across from me, pressed tightly to the wall. "She may be an heir but she's not powerful enough to be queen. A true queen can utilize the crystal. Get her out of there if you want her to live."

I assumed that they couldn't step any closer to help me, and Selene was just watching from the sidelines as usual. Ignoring all the others, bending down I easily scooped up her heavy wolf body, trying not to trip on the clothing dangling from her. Making quick strides, I handed her off to a waiting council member, who carried her out of the room to seek medical treatment.

Then I faced the council. Well ... crap. That was a hard act to follow. If I was nervous before it was nothing compared to what I felt now. Yet some deep part of me was thrumming with excitement, as if the crystal was calling to me. My heart was pulsing in time with the energy coming off of the crystal.

"Please hurry, Arianna. We cannot be near it much longer," Torine said. As I peered closer at them I noticed their complexions were ashen, their faces glistening with sweat. I nodded and made my way over to the crystal.

We had a saying in our culture: you were either born to be a queen or you weren't. It was in your blood. Not every heir could be queen and now I understood why. And the fact that I had no control over this actually brought me a sense of relief. I could just let it go. Trudging back through the heavy magic, I let go of all expectations of the outcome. What would be would be.

My hand hovered a few inches from the crystal and I saw the tiny blond hairs on my arms standing up. It felt like the magic was seeking me, searching for an outlet, and in that moment I *wanted* to touch it, I *needed* to. With one last deep breath I reached out and placed my hand on the crystal. The second my hand wrapped around the cool shimmery stone, a hot mass unfurled within me. As if a well of energy had been caged inside of me and was now free. A fizzy burning encompassed my entire being.

The air around the crystal popped, and the crystal flared with magic then. Everyone else in the room gasped. I couldn't speak, couldn't even pay attention to them because I was too busy staring at the wall in front of me and the shimmery multicolored flowers that had appeared there. Like some mirage, the images swirled and changed, so fast I really couldn't tell what half of it meant. Red splashes, blue water, flashes of a land filled with green and life.

More of the energy filled me up and I wanted to place my other hand on the crystal, to hold it forever. I felt the power coursing through my veins and it was like I had drunk ten energy drinks.

My blood burned, and for some reason I felt the red lineage of my birth very strongly, the way I always did when I'd been close to the Red Queen. I would swear that some of her essence lingered in this room, in the power. Lilac. I could smell the lilac perfume she always wore.

"Enough!" Torine shouted, and broke through my trance. Dropping my hand, I turned to face them. The entire council and Selene were on their knees, panting, almost as if they were genuflecting to me. Each of their faces were a mix of expressions. Some held wonder, some awe. But there were more than a few creased in fear. The power of the crystal was still pulsing at me, calling to me, and I physically had to fight the urge to touch it again. When my eyes finally dropped down, I had to blink a few times to clear my sight. Was that ... my entire body was glowing in a purplish hue. Every part of exposed skin softly twinkled.

"You passed," Torine said, and just like that the second task of the Summit was done.

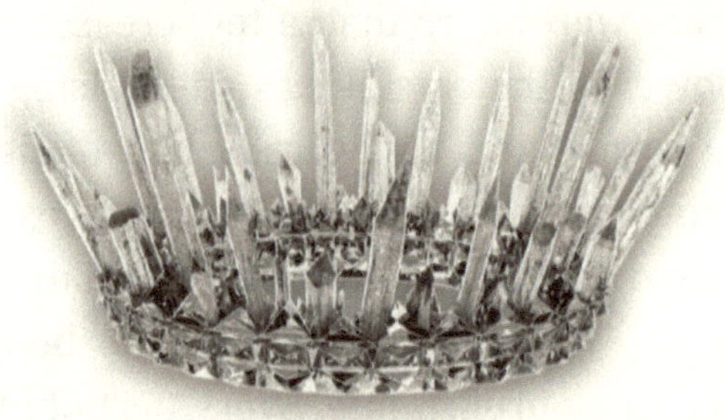

Chapter Five

Dangerous waters surround the Island.

AFTER THE TRIAL I was ferreted by Calista straight back to my suite. She'd wanted me to fill her in on everything that had happened, and I knew she hated that she hadn't been able to be in there. I wasn't supposed to share this with anyone, but I was so done with secrets. I could trust my advisor, and I was telling her.

Of course, then I had to try to put into words what had happened. How I'd felt. I wasn't sure there was any way to adequately describe it. I knew the mecca was powerful, but that had felt like so much more, almost as if it was the very essence of what kept the earth alive, that without it the entire world and universe would cease to exist. But that wasn't right. The magic gave us power but it wasn't the source of the earth's life. Right? My thoughts had been so clear when I was touching it, but now they just didn't make sense.

"Unbelievable," Calista said, when I finished my stumbling explanation. "Well, the entire castle is buzzing with news from the trial. The council are saying there's never been an heir who connected to the mecca the way you did."

I shuddered. "It was so weird, almost like it was projecting through me, sending messages and other information."

Calista was swiping through her tablet like a speed demon. Talking just as quickly as she ran through the information. "Breanna is okay, but she's been dismissed back to her borough. A failed heir. They are discussing whether she is strong enough to even remain as the alpha of her pack. Trial three is tomorrow. Since there are only two heirs left, the points are what is most important now. The higher your points, the more benefits in the final battle. Weapons. Magic. And all the rest. You have a reasonable lead at the moment, but you cannot let Selene take that from you. She's a formidable fighter, and completely devoid of honor. She'll do anything to kill you."

I started pacing, trying my best to listen to her advice. I knew I should be paying closer attention – this was all important information and I could easily be killed in the final battle – but the rush of blood inside of me was taking all of my concentration.

"Oh, and Violet has returned to the Bronx. She's examining the body of the female attacker who was killed at our vortex. She'll be here by nightfall to give us her thoughts in person. She said it's not safe to relay messages any other way."

My heart fluttered with joy. I missed my best friend so much. We were never apart for long, and I couldn't believe she'd been away when the queen fell and the Summit started. Beside the one allowance of the bear king's advisor, Gerald, the royal residence was locked down to new people. Which wouldn't matter much to Violet, no one stopped magic born from doing whatever they wanted. Only the queen had any hope, and right now we were missing one of those.

"We should go over fighting strategies, practice with multiple weapons," Calista said, and I was just nodding as a crushing exhaustion hit me, like I hadn't slept in a week.

As my head fell, I tried to grasp onto my energy and I realized I could still feel the mecca inside of me, filling my blood and somehow draining my energy. How was it doing this?

"Sure ..." My voice was dreamy. "After my nap." I shuffled back to my room, passing a bewildered Calista. I wasn't one to really take naps, but ever since entering the Summit I'd been so damn tired. Maybe this sort of magical drain had been going on for a lot longer than I thought.

I didn't even have the energy to kick off my shoes, the second my head hit the pillow I was out. My sleep was peaceful at first, but then flashes of images started haunting me.

Fields of beautiful flowers as far as the eye could see ... I was running through them like a carefree child but then I dreamt of my Red Queen's white lynx covered in blood. So much blood. That's when the flowers began to die and I felt like I couldn't breathe. My heart was breaking. So much pain.

"Arianna!" I felt a light smack on my face.

I gasped, sitting up. Calista stood over me holding her knife, eyes wild.

"What?" I surveyed the room for a threat.

Calista didn't speak for a moment and just stared at me. Finally she relaxed, putting her dagger back into her boot. "You were whimpering, moaning, then you screamed. I ... your skin was glowing purple. I thought it was a magic spell dream. I called Violet. ..."

I swallowed hard, throwing the sheets off. My limbs were trembling as I inspected my skin, which now looked fine.

"Not a magic dream, just ... a dream."

Calista didn't seem convinced. And I wasn't so sure either. It wouldn't be the first time rival magic users had possessed queens in their sleep. And there had been slivers of eeriness to that dream, but I was still sure it had not been from any of the magic born.

I stood, meeting her eyes, my limbs solid again, the last vestiges of the dream dissipating from my mind. "I'm fine," I said firmly, and let my alpha power leak out the tiniest bit. "I'm sure it's just an overflow of all the mecca energy I absorbed today. It was bound to affect me in some way."

She lowered her head, relaxing a tiny bit. "Still, I would feel better if you saw Violet."

My heart perked up. "Is she here?"

Calista nodded. "You've been asleep for four hours. When I couldn't wake you–"

A grin lit up my face. Seeing Violet was exactly what I needed. "Where is she?" Technically, she wasn't allowed in the castle until the Summit was over. Not just because of the lockdown, but also because this was still Sabina's magical territory.

"On the roof waiting for you," Calista said.

I tore out of the room and opened my front door. Ten of my guards stood at attention in the hall. They straightened even more when they saw me.

"Ben, Victor, Derek, I need you to accompany me to the rooftop, please." Those three of my dominants stepped out of line and nodded.

"Your Highness, three is not enough," Monica said, her voice strong but respectful. She was the overprotective one and I appreciated it.

I leaned in to whisper, "I'm meeting Violet."

That was all that needed to be said. She stood back against the wall and nodded. No one would get the drop on me with Violet around. She was the most powerful magic born we had ever seen. I didn't want to take all of my guards and make a big scene with a large procession gallivanting through the halls. I was hoping for a stealth mission to the rooftop and back with no witnesses.

Ben took position in front of me and Derek stepped in line to my right as Victor slipped in behind me. Now that the heat of Derek's arm was pressed to mine, I was kicking myself for this awkward lineup. Derek and I had had a summer fling two years ago and I broke it off because I just didn't feel the spark that I thought you should with a mate or life partner. I could tell from the way he looked at me and stepped in line next to me that he wasn't over it. He was gorgeous and one of my best hand-to-hand fighters, as dominant as they came, but when it wasn't there it just wasn't there. You can't force love, it just happens, right?

I forced myself to focus as we traversed the halls. Ben wouldn't have taken the lead if he hadn't memorized the entire layout of the castle. Ben was my smart one and I had no doubt he'd stayed up all night learning at least five different evacuation points in case of an attack. After getting into the empty elevator and using a key, we took a short ride to the top floor. The doors opened to reveal the beautiful rooftop patio.

I had only been here a handful of times for various parties and meetings the Red Queen hosted. The perfectly trimmed tall hedges were designed to provide complete privacy, even if there weren't many prying eyes at this height. My favorite part was the way the small white string lights reflected on the travertine floors. It was magical, and if I became queen it would all be mine. Although, I wasn't sure I really needed anything this luxurious – don't get me wrong, I loved the finer things in life – but at times it all seemed a little excessive. But it was part of the royal life and I didn't get a choice. The royal residence had stood in this spot for over a century, and would be here for hundreds more.

My guards fanned out, doing a sweep of the deck before allowing me to step fully out into the open. I knew Violet would not be seen until she wanted to. Once my guards came back and told me that no one was here, I instructed them to stay put and stepped out into a more private area, though still where the guys could see me.

Taking a deep breath, I exhaled using the unique whistle code that Violet and I had made up when we were twelve. We had been heavily loaded up with sugar after eating a pint of chocolate ice cream each, and decided we needed a secret call. We still used it today.

Poof. Right before my eyes Violet appeared.

"Jesus, Vi! You scared me." I'd been expecting it. She was nothing if not a master of the sudden appearance, but my body involuntarily reacted. She grinned, quite pleased that she could still catch me unawares like that. Violet was sadistic at times. She loved scaring me.

Stepping a little closer I couldn't stop a true smile from ripping across my face. She looked radiant as usual, wearing a purple silk medieval dress. Violet loved the Renaissance times and dressed like she had just left one of their weekend fairs. We stood at almost the same height, although her wild white mane of hair made her seem a tad taller.

For the first time in days I felt at peace. Violet had always soothed the energy inside of me, almost like we were synced somehow. She still hadn't said anything. Her eyes, the palest of blues, only a shade above white, were staring so hard it was as if she was trying to look through me. Her eyes widened then, and as she lifted a hand toward me it glowed softly in the dusky light. There was an odd expression on her face.

"Ari, your energy has changed … I've never seen this much magic on a person before. You're lit up like a vortex." Violet was never one for subtlety, and I appreciated it, but she had me worried.

I felt fine after my nap, but there was still some of the mecca moving beneath my skin. Actually, fine was probably a lie. I felt amazing, strong and powerful, like I could actually do magic or something. My energy was all over the place, as high as a kite one minute and the next back in the dirt.

Violet narrowed her eyes on me. "What happened? You need to tell me everything."

"Firstly, tell me about the one who attacked us in the Bronx. Was she a spelled bear?"

Violet's eyes darkened, and she stared straight at my forehead, like she could see the honor marks, despite them being washed off yesterday. "Human, Arianna. No matter what way I tested her the end result was human. Not bear. Not wolf. And not magic born. In truth, her energy was very hard for me to find, and if she had been spelled before – during the attack – it was gone by the time I got to her."

Dammit! Violet had been my best hope to figuring out this entire mystery. Could the bear advisor be right? Could all of this be the fae, and were they actually strong enough to hide from Violet's brand of magic? Why would the Tuatha de Danann start to interfere on Earth again?

Violet stepped even closer to me and I knew she was waiting for my part of the story. Lowering my voice so no nearby shifter could overhear, I quickly detailed everything that had happened, from the moment I woke to the toll of the bells, to the mecca crystal, and the dream I'd just had. I held no information back, except for the specifics about the fae. That information was still too new and shocking for me to truly comprehend. Plus I felt it was unwise to risk Torine hearing about my disregard of his order. No doubt the council would find a way to disqualify me from the Summit. So for now the fae information would remain secret.

As Violet pondered my story I took in her unique beauty. When we were kids she tried to make her white eyelashes black with mascara, and we even tried putting base makeup on her face to counteract her paleness, but all it did was make her orange. Eventually she accepted her uniqueness, and other than a hint of shimmering eye shadow and pinkish lip gloss, she was all natural: long silky hair so white it looked like a wig, skin the color of porcelain, and arresting crystalline white-blue eyes, so mesmerizing.

She took my hand, surprising me. Violet wasn't much for physical touch. She took on too much of the person's emotions and baggage. She only ever touched me, and it was still rare.

After a moment she dropped my hand. "When the queen fell I immediately went into a meditation," she said.

Meditation to Violet could mean anything. My guess was that she had astral traveled here to New York to see what was going on. I still didn't know all that she was capable of. Most of it had no easy explanation, and I think sometimes her abilities scared her, so she wouldn't speak of them. I nodded for her to continue.

"What I saw... the entire world dimmed, like a light had gone out."

That made sense. The queen held the mecca for all of the shifters. When she died the power dimmed, and now it was leaking everywhere.

"BUT..." Violet put up a finger. "Then it flared. It flared to life so hugely that I was kicked out of my meditation. Now..." She spun around looking at the city, seeing a world of energy that I couldn't see. Then she faced me, seeming more serious than ever before. "Now it's HUGE. It's bigger than before. It's everywhere."

I furrowed my brow in confusion. Okay ... I wasn't sure what to say about that, but Violet and I had not been alive the last time a queen had fallen, so maybe that was normal.

As if she read my thoughts she shook her head. "I've read the magical history books. It's never happened before. The past magical users always recorded that the mecca dies down with the death of the queen and only rights itself after coronation."

I looked around at the unseen energy that she spoke of. "Is it dark, this new energy? Do you think it can harm me? Or anyone else? We basically touched the mecca today, and it was so much bigger than I'd expected."

Maybe Calista was right and I had been magically cursed. But Violet shook her head immediately. "It's the purest light I have ever felt, and I can't be sure of course, but you are connected to it, and in a way I've never even seen with the Red Queen."

My mouth dropped open. Before I could speak I heard a door slam and I turned to see Selene and a single guard walk outside giggling and holding hands. The second she saw me she threw her guard's hand away and stood at attention, her snake coiling around her arm. Typical Selene. Not even the Summit could make her keep it in her pants. Sure, shifters are hot-blooded and highly sexual, but come on, there's a time and place for that.

I turned, but knew what I would find. Violet was gone and I was left with more questions and worries than I had before.

A glint on the ground caught my eye and I smiled, picking it up. A button. I had never left New York City. Heirs were not allowed, so whenever Violet was made to travel she brought me back a souvenir. I had them from all over the world. Now I had a *Mind the Gap* button from London. Everyone needed a best friend like Violet.

"Missed you," I whispered into the night air, hoping it would carry to wherever she was.

When I turned back around, my three guards were there and so was Finn. Selene continued to glare at me until we stepped into the elevator. As the doors closed I reached down and scratched Finn behind the ears where he liked it. He wouldn't do it in front of my guards, but if we were alone his back leg would be twitching.

Where did you go? I had a crazy dream Calista couldn't wake me from, I told him.

He looked up at me with his wise eyes. *I know. I was stuck in there with you.*

I frowned. *My dream? Do you always see my dreams?*

Never, he replied calmly.

I sighed. Another worry to add to the list of things I didn't want to think about right now.

"Poker night?" I asked my guys as the elevator descended. They all grinned. I needed to have some fun tonight. And possibly a bottle of red wine. But I knew Calista wouldn't allow that. Not during the Summit.

"One game of poker. Do you hear me? ONE GAME," Calista said as we crowded around the table thirty minutes later; Monica was dealing.

Three hours later, Calista was clutching her cards tightly, staring at Ben with a perfect poker face. I grinned. I loved seeing Calista like this, with her guard down and having fun. No wine for me but tons of chili cheese fries and poker. At 11pm my advisor finally kicked everyone out and we wished each other a good night. The way her eyes tracked me back to my room I knew she was worried for me. We didn't know what tomorrow's task would be yet. It could even be the final battle if the council decided to hurry things along. Which meant tomorrow might be the last day of my life. At least I'd had one last night with my pack.

That night I had a dreamless sleep, and woke early to the smell of bacon. Calista knew how to get this heir out of bed. Food. Every time.

I showered quickly so my hair would have time to air dry, and when I came out to have breakfast was delighted to see Violet sitting at the table with Calista.

Violet got right to the point. "You think Selene is banging that guard?"

I laughed. There was no protocol with Violet. She would never bow to me, never call me "Your Highness," and I loved her for it. She was the one normal in my life. I saw Finn under the table and Violet's bare feet stroking his back. She was the only person he ever let touch him except for me. He told me once that her touch was akin to feeling buzzed or drunk. Blissful. It made me wonder if Finn had ever gotten drunk.

"Totally. Who isn't Selene banging?" I said with a shake of my head.

Calista huffed at us. "Your language is unbecoming of an heir and future queen."

Violet grinned and blew air in Calista's face, who was sitting directly to her left.

Calista looked alarmed and started rubbing her ears. "Don't do that!" she shouted frantically.

"What did you do, Vi?" I scolded her as Calista became more panicked.

Violet rolled her eyes. "I'm just playing. I took her hearing so she didn't have to listen to us being unbecoming."

I choked on my laugh. "Give it back. You know she hates magic."

Calista was like family to Violet. She would never harm her, but she definitely liked messing with her. Leaning forward, Violet blew in her face again and Calista glared at her.

"Just playing, Cal," Violet said. Then Calista did the most awful thing you could do to a person – she stole the bacon off Violet's plate and popped it in her mouth, grinning. Violet just winked. They totally loved each other.

"So what's on my agenda today? Go for a little stroll in Central Park? Do some shopping? Fight for my life?" I realized then that I was nervous. This was becoming a daily occurrence. But with the crown so close now, the pressure was really on.

Calista cleared her throat. "The council has decided that there is to be one more task before the final battle – which will probably be tomorrow."

Violet pulled a small object from her pocket. "Or it could be tonight. Which is why I'm here now." She placed a glass vial on the table. It had an ornate gold stopper, and the fluid inside glowed with a purple hue.

"What's that?" I asked her. Knowing Violet, it could be anything. Violet only needed four hours of sleep a night. She had way too much time in the day and was always making potions and practicing her spellcraft.

Violet leaned in closer: "Besides what their points give them, heirs are allowed to bring one weapon of their own into the final fight. It needs to be this."

Calista spit her water out, spraying the table. "You expect me to let her go into a fight to the death against Selene carrying a tiny glass vial! You're mad!"

Violet stood, her chair skidding on the tile floor, and faced me. "You know how I get those feelings?" she asked me.

Oh lord. Here we go. If Violet had gotten one of her "feelings," there was no way I could talk her out of this.

I indicated the vial. "What is it, Vi?"

She swallowed roughly, getting herself under control. "It's anti-venom for Selene's familiar."

I opened and closed my mouth a few times, words failing me. Larak was one of my biggest worries. He had been known to kill with one bite, and familiars were allowed to fight in the final battle. If Violet had a "feeling" I might be bitten, then I needed to listen.

"How did you get it?" As far as I knew there was no anti-venom for the magical snake, unless…

Violet grinned. "Last night, after you left the roof and Selene was busy with that guard, I took a little sample of the slimy creep's venom and spent all night making this tincture."

Took a little sample? One did not simply take a sample of Larak's venom. She must have magically bespelled the reptile and sucked it from the fangs.

I didn't even know how that was possible. No one understood the magic borns' powers. They didn't have wands or crystal balls. They simply were able to manipulate the mecca energy. Sometimes things worked for them, other times it didn't. But besides the queen they were the only ones who could utilize the mecca.

"Are you sure this is not going to backfire on you and somehow put your life in danger?" I was very serious as I faced my best friend. I was standing now too, my wolf demanding I get up.

Violet just chuckled. "Of course not. You know me. I always cover my tracks."

We remained in a stare-off for many minutes, but as always her eyes were eventually too intense to stare directly into – which she used to her advantage often, declaring herself the stare-off winner every time.

Finally I sat. "Okay." I breathed and clutched the vial to my chest like a life preserver. Going into a final battle with no weapon wasn't exactly smart, but it wasn't the first time. I'd once won a dominance fight using a brick I'd picked up off the ground. I could be scrappy if I needed to be, and I was one of the best at disarming and stealing weapons. Violet wouldn't press this upon me if she didn't think with total certainty that I would need it.

Plus, if I won the task today, I would probably have enough points to be granted an additional weapon. Which was all I needed.

Violet disappeared again when the guards arrived to let us know we were needed in the main Summit hall. It was time for the third task. Not knowing what to expect, I dressed in my red uniform, cuffs on, weapons hidden about my body, my hair in its traditional braid crown. The snake anti-venom was tucked away in the safe inside my room. Selene or her familiar wouldn't risk attacking me until the final battle. It would be too easy to trace it to her and she would be executed for treason. That's why we had rules about attacking heirs during the Summit. In the early years, plenty of the heirs were killed in the first few days. Sneak attacks. Which was not how it was supposed to work. A true queen won through trial, not because she was the sneakiest and most underhanded. There was no honor in winning like that, and the council was all about honor. My people remained close as we made our way through the mansion's maze of floors and halls. I never saw any of Selene's dominants or guards; she was probably late again.

Sure enough, as I stepped into the huge room, many of our pack members were already gathered but no purple heir was in sight. The council members were standing in their usual spot, the white magic born of Manhattan at the forefront.

Sabina gave me a gentle nod, and I was reminded of how different she was to Violet. My friend had rough edges, and was sometimes hard to handle, but her heart was pure gold. Sabina was refined and smooth, like a diamond polished to perfection, but there was also a coldness that lingered beneath her skin, like sometimes she let the power control the shifter and not the other way around. She was a lot older than Violet, at least a hundred years if the gossip was true. She'd been the Red Queen's friend, and I wondered how she was containing her grief.

My group had paused on the edge of the dais. Torine noticed me there and waved me up to stand with them. Calista and I exchanged a single look before she gave me a nod and I was on my own. With a deep breath I strode forward and took my rightful place at the head of the council, Finn by my side. I wasn't quite queen yet, but there was something in faking it until you made it. I needed the extra boost of confidence, especially after Violet's revelations about the mecca. The buzz of energy beneath my skin was almost unnoticeable today, but I still felt different. Restless.

Sabina was still staring at me. Could she see the mecca's changes also? Was she also wondering why I seemed to be connected to it?

The magic born almost looked like she was going to approach me, but thankfully Selene chose that moment to enter the room, her entourage of twenty making a big show of pushing shifters to the side so she had a clear path.

"Nice of you to join us, Selene," a council member reprimanded her. "Kindly hurry yourself to stand with Arianna. We have a task to get underway."

The slightest of pink tinged her cheeks and I could almost see the retort she was holding back. She didn't waste any more time, though, reaching my side in seconds. She could haul butt when needed.

Someone other than Torine took the floor this time, Glenda, the second oldest of the queen's council. "Thank you all for being here. This could be one of the most important trials of them all." She had a commanding presence – her hair a deep carrot red, her eyes bronze – and a no-nonsense attitude. She had been my tutor for a short time in my youth.

"Sabina, if you could do the honors," she said, turning to the magic born. "It's time for the gods and the mecca to decide on the final task before the battle. The points that will be earned today will be instrumental in ensuring weapons and other advantages for one heir in the final battle."

The magic shifter wasted no time, unleashing her power and repeating her actions from the previous time she'd called the scrolls forth. Glenda was the one to stare out into the high ceilings, and eventually call a scroll down to her. It felt like she took years to finally unroll it and read from the parchment.

"Scavenger hunt through the Island," she shouted out into the large room. All of our people erupted into conversation, some cheering and others groaning. I swallowed roughly, and wiped my damp palms on my pants.

This wasn't one of the worst tasks, but it wasn't an easy one either. It would require us to leave the boroughs and head to the Island, alone, no guards or help from outside sources.

The Island, a stretch of land below Brooklyn and Queens, was technically a neutral zone. This was where we held most peace Summits, with one side of the land containing a residence for the wolf queen and the other side a mansion for the bear king. There were often bears there, which could be a worry right now. The fact that we had no queen, the mecca appeared to be leaking, fae might or might not have been involved in all of this, and the bears were still not to be trusted ... led me to believe this could be far more dangerous than a simple scavenger hunt.

"Heirs," Glenda said, "you have ten minutes to prepare yourselves. You're allowed as many weapons and as much food as you can carry, but do not weight yourself down too much. There is a single item that has been hidden away. The first to retrieve it wins. You have twenty-four hours to complete this task."

Noise erupted again and I quickly hurried down to find Calista and my guards. My advisor pounced on me immediately. "I've already sent some of your people back for supplies and weapons. You need to spend the next ten minutes studying this map closely." She whipped up her tablet and I could see quite a detailed map of the Island. There were plenty of landmarks, and I knew some of them might come in handy.

I had always been a quick study, and I had been to the Island plenty of times, although the trip in my fifteenth year stood out the most. Nothing like your first kiss from a bear to really get your heart pumping. I still hated that it affected me so much. At fifteen he'd been small and not at all intimidating. He'd also been kinda charming, and very funny.

I pushed the memories aside, needing to focus. No matter how many times I tried to forget that bear, every time the Island ever came up I was thrown back to that night, to the summer festival, the stars, the warmth of his lips on mine...

Focus, Arianna!

My eyes ran across the map multiple times. I used techniques I'd learned from Calista to imprint the image in my mind. She had a naturally photographic memory. For the rest of us, we had to do what we could.

"Take note of exit points in case of ambush," Calista whispered. "Water sources, if you need to hide your scent."

She continued on and on, pointing out everything. I had noted most of this already, but this was another one of her techniques. Apparently talking things out loud, or listening to someone else doing it, jogged the brain. I'd be more inclined to actually remember what was said rather than what I saw on the paper.

"Three minutes," Glenda said, her voice echoing across the crowd.

My head spun to the entrance, relief coursing through me as two of my guards dashed into the room. They held a medium-sized backpack, the sort which strapped across my waist and chest, and would be secure when I ran.

"We gathered just a few energy bars, water, and some other first aid supplies," Monica said. "Weapons include two guns, two blades, and a few other smaller pieces. The pack should not be too heavy for a full day of movement."

I nodded my thanks, taking only a second to zip the compartment open and assure myself of the inventory. It wasn't that I didn't trust my people, I mostly did, but as an heir I could never be too careful.

Once I slipped the pack on, Calista helped me tighten it across my chest, and then it was time to move out. I knelt quickly to hug Finn. He would remain behind; there were to be no familiars on this journey.

Stay safe. I will come if you need me, no matter what the rules say. He nuzzled into me, his giant form blocking out all those around me. *If anyone hurts you, I will kill them.*

I got your back too, friend. Stay safe while I'm gone, I told him.

One last hug and then I had to leave him. It was kind of painful to know he couldn't actually be with me for this task. I'd bet Selene was struggling even more. She was never away from Larak. The two of us followed Glenda and Torine from the royal mansion. The other heir also wore a backpack, although hers was larger and quite a bit bulkier, which probably meant she had a ton more weapons and supplies than me, but she'd also tire faster and be hindered more in pursuit situations. It was hard to know what was right, because at the moment we didn't know what the item was. Or where on the Island it might be located. The council was sure to make it difficult, but how difficult was the question.

The streets of Manhattan were busy, humans scurrying about without a single clue of the trials going on in the shifter world, a world that existed beside their own. We had to pass by the industrial building that magically hid our mecca, and as the energy closed around me my pulse elevated and my eyes closed. The mecca was so strong, calling to me, and I wanted nothing more than to step into its energy.

"Are you okay, Arianna?"

This was the first time Glenda had acknowledged me in a familiar way since the beginning of the Summit. It wasn't good form to show any sort of favoritism toward one of the heirs. No council member should show preference.

"Yes, just ... the mecca feels quite strong. I thought the queen's death would weaken our power until the balance was restored."

Glenda and Torine exchanged a single glance, one which was filled with creased eyes and furrowed brows, but then both of their expressions wiped clear as if they were completely unconcerned.

"It'll all be back to normal once the new queen is crowned," Torine said, trying to act all fatherly as he patted mine and Selene's arms. "The power is searching for the link to it and our people."

Yeah, we were totally getting the "all is well" speech, and even Selene seemed to know it. The council should be filling us in on whatever was going on, it was going to be one of our problems very soon. But no. As always they liked to keep information within their little group.

I managed to push thoughts of the mecca aside as we strode further from it. The energy seemed to have attached itself to me, but eventually the tingly sensation died off and I forced myself to focus on the task. I had to find the hidden item on the Island because I was determined to go into the final battle with every advantage.

We reached the second royal garage – the main one was within the queen's residence – but none of her vehicles could be used during the Summit; they were all being investigated. In fact, all of them would be replaced before the next queen took power, like a clean slate. A driver was already standing beside a limo and I recognized him as a member of the royal guard.

Selene and I paused, waiting for final instructions from the two council members.

"Here are the details of your task," Glenda said, handing a rolled scroll to me, and then one to Selene. "Do not open it until you arrive on the Island. The task officially begins when you step foot onto land. Once you are there, none of us will be keeping track of you. This is a race to be the first back with the item. That person is the winner for this task, no matter what happens during your time on the Island, so take care. Avoid humans as much as possible, because they do populate the area. Good luck."

Great, so if we were ambushed by bears or some other enemy, no one would know.

Here's hoping the council had a bunch of "of age" heirs secretly stashed away, because they were down to two here, and who knows if either of us would survive the next few days.

Nothing more was said as we entered the vehicle, Selene and I choosing to sit at opposite ends, both of us staring out the window. It would take us a bit of time to make it through the traffic of New York and reach the Hudson River, where the private docks were. This was where the royal ferries were moored. Plenty of time to think and wonder what I was going to find when I opened the scroll clutched in my right hand. What impossible task had the council set for us?

Chapter Six

A bear load of trouble.

THE BOAT TRIP took a long time, but eventually it arrived at the Island, dropping us right onto the beach. Selene took off in a flash, and I knew she was hoping to get away from me so she could read the task and formulate a plan without me following. Like I would follow her anyway – I preferred to think for myself. As the sand squished under my boots, I took a second to inhale the salty air. This place was beautiful, an oasis of sand, salt and sun. I could see no one around me, and felt safe to unroll the scroll. Holding it between both hands, I quickly ran my eyes over the slanted writing across it.

Enter the bear king's mansion on the island and retrieve the miniature mecca crystal stashed there, usually near one of his advisors. Use cunning. Use stealth. If you are captured, your life is forfeit to the bears.

Holy shifter babies. Was the council for real? Did they want to start a war? Both the bears and the wolves had multimillion-dollar mansions on the Island. It was the one place we could be in peace and meet at the yearly accords or the summer festival without bloodshed. This would ruin all of that if Selene or I were caught, especially because we were both armed to the gills.

What would Calista do? I ran through all strategies in my mind. How far to the bear king's mansion on foot? Were there any holidays or occasions that would mean the bear king himself was in residence? I didn't even know what he looked like. Gerald was the first bear I had met in years.

I focused my breathing as a plan came into mind. Adjusting the straps on my backpack, I took off running toward the large blue beachside residence perched atop the cliff. The bear king's mansion was on the opposite side of the Island to the wolves' residence. It was a steep hike on foot but I would be fine. Was Selene ahead of me? It didn't matter. I just needed to focus on getting the job done. As I reached the thicker trees that signaled I was heading in the right direction, I saw two friendly humans coming out of a hike. They smiled at me.

"Great weather," one of them said.

"Mmmhmm," I replied, and smiled, walking past them quickly.

Humans found it difficult to be in my presence for too long. As an alpha, the power of my wolf made them feel uneasy ... threatened. Then add in that I was an heir and the small connection to the mecca within me was enough to make them sick if they remained in my presence too long. Once a human woman on the train had vomited right at my feet. She'd sat too close to me for an hour-long ride. Since then I avoided public transportation. Submissive wolves were sent to deal with any human drama. They were tolerated much better by the humans.

It was a brisk hour-long hike before I finally reached my entry point to the bears' residence. I decided to go the more difficult of routes, which I knew was less guarded than some of the others. Of course, this required me to rock climb up a massive cliff, which would bring me to the back of the mansion, which faced the water. This section of the building was pretty much floor-to-ceiling windows. I'd have a clear view of how many bears were inhabiting the place. If I'd have taken the front entrance, which was where their cars were parked, I would have had to deal with a multitude of guards, and a ten-foot-tall electrified fence.

So cliff face it was. I climbed silently but with swift movements. It still took me at least twenty minutes to scale up, and as I reached the edge I popped the very top of my head up to see over. The immediate area looked clear, so in one rapid movement I launched myself up and over onto the flat ground. Without pause, I rolled myself across to take cover under a large fragrant rose bush.

Letting myself catch my breath, I slowly unhooked my backpack, going over my next moves in my head. My plan was somewhere in that fine line of genius or completely crazy. Removing the knife from my boot, I slipped it into my bag and then covered the entire pack with greenery. My bag was now camouflaged ... and I was about to infiltrate the bear king's Island mansion unarmed. I was hoping it was the right choice, because the reality was that if I was caught and it looked like I had any intention of harming the king's people, I would be put to death straight away. If I were weaponless and simply looked like a spy or thief, I might keep my life. I think the council would appreciate my thinking on this – trying not to incite a war. I doubted Selene was so thoughtful.

Oh man, I missed Finn. He'd have been able to scout around for me. Despite his massive size, if he didn't want to be seen, he wasn't. Not able to stall any longer, I slowly inched my head up and surveyed the home. The estate was far back on the property, but from my current location I could see two men inside the living room. The double back doors were open, white gauze curtains flowing in the wind, letting the sea breeze into the house.

Were those the bear councilmen? My council had directed us here and said the mecca crystal was near one of these bears. So hopefully I'd luck out and find it on my first go. The backyard appeared to be empty, and there was a lot of foliage scattered about that should give me cover on my way to the mansion. Just as I was about to dash across, I saw Selene lying on the roof, inching forward in an army crawl. Dammit!

Wasting no time, I sprung from my bushy hideout and hit the ground, staying flat as I crawled my way beneath plants and trees. I wanted so badly to shed my clothes and shift to my wolf. To have her nose and her eyes ... her instincts. But it would be much harder for me to retrieve the crystal, and shifting took time and would leave a magical trace that could easily be detected. I couldn't risk it.

I crawled slowly along the perimeter, not caring that I was covered in sand and dirt and had a small cut on my elbow. My plan was to get to the side of the house and then sneak in through a window. I was pleased to find that the closer I got to the house, the more I felt ... a tingle, a magical beacon. The mecca crystal, no matter how small, was calling to me.

I inched closer until I reached the side of the house, where there was a study visible through large double windows. I could see full bookshelves; the window was cracked open. That was my entrance. Rolling out from under the bushes, I popped up and was almost at the side when a voice sent my entire plan crashing down.

"Well, well, what is a wolf heir doing on the bear king's property?" The voice was husky and deep and I was so royally screwed. Pun intended. I had been seen. If I ran, the guard would sound the alarm – I needed to talk my way out of this situation, running was not an option. Turning slowly, I opened my hands to show I wasn't armed. He already knew I was an heir, he must have recognized my insignia on my shirt, which would hopefully buy me enough time to plead my case.

Unfortunately, by the time I finished spinning to meet my fate, no plan had formulated in my head. Looks like it was the good old "wing it and hope for the best" plan. Some freaking queen I was going to make.

When the male came into view, I was a little taken aback. I'd expected it to be a guard, multiple guards actually, but it seemed luck might be on my side after all, because the giant of a bear standing shirtless before me was definitely not a guard. He seemed to be the gardener, right down to the pair of shears in his right hand, hanging non-threateningly at his side.

I took a second to admire the view. Because a view like this was made to be admired.

He was one of the hugest males I'd ever seen, topping out close to seven feet. He had heavily corded muscles and darkly tanned skin. Someone clearly used to being outdoors, lifting heavy stuff, swinging an axe ... maybe. With his wild dark hair and neatly trimmed but still sort of scruffy beard, he was every girl's woodcutter fantasy come to life. And his eyes, holy crap, his eyes were like molten copper, swirling as they remained locked on my face.

I realized I'd been standing there gawking like a pup with her first crush, and that was no way for a queen to act. I needed to talk my way past the gardener and then grab that crystal before Selene got there first.

He showed no discomfort to find a wolf casually strolling around his king's territory. His stance was relaxed, although his face and eyes were harder. He tilted his head to the side, and as those unique eyes caressed my features, the swirling depths deepened and his clenched jaw relaxed. His lips quirked into a smile.

"You," he whispered, and chills ran up my arms.

He said it like he knew me.

"I ... I'm unarmed, and this is not an act of war. Our queen fell and..."

He took three quick paces toward me and I tensed, readying myself for a fight. I didn't need weapons to kill a man. I'd done it with my bare hands many times. Despite the fact we were gifted dominion over our boroughs as heirs, you still had to prove yourself. You still had to be alpha enough. But this was one of the largest men I had ever seen. If he wanted me dead, there was no doubt he could make that happen.

He hadn't raised any alarm yet though, which gave me some sense of comfort. One on one was much better odds than the entirety of the king's army.

He cast me in shadow as he closed in, seemingly even more massive than he'd looked from across the way. My breathing slowed, every part of me focused on the incoming battle. Then he shocked the hell out of me.

"I never forgot that kiss," he said, his arm snaking out to curve around the back of my neck.

My brain tried to process his words and actions at the same time. What in all shifter gods was he doing? What kiss?

My next barrage of curses was hushed as the bear's surprisingly full lips crashed into mine. For a second the world stood still. I forgot who I was, what I was doing here, and the fact that hot-as-woodcutter-man was a bear. Energy sizzled between us, so intense that I was either going to collapse or drown if it didn't ease.

Desire like I'd never known unfurled in my chest and continued downward through my body. I fought for clarity, drawing on every piece of training I'd ever had in my life. He was a freaking bear, I was a queen heir, this could not happen! I started to growl, and just as I was about to bite his tongue off, he pulled back, grinning.

It was then that I realized exactly who the royal gardener was, why he acted so familiar with me. It had been the dimple that jogged my memory, a dimple that was barely visible within his dark facial hair.

"You…" My voice was hard, but still much breathier than I liked.

It was the same bear I'd kissed at fifteen on this very island. Of course back then he'd been only a little taller than me, and baby-faced. Now he was hard and all man. And he'd just kissed me … again. My right hand came up and smacked him solidly across the face. I'd practically had to jump to reach it, but it was still so satisfying.

He had no right to touch me, and I didn't appreciate the manhandling, no matter how satisfying the kiss was. In the back of my mind I was reminded of the wolf council's words: if we were caught here, we belonged to the bears, and they could do what they wanted with us. Yeah, not okay with me. No bear got to kiss me, or make my body ache – not allowed.

Unfortunately, my slap hadn't seemed to deter him. If anything, his eyes were twinkling as they continued to hold me captive. Over his shoulder a streak of purple caught my attention. Selene was running through the yard clutching a stone in her hand. *No!*

Dammit! This distracting, giant gorgeous idiot had just cost me the third task, and I still wasn't in the clear. Not only was Selene going to win the points and have the advantage in the final round, I was still stuck here at the mercy of a bear.

"Who's that?" I said, bringing the other heir to his attention.

With the smallest of smiles, he turned to stare straight in the direction Selene had dashed, as if he'd known she was there all along. In a burst of movement he took off after her, and he was fast.

"Wait right there," he called back to me, his voice low and gruff.

Yeah, for sure, woodsman. Idiot.

Without hesitation I took off, leaping across multiple obstacles and not letting up my pace one bit. I heard a shout, but there were no other sounds of pursuit; the gardener had chosen to run down Selene. I doubted he would catch her; she had a decent head start and was probably already halfway back to our meeting spot. I ran as fast as I could to the cliff face again, unearthing my pack and all but falling back down the cliff, getting a nasty gash in my left elbow. It would heal quickly though; I was more worried about being caught.

Luckily I did not see any more humans on my trek back to the meeting point. I was surely a disheveled mess right about now. When I reached the thick trees of the cherry grove, Selene was already waiting for me.

She had a leather pouch in her hand and was grinning from ear to ear. "Thanks for making out with that mammoth bear. You really gave me the extra time I needed to get in and out."

My blood boiled as disappointment and rage flooded through me. Now it looked like I was some stupid, hormone-driven wolf who couldn't keep it in her pants long enough to try and become queen.

"Not that I can blame you," Selene continued. "He was probably the hottest guy I have ever seen. Yummy."

"He attacked me!" I said, my voice hoarse.

Right ... crap. My mind knew the truth; he had initiated the kiss but I had liked it. For the love of all things shifter, why? I'd been attracted to that male when he was scrawny and underfed – and now ... definitely not scrawny. And where in all the hells was his shirt? Seriously, you can't just surprise a woman with a body like that and then kiss her. It just wasn't done.

I should have kicked him in the jewels; my slap was nowhere near harsh enough. Shaking it off, I followed the still-grinning Selene out of the woods. I knew by this point the advisors would be watching through Sabina. They would know she'd been the one to retrieve the crystal first, so I couldn't steal it from her. I had lost fair and square. Damn that bear!

"There is no point stressing yourself over this." Calista was trying to appease my anger while I took out my frustration on a boxing bag. "Things happen. Selene has the advantage in the final fight, but you are not without plenty of skills of your own."

Smack, smack, smack. Each thud was cathartic, right up until the bear's face flooded back into my mind. "It wasn't just that she won," I said, huffing between words. I wiped at the sweat coating my forehead, before spinning out and kicking the heavy weight. The bag swung out and back for my next kick. "I let him kiss me. I just stood there for at least thirty seconds and enjoyed every freaking second."

What was wrong with me?

Calista chuckled, and I immediately swung my head around to nail her with a glare. This was so not funny, and as my advisor she should be appalled by my actions. I was a queen heir to the wolves and he was a bear.

"Arianna, you're a hot-blooded female and it has been a long time since you had any sort of regular partner. You neglect that part of your body and life because of duty, but the blood of shifter queens run in your veins. You're sensual, and need someone to kiss you like that every single day."

I was no longer kicking the bag. She had caught me completely by surprise. I didn't know what to say. Calista was always nudging me to take a mate, to settle down and do the whole ... relationship thing. I grew up with a mother that chose a breeding partner for sperm so it hadn't exactly put the greatest example in my mind.

"Just next time, please ... not a bear, and not during the Summit." And my advisor was finally back. "I need your focus for just a little longer, we have a throne to win. And our strategy must be absolutely bulletproof for tomorrow. Selene cannot become queen. She is not worthy."

I rested both of my gloved hands against the bag, sinking into it as exhaustion washed over me. It had been a big day, but my stamina was usually better than this. For some reason I was just wrecked. Every day of being this close to the mecca was changing me. Its energy infiltrating my body.

"Has there been any word on the mecca?" I asked, lowering my voice. We were alone, my guards spread out the perimeter, but you never knew who was listening. "Every day it feels even stronger to me, more out of control."

Calista had her tablet out in a flash; that thing was pretty much an extension of her hand.

"Nothing official, and honestly, until Violet mentioned the change I never even noticed there was anything up. I can only just sense it now."

"It's so strong for me," I murmured, holding my hands out like I was actually running it through the power. It felt like it was swirling around me.

"Must be an heir thing," Calista said, shrugging.

I'd have asked Selene, except she was not my favorite person today, or any day really. I couldn't lose to her tomorrow. No matter what happened in the battle, I had to take her down. An entire race of wolves was counting on me. Not to mention I wasn't too keen on death.

Calista signaled to my dominants. "We should head back to the suite. I have a bunch of schematics to go over with you, and we should discuss all the possible scenarios for tomorrow."

I nodded, already unstrapping my wrists. My body ached, and I knew I'd pushed it too far. After arriving back to the main hall, and having to watch as Selene was awarded the points, gold, and spell book, I'd come straight down here. I must have been hitting the bag for two hours at least, and still tension rode my body.

Damn that bear.

Violet was in my suite's main dining room when we trooped in. A few of my dominants stopped to chat with her for a minute before settling into their normal positions. Poker was definitely on the table again tonight, but probably not for me. No doubt Calista would have me studying.

"Feel free to jump into the first few games," she said, shocking the hell out of me. "I need to discuss a few of the Summit rules with the council. They have to give me some more details about tomorrow. We'll get started when I return."

I was pretty much bouncing in my chair, and Violet threw back her head and snort laughed. "Girl, you are seriously like an excited puppy right now. Anything to get out of work."

I stuck my tongue out, in full queenly glory. "It's been a crappy day. I'm excited for a bit of fun before figuring out how not to die tomorrow." The logic and skills required in poker calmed me—or did until I was two margaritas in and Derek started suggesting we start playing strip poker.

As if he heard that thought, his eyes met mine.

Calista's words earlier had shaken me. She was right. I needed a relationship, a regular partner, someone I could depend on and trust. Why couldn't I feel the sort of passion for Derek that damn bear had made me feel with one stupid kiss? Derek would have been perfect as a partner. That was the reason I'd already tried to make it work. But to no avail. I just couldn't seem to be like my mother, or the Red Queen. I couldn't have the convenient male because it worked, I wanted more. I wanted epic. To feel every single emotion, even if some of those were dark and scary. Safe did not interest me. Love was huge and crazy, or so I had been told, and I wanted that.

Violet snorted again, before winking at me. The look on her face ... I was ninety percent certain she could actually read thoughts. She gestured for me to take my place at the table and we ended up with eight in for the first round. The rest of the guards were on duty, but would swap in and out through the night. Some would sleep and the others would gamble. Not much else to do while trapped inside this mansion, and it kept morale high.

I took a second to really see the shifters around me. I'd been so caught up in the Summit and the queen's death that I felt I'd barely had any time with my friends. My family.

First was Monica and Jen. Those two were dominant, best friends, and laugh-out-loud funny with their inappropriate comments. They even looked similar, both small, with ashy blond hair. Jen's eyes were gray, darkening to blue when she was angry, which was a lot more frequently than the more levelheaded Monica. She was both protective and calm. I always knew she'd keep a level head in any situation, and that's how she'd made it into my inner circle of guards.

Next to them were the triple threat. Ben, Derek, and Victor. Those three had each been adopted into a shifter family in the Bronx, and grew up as brothers, and were fiercely loyal. Derek was the most stunning of the three, with his multiple-hued hair and dark green eyes. He had all the attributes of a good mate: strong, alpha, respectful, intelligent, and brave. But I also found him lacking in some depth. I was an alpha and heir, I was used to people obeying my orders, but I knew the mate for me would have fight in him, would call me out on my crap, because sometimes I was completely full of it. Derek deferred to me a lot. I needed more than that, and was hoping it was out there, and not in any sort of bear-like shape.

Ben and Victor were like brothers to me. Those two were in the dirty-blond range, handsome and tall, but with less brawn and more brains than your average wolf. Each could definitely hold their own in any fight though. All of my dominants were highly trained, extremely intelligent, and had proven their loyalty to me more than once. I loved them all, and could only hope I would still be here next week to continue our poker nights.

The final of the six was Blaine. Very alpha, very dominant. He was the same age as me. His mom had been best friends with my mom, and together with Violet the three of us had wreaked havoc over the Bronx. I'd been missing his company lately.

He pushed back his auburn hair, letting it fall in disarray to his shoulders. "You need another haircut," I said, nudging him. "Although it's looking mighty pretty."

He shrugged off my good-natured ribbing, a grin shooting across his face as he dealt the next round of cards. "Don't think you're going to distract me with all your sweet talk, Your Highness. I don't care how close you are to being queen, I'm still taking all your money."

I returned his smile as everyone began to fight over whether Violet should be allowed to play or not.

Jen jokingly glared at the magic born. "She magicked her cards into all aces last time!"

Violet pursed her pale pink lips. "I fessed up to it later."

Monica grumbled. "Three hundred dollars later."

Violet rolled her eyes and held up a palm. "I solemnly swear not to magic the cards." A fine mist leaked from her palm, hushing everyone up.

"What's that?" Monica leaned closer as the mist settled over the cards.

Violet shrugged like it was no big deal. "Just bespelled the cards so that they can't be magically tampered with."

All six sets of eyes looked at my best friend in awe. She didn't even realize when she was being a fascinating creature.

Finn linked to my mind: *Let me inside.*

I stood, excusing myself, and told my door guard to let Finn in. I was preparing myself to give him a good pat down, maybe some bacon. I hadn't seen him all day. But when he walked through with windblown fur and a wild look in his eye, I knew something was wrong.

He trotted in and walked back to my room, passing the poker-playing group without a word. He didn't even nuzzle Violet's outstretched hand.

My friend looked concerned as she followed him with her eyes, before turning back to look at me.

"Just play without me. I'll go and see what is up with him," I said, moving swiftly toward my room. I knew my familiar, and something definitely had happened.

The second we were alone I knelt down and met the eyes of my dearest and closest friend. Calista, Blaine, and Violet meant everything to me, along with the rest of my dominants, but Finn was much more. At times I couldn't tell where my soul began and his ended. We were one, like my own wolf.

"Tell me everything."

He nodded. *I went back to check on Winnie and to spend the day in the Bronx with her and Rhett.* My stomach knotted when he said Winnie's name and spoke of Rhett, her red fox familiar.

"Is she okay?" I nearly choked on the words.

Finn hushed me with a headbutt. *She's fine. We had a good day, and when I was leaving to go to the vortex ... I was followed.*

Finn and all other familiars could use the vortex as we could. They could harness the mecca for small amounts of time.

"Followed by who?" I said out loud, already pacing.

Was it the bear? Did he come seeking retribution?

There was a woman following closely behind me the moment I left the apartment building. She looked and smelled like a human, so I didn't worry too much about her. She was walking with a golden retriever, who strangely enough didn't seem to be frightened of me.

I was getting a bad feeling about this story.

When I reached the building for the vortex, she kept walking straight, so I figured it was just a strange coincidence, one of those rare humans who aren't repelled by the energy of the mecca. But then, after entering the building, when I was standing a few feet from the vortex travel disc, the woman's dog burst through the window, shattering it, and as it came closer to me its illusion dropped and I saw its true form. A lioness.

My breathing stuttered. "What are you saying?"

Finn looked at me in a way I would never forget, like the whole world had changed overnight.

That woman had a familiar.

A familiar! That wasn't possible. Only heirs had familiars. Not humans. Not to mention there was no account of a lioness that I could recall. "Do you think it was a bear heir?" We didn't exactly have tabs on all of them. Any of them really.

Bears only have male heirs. Just as wolves only ever produce female heirs.

Finn surprised me with this hidden knowledge. Well, maybe not hidden, but I never knew that. Okay, where did that leave us? With a female wolf heir that lived in hiding? But why would she? And why was she there following

Finn? Part of my training was to memorize every single heir and past heirs, and all of their familiars. I had never even known a lioness was possible. It was usually birds and other forest creatures, nothing as exotic as a lion.

I reached out to pet my familiar's thick fur, deciding there was nothing I could do about it today. The Summit would wait for no one, so I'd have to push it to the side and focus on myself.

Tell no one of this. I'll deal with it when I'm queen.

Finn nodded at me.

The council would have to tell me everything then. They liked their secrets, but I would accept none of that. Funny that right at the moment I realized how badly I wanted to be queen was also the moment I started to see how much of a mess our world was in. The next queen was going to have a hell of a job in front of her. God help us all if it ended up being Selene.

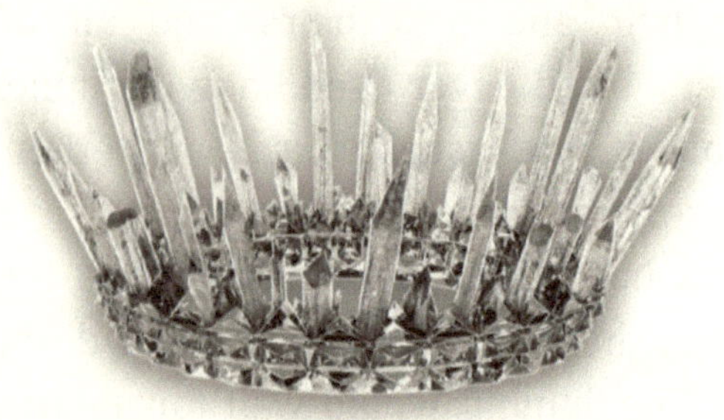

Chapter Seven

Two strikes and you're dead.

CALISTA SPENT THE rest of the night drilling battle strategies into me. The council had told her that the final battle would take place in the queen's basement gymnasium, and that Selene would be awarded two weapons because she was five points ahead of me. The Island challenge had given her the slightest lead. I would only be permitted one weapon, which was to be Larak's anti-venom.

Familiars were required to fight.

By the next morning I was sore and tired. I could barely sleep thinking about what Finn had told me, not to mention stress over the upcoming battle and that damn bear. My mind was racing and I wished someone would invent an off button. A knock at my door had me standing at attention, Finn at my side. We were ready. Finn wore his custom leather and gold saddle, as I often rode him when we went into battle simulations. I donned my golden arm cuffs and stainless steel long sleeve chainmail shirt, which went from my neck to my hips and would hopefully keep me from getting gored alive. Selene was one of the best swordswomen in New York City, but I was pretty darn good with weapons myself.

If only I had one to take with me.

My eyes flicked back to my beloved sword resting in her sheath on the bed, not strapped to my body where she belonged. She was a beauty, as long as my arm, with super sharp double edges, gold inlaid filament, diamonds across the hilt, and my name carved into the handle. I'd trained long and hard to make my sword and I as one.

Pretty sure she was sad about not being in this fight too.

The door opened suddenly and I turned to see it was Violet. I relaxed a little, glad that my best friend had come to see me off. "Hey, I thought you were a council member ready to escort me."

Violet ran a hand through her silky hair. "You're going to be fine, Ari. You're like ten times the battle strategist of Selene. She's probably going to stab herself and end it all before it's even begun."

I laughed. That was a nice thought, but unfortunately we both knew Selene was a worthy opponent. Utterly ruthless.

"Oh, and by the way," Violet continued, "can I just say that poker is no fun if you can't cheat."

I laughed again, thankful that she was attempting to take my mind off the last task.

"Maybe we should get all of the magic born together one day and you can play magic poker," I said, winking.

She smiled, her face lighting up at the thought, and just as quickly her face became serious.

"You have the anti-venom?"

I nodded. It was tucked in a small pocket of my black pants. Easily accessible. Violet seemed satisfied with my answer. Part of me wanted to ask her if she was sure I needed this over my sword, but I trusted her.

She must have seen my hesitation. "I've seen Larak kill a grown man in sixty seconds with one bite. Your blade can defend your life, but this anti-venom can save a life. Yours or Finn's."

Oh God, I didn't think about Finn getting bitten. Violet was right. This was my greatest weapon. I moved in then to hug her, and for once she didn't even tense up, she just hugged me back. I let her lemon and sage scent wash over me.

"I love you, Vi," I whispered, and then pulled back.

She gave me one of her wise looks. "Save your goodbyes for another day. Your journey doesn't end here."

Suddenly Calista was at the door. "It's time."

If I thought I looked like crap, it was nothing to how my advisor looked now. Her hair was strewn all over and she had deep dark circles under her eyes. Her shirt was barely tucked in.

Stepping in line beside her as my guards led me away, I whispered, "You look like hell."

She gave me a tight smile. "I didn't sleep much."

Poor Calista. She had waited her whole life for this. The entire duty of an advisor was to get their heir to the throne. This was her big moment. I stopped in the grand hallway just before the elevator and faced my loyal advisor. "Calista, I won't let you down."

She gave me a smile and broke protocol, pulling me into a hug. "I'm not worried about that," she whispered. That's when it hit me. Calista was afraid I would die.

The queen's *basement* was grossly misrepresented with that name. It looked nothing like a basement. With travertine floors, fifteen-foot ceilings, and mirrored walls, it was more akin to a fancy ballet studio. I stood at one end of the long fifty-foot room, facing Selene at the other. The tall golden chandeliers that hung overhead were in such stark contrast to the death that was about to stain this beautiful place. Did blood even come out of travertine?

Calista was at my side, giving me last minute instructions, her voice harried, eyes wild.

I gave her my best reassuring smile. "Don't worry, Cal, I got this."

She sucked in deeply, and a semblance of calm washed over her delicate features. "Yes, you do. Say the words for me."

I shook my head, but complied.

"I will win this final task. I will become queen of the wolf shifters. Selene is as good as dead."

My advisor looked pleased. My voice had been strong, no hesitation. All of my nerves and fears from earlier were pushed aside as I focused myself. This was the final test and I would not fail.

Torine walked to the middle of the room then, and without saying a word had everyone's attention.

"Welcome to the final task of this royal Summit. There are two worthy heirs remaining today, and when one falls, the other will become our new queen." He turned as he spoke, taking in the many who had gathered around the edge of the room. "A queen must be smart, loyal, wise and above all FIERCE!" His voice carried throughout the area. "In this final test we will see who is the fiercest of all. The first to dominate in battle will become queen. Selene of the Purple Hearts pack, prepare yourself."

She was moving, her snake coiled loosely around her right arm. In one hand she held a mace, the spikes glinting in the light, creating a mirrored reflection on the ceiling. In her other hand was her sword, long and sharp and serrated at the tip.

"Arianna of our beloved Red Queen's line, prepare yourself," Torine shouted.

With a rush of adrenalin, I hopped onto Finn's back. This final task was one with no rules. It was a fight to the death, plain and simple. As Selene and I moved into the center of the room, facing off against each other, I noticed Sabina stroll into the basement. She stood against the far wall before inclining her head in a slight dip at Torine. What was a magic born doing here? Never mind, I couldn't worry about that.

After everyone had cleared the way, Torine yelled loud and clear: "Begin!"

And that was it. I had begun the fight for my life.

One good thing about Finn and me, we usually chose to speak to each other in words, but we didn't need to. In times of battle he could link with me and read my thoughts, get pictures, and have a clearer connection so that our moves were effortless.

Finn took off at full speed with me holding onto the saddle, my metal arm cuff out in front of me like a shield. All Selene could do was wait. She just stood there, weapons ready, until we neared.

I had to be clever in my attack. Without a weapon I would be relying on Finn's strength and the hope I could maybe knock the purple heir down and steal one of her weapons. Finn's growls increased as we closed in, and Selene responded by swinging both of her weapons around and settling into a fighting stance. Her sword was held with just enough height that it would eviscerate my familiar if he didn't change trajectories. I sent him some images of what I planned, and just as he was about to leap onto Selene, he ground to a halt and I used this momentum to fling myself up and over her.

I twisted in the air, flipped myself around and landed behind the purple heir in a crouched stance as Finn remained at her front. Selene's head swung back and forth between us, her snake curling across her neck and hissing in my direction.

Finn and I would attack as one, one of us to be the distraction while the other got a weapon. Selene flung her arms wide and pointed a weapon at each of us. Deadly still, but there were weaknesses now for us to exploit. Her middle was completely exposed and her focus was scattered between two points.

I growled, and she tensed, her eyes narrowing on me, before they ran up and down my body. I could tell it was worrying her that I had no visible weapons. Her fear of my unknown weapon was almost as good as a weapon itself. I growled again and pretended to reach into my back pocket. She tensed, and turned her body further in my direction.

This was exactly the opening Finn needed. He launched himself forward and Selene shrieked as he clamped his strong jaws down onto her arm, crushing the armor. She dropped the mace, unable to hold onto it after the force of his blow. Larak came at me then, the snake strong enough to launch himself out quite a distance, his focus on protecting his heir.

But I'd seen it coming and was able to dive and slide underneath his big body, moving fast enough that the fangs missed me. With Violet's warning strong in my mind, I was being extra observant of the snake. Selene had clearly decided to use Larak as her number one weapon.

I avoided his first strike, but knowing he was coming at me again, I closed my hands around his thick tail – my fingers were barely touching, that's how huge he was – and I flung him as far as I could across the room. I heard Selene's hiss, but there wasn't much she could do while dealing with Finn. My familiar darted away then, her mace clasped in his strong jaws.

Selene was struggling with her crushed armband, but that didn't stop her kicking out at me.

"Think you're so great that you don't even need a weapon, Arianna!" She was angry, her hair flying in disarray, her eyes crazy. She followed her kicks by swinging her sword to where I'd rolled across the ground. She was fast and I felt the slices across my back, but thanks to my chainmail they were not deep. I didn't stop rolling, knowing that if I wanted to keep my life I needed to keep moving. "What did you bring instead of a sword?"

The mystery was totally freaking her out. Thank you, Violet. She had doubly helped me today.

I was still rolling, picking up speed so I could get out of her path. Halfway across the floor, I popped up to my feet, ignoring the ache in my back as I settled into a wider stance to face her. I could feel the wet trickle of blood from my small cuts but ignored it. They were nothing. I'd had worse shaving my legs.

By this time Larak was back on her arm; her slimy familiar was fast. She had slowed her pursuit of me now that I was up and able to return the attack, which gave Finn time to drop the weapon into my hand. I felt relief when my fingers flexed around the solid handle. The mace wasn't my preferred weapon, but it was better than nothing.

Selene stepped closer again and the four of us were in a faceoff. Larak hit the ground so he could challenge Finn. I sent one last warning to my familiar to be careful of that snake, then I focused on Selene. She had a greater reach with her sword, but this would be a much more even fight now.

She struck out at me and I lifted my weapon to meet her halfway. The clank of steel was loud, echoing around the room. The mace was top heavy, and while it landed a heavier blow, was not as quick or smooth to swing in this sort of swordplay battle.

"You're too weak for the mace," Selene sneered, as she performed a complicated series of slashes and jabs with her blade. I only just managed to block most of them, and there was no room for me to attack. Only defend.

From the corner of my eye I could see Larak and Finn locked in battle. My familiar had his jaws wrapped around the back of the snake's neck, preventing him from using his venom-filled fangs – which were the length of my index finger – but Larak's long body had encircled my wolf and was squeezing him tightly.

Selene slipped past my defenses then. Even though I saw it coming and managed to dodge to the side, she landed a decent slice across the side of my neck. Luckily my chainmail top was high-necked, but even so, I felt blood trickle down my chest. I forced my full focus back to her, and as she sliced out again, I stepped into her body, dodging the blade, and slammed the mace upward. It grazed the side of her head, taking away a chunk of hair and leaving her stunned.

She'd not expected the direct attack; I'd been on the defensive the entire time. No more though. It was time to win this. I was close enough now for hand to hand, so I dropped the mace and used my favorite move, the spinning heel kick, and as my foot connected to her wrist I heard a distinct crack, and she howled.

My wolf surged within me, urging me forward. There was no room for weakness. I needed to end this. I swung out and she blocked with her good arm, the other cradled close to her body. I had definitely broken her wrist. We sparred back and forth for many moments, both of us injured but neither slowing. I could tell her wrist was starting to recover, but even with shifter healing it would still take a few hours. I needed to end it now, while she was weak.

I went in aggressively, Brazilian Jujitsu style, hands up to protect, and lots of kicks and elbows. Selene was keeping pace with me, so I jabbed out and clipped her injured wrist. Her face creased in pain, and I used that moment to knee her in the gut, knocking her down. She hit the ground hard and I was over the top of her in seconds. My elbow cracked her in the temple and the impact rolled her eyes back in her head. She bucked a few times, but I didn't let her up.

I wasn't keen on literally beating her to death, so instead I let my hands settle around her throat, and with a deep breath I was just about to twist and sever her spine when a magical essence washed over me and I was frozen in place. My wolf and I screamed at this loss of control. What was happening? Were we under attack from the bears? Or the Tuatha de Danann?

My pupils were able to dart around still, and from what I could see Finn and Larak were not moving either, nor were the observers across the room.

A deep voice echoed around us all. It was Torine.

"We are calling an end to this task of the Summit due to the obvious fact that Arianna is the clear winner and our new queen. Selene is the backup heir. In this time of turmoil, we think having a backup to step in should anything happen is a good plan. Especially as there are no heirs of age at this time for another Summit, and the weakness can no longer linger through our packs."

My wolf and I calmed somewhat, even though I was still annoyed by these actions. Why didn't the council tell us that was the plan? No doubt they wanted to make sure one of us could kill the other, and that's why Sabina was here, to lay the magic freeze over us just before the kill.

I was a bit relieved that I didn't have to kill anyone today, though knowing Selene was my backup wasn't exactly a comforting thought. She was determined to be queen, and no doubt she'd be waiting for someone to off me so she could step in.

The magic around us eased, and a force lifted me up and deposited me away from Selene. Where was the trust, people? I wasn't going to kill her now ... well, probably not.

Finn ran to my side and I sank down, threading my fingers through his fur.

You fought like a true queen, he said to me. *Down and dirty.*

I had to chuckle; he wasn't even kidding. I'd completely forgotten the weapons after a while, knowing I couldn't best her swordsmanship with the mace, and just went for the brawl. Quite satisfying actually.

Something impacted Finn then, hitting him hard enough in the side that both of us stumbled down.

"Larak, no!" Selene was screaming at her familiar, and I was just turning to see what had happened, when Finn collapsed beside me.

The huge snake rose up again, preparing to strike a second time. Thankfully, Selene got to him first, and with a shout threw herself onto him and stopped his strike.

I was panicking, my hands running across Finn as he wheezed at my side. I could hear the noise, the chaos around us, but I was detached, my body in full lockdown panic mode. Larak bit Finn, oh my God.

"Someone save the familiar," I heard Torine shout.

A queen without a familiar was no queen at all. If Finn died, I would go crazy until I was no longer able to function. We were soul bound.

"Treason!" Calista shouted from the door. She was right. I had just been declared queen and

Selene's familiar had tried to kill me. Luckily I had the anti-venom. Thank you, Violet.

The foam was already forming along Finn's jaw; his eyes were glassy as I dug deep into my pocket for the vial. I was shaking, almost dropping the precious liquid as I finally freed it.

"Hang on, old friend," I said, trying to be as reassuring as I could. I really just wanted to scream and howl and cut that snake into a million pieces. "I'm going to save you, you'll be fine."

Larak must have given him a huge hit of venom. My wolf's heart was already stuttering as his blood started to boil within. I could feel what Finn was feeling and it was awful, pain like I'd never felt before, burning in my chest.

Someone dropped at my side, and I was just about to lash out when my limbs froze. It was Sabina. "Let me," she said. "I can get it into his bloodstream faster than you."

She must have known what it was, because as soon as I dropped the vial into her hands she uncorked it. As the liquid emerged upon a magical wave, she whispered to it, and it shot straight toward Finn's heart. He jerked as it entered, soaking through his fur. His low whimpers were killing me.

I knew Selene and Larak were being completely ripped a new one from the council, but there'd be no real punishment. Selene was considered royal now, a spare heir. Which gave her power over the council. Plus she'd argue she had nothing to do with it, that the snake hadn't understood the battle was over. She'd also mention how she'd jumped on him and stopped a second attack. Very convenient, right? She was great at the lying and deception thing.

I held my breath, running my hands across Finn's soft white fur, as I waited for the antivenom to kick in. What if Violet got it wrong? Or if Larak and Selene had done something to ramp up the potency.

Calista, who appeared from somewhere, broke protocol and draped an arm around me, hugging me close. I'd just become queen, every heir's dream, but I couldn't have cared less.

Finn's heart started to race then, and I swear the heat pouring off him was akin to a lava field. The venom was literally cooking him from the inside out. Tears poured down my cheeks as grief consumed me. To see him suffering like this was worse than if it were me. I wished it had been me.

I was going to kill that snake, in slow torturous slices of my blade.

Finn growled then, and it seemed a little less weak then before. Sabina dropped her head down and whispered, "Eraticata" as a slow stream of silver fluid dribbled out of Finn's mouth. "It's working," she told us. "You're very lucky to have had anti-venom for Larak. Nothing I could have done today would have saved your familiar."

A sliver of hope struck me, and I promised I would give Violet anything she wanted in the world for this. She had saved my life, even if it was in a roundabout way. Finn was my life.

I could feel Finn getting stronger, and I stayed by his side until he could stand. Only then did I stand as well.

Tears stained my cheeks, crusty blood stuck to my body from my neck to my elbow, and I held Larak in a murderous gaze.

Torine met my eyes and nodded. "Long live the queen!" he yelled, and everyone in the room chorused his words. Even Selene. She had to. I was her master now.

That night I had Calista email Selene a copy of a menu from a restaurant in Arizona. They specialized in serving deep-fried snake. I wanted to make it clear that if Larak went anywhere near Finn or me again, I would have the palace chef serve him for dinner. I also issued royal orders that ejected her from the Manhattan borough and forced her to take over the Bronx. On one hand I hated to have Selene in my old territory, but on the other I refused to rule Manhattan with her so close by. Not long after this I received word that Selene had exited the palace.

"She's going to the Bronx?" Calista asked me.

I took a deep breath, running my hands over Finn. I'd barely left his side since the last battle. Violet had appeared soon after he received the anti-venom and helped us get him back to my temporary suite. She was now allowed free run in the castle. I was the new queen, lockdown had been lifted, and Sabina would no longer be the magic born of Manhattan.

I was so relieved Violet was here. She was going to stay by Finn's side tonight just in case he had any setbacks from the venom.

"Yes. Can you let all of my main shifters know they're moving to Manhattan," I said to Calista, relieved to see her tablet already out and her fingers flying over it. "I don't want Selene anywhere near me, and unfortunately the Bronx is the only territory I can offer her."

I regretted that some of my wolves would be left under her control, but unlike the Red Queen, I'd be keeping an eye on Selene. If she stepped out of line, I would crush her like the devious little worm she was.

"I've already started organizing the castle," Calista said, her laser focus never moving from her device. "We will have more than enough positions for all of the wolves you're transporting to Manhattan. You need to screen all of the queen's current guards and staff, decide who you trust enough to keep around, and relocate the others."

And so it began. I was not going to have much of an adjustment period. Coronation tomorrow and then straight into the fray. Wow, I was actually going to be the queen of the wolf shifters.

I both anticipated the coronation with almost crazy levels of excitement and feared it for the seriousness of its ritual. I was told it would be held with a very special attendant, the bear king. It was one of our oldest laws that the bear king be present to witness the coronation of a new queen, and that afterward we have peace talks and hopefully form a new agreement between the two current monarchs. I was kind of looking forward to meeting the king. I hoped he brought Gerald and that we could discuss going after the Red Queen's killer together. Maybe he had learned more about the fae and their possible threat. I hadn't forgotten that I had three deaths to avenge.

My fears stemmed from the fact I would have to join with the mecca in front of all my people. This was the most important of steps for the new queen to take. This joining was the cementing of the power in the boroughs. I would then begin to filter the mecca's massive energy and send it out into my people around the world. We had been weakened for a week now, which might seem like a short amount of time, but ... a lot can happen in a week.

The mecca was unstable, changed since the Red Queen fell, and who knew what was going to happen tomorrow when I took that final step to being queen.

Violet, who had briefly stepped from the room, returned and crossed back to Finn's side. She held a vial in her hands, the liquid a murky pink color. "This will help him get some sleep," she said, her voice low. "The anti-venom almost wasn't strong enough. Larak threw everything he had at Finn."

My heart stuttered, and it was only my rhythmic patting of his warm body that allowed me to keep myself from falling apart. Violet leaned down and I watched the liquid flow into my familiar. Almost in an instant he relaxed, and I could feel the tendrils of pain within him ease. Not much on Earth could hurt a familiar, but Larak was not from Earth; he was from the same world as Finn and his venom was deadly.

"I don't know how to thank you," I said to Violet. "I love you, you know that, right?"

She shrugged, giving me a wan smile. She'd been worried for us during the fight, and I could see the toll it took on her. "You don't have to thank me, I'd do anything for you two. Sometimes I just wish these powers were more predictable."

Violet didn't like to talk about her powers much. She confided in me once that it alienated her when she just wanted to feel normal and accepted. But since she'd brought it up, I decided to push her a little more.

"Vi, what exactly did you see? Was it the actual future, because I never knew you could do that? Did you see Finn get bitten?"

She froze, and I wondered if she would answer or brush it to the side as she was known to do when things got too personal. When she looked up at me her eyes were even more unnaturally pale than usual. "Sometimes I get flashes, other times it's just a sense. Either way, the future can change in a blink, so you cannot put too much faith in the visions."

That was all she said before joining me in stroking Finn's luxurious white fur.

Well, what do you know. I think my best friend had just admitted that she could actually glimpse the future. I took a moment to really look at her familiar face, all of my love pouring out in the next words.

"Hey, Vi?"

She looked up at me.

"Want to be my palace magic born?"

Her face lit up and she actually jumped up off the couch. "Take over Sabina's job?"

I laughed, letting some of my happiness out. "Yes. I respect Sabina but she isn't you."

Violet looked overjoyed and I didn't realize until now how much she must have been waiting for me to say that. Being the palace magic born was like being queen of the magic borns. I would give Sabina a good severance package, let her go with grace. She would have her choice of alphas to lead with. She probably wouldn't even be surprised, as Calista had just pointed out, it was commonplace that a new queen changed staff when she took office. My only stipulation would be that Sabina could not join the Bronx borough. Selene was not getting her hands on a magic born. She was dangerous enough as it was.

That night, as I finally got into bed, ready to pass out for a few hours of blissful unconsciousness, I found myself reliving everything from the last few days. One would think that the strongest image would be the moment I became queen, but unfortunately for me that would always be tinged with memories of fear and pain. Of almost losing my soul. My Finn.

Rather I focused on the woman and her lioness familiar who had stalked Finn. Her presence had not been a worry I could deal with in the midst of the Summit, but now it couldn't be so easily pushed aside. As exhaustion pressed on me, and I sank deeper into the world of sleep, I let my mind touch on Finn; I'd almost lost him today. I was reassured to feel his warm presence through our bond; he was alive and would fully recover. Thank the gods.

I was going to be queen!

Again this thought had me in a mess of emotions, my stomach tied up in knots. Wanting to be queen, and then actually living it day to day, were not even remotely the same thing. I wondered if I would do the Red Queen proud, or crash and burn.

Of course my last thought, as darkness descended across my vision, was of that damn bear gardener, and that brazen kiss I couldn't seem to forget. No matter how hard I tried.

Chapter Eight

The darkness in the deep.

THE NEXT MORNING I was awoken by a neurotically happy and bubbly Calista.

"It's your coronation! Good morning!" she squeaked, throwing my curtains wide.

I groaned in bed. My wounds had been tended to after the battle but my body still felt like it had been hit by a truck. I needed food, tons and tons of food.

"Feed me," I croaked. "Or I'll have you beheaded."

Calista laughed. "Not even queen yet and already evil. Well, Your Majesty, I have a five-course meal waiting for you. Violet was just tucking into the bacon and egg burritos."

I shot out of bed and tore out of the room just in time to see Violet's hand frozen midair as she looked at me.

"You would dare touch your queen's breakfast?" I said in a heavy British accent, and Violet busted out laughing. Calista followed, her laughter light and infectious.

This is what I needed, lots of jokes to break up the nerves that had settled in my gut. And lots of bacon, always bacon.

Violet took a bite and grinned at me as I sat beside her and was relieved to feel Finn relaxed by my feet.

I love you. I said simply.

And I you.

The rest of us didn't talk, we just ate, moaning and nodding at the amazing array before us. Eggs Benedict, spinach and mushroom quiche, crown-shaped pancakes to honor my coronation. This palace chef was definitely NOT getting replaced. In fact I decided right then to give him a raise. I could feel the aches in my body healing faster as I consumed more calories.

I looked at Violet then as we lay back in our chairs nearly panting and stuffed with food.

"You know what I hate about living in the city?"

Violet shrugged. "There's nothing I hate about this city."

Violet loved New York, its noises, its smells, its concrete jungle. Not to mention she could stroll around in her Renaissance outfits and no one even blinked an eye. She fit here. Always had.

"As a shifter, I'm always wanting to break free of my human skin and run. I have these dreams where I'm running through fields of flowers as fast as I can. You can't do that here."

It happened every so often when one of the wolves lost control, but it was forbidden. Humans were already too aware of us, and they did not need to start fearing the beasts that lurked in plain sight all around them.

Violet got that look on her face then, the one which when we were ten definitely meant I was going to be in big trouble. Queen heir or not.

"What?" I said. "Spit it out."

"I think I know a way we can run in the city."

I raised an eyebrow as my best friend stood and pulled a book out of her messenger bag. It was one of the spell books I had won from my first challenge. I could see some little pieces of paper acting as bookmarks and knew Violet had been studying it closely.

She flipped it open, turning a few more pages, before stopping on one near the center. She nodded. "Yep, I can do this."

I stood and peered over her shoulder. The text was unreadable, all dots and swirls and runes. "Can you read that?" I asked, bewildered.

She nodded. "Can't you?"

"Nevermind. What's it say?"

She set the book down and faced me, grinning. "It's a transmutation spell to make our wolves look like ordinary animals. Dogs, rabbits, butterflies."

"Whoa," I breathed. That was a magic Finn instinctively could do, mutate himself slightly, but no one knew how the familiars got the power. I'd never seen a shifter do it.

"I'm not sure I can easily do a butterfly, but I could turn us into two dogs."

I grinned. A run through Central Park? That was exactly what I needed to calm my nerves before the coronation.

"Do it," I told her. Normally the Manhattan pack went on runs outside the city. Huge buses left three times a day for any who needed to get away and shed their skin. As an alpha and heir, I was more in control of my wolf. I could go months without a shift if I had to, but it wasn't good for either of us. Since the buses weren't an option for me ... if Violet had a way for us to escape inside the city, I was going to take it.

"Stop right there!" Calista shrieked, and we both turned to face her.

"You will NOT experiment with new magic on the queen."

Violet rolled her eyes. "We're just going for a run, it'll be fine. I know I can do this. It's simple really, I can't believe I didn't realize it before."

But my advisor shook her head. "Try it on me first," she instructed as she began to undress.

Violet threw her arms up. "Fine."

Twenty minutes later, four of us were in our magical doggy disguises, and I had five of my royal guards leading us to Central Park. Calista, Violet, Finn and I were frolicking through the streets of Manhattan, followed closely by my guards, who were looking like New York City's hottest dog walkers. Derek had wanted to run as well, but I couldn't afford to lose all my dominants. Unfortunately I was queen now and people would want to kill me. So Derek had to be a walker, along with Ben, Victor, Blaine and Monica. They held our leashes loosely, which was always best when you were dealing with wolves. Even with the logical human side of me in place, I hated being caged and would fight. Instinct could only be pushed down so far.

It was still early and not many people were on the sidewalks, only a few joggers and the random girl doing the walk of shame. I looked over at Violet, who was a beautiful tan Labrador, and had a sudden thought. Maybe this was the spell that woman was using to disguise her familiar. That meant she had knowledge of old magics, and also had a powerful magic born at her disposal. Before I could think more on it, we entered Central Park. The guards unclipped our leads and Finn took off running. Grinning, I followed him, with Violet and Calista hot on my heels.

Despite the fact we looked like dogs on the outside, on the inside it was the same as always when I shifted to wolf, the animalistic side of me rising to the surface, the less complicated emotions, the freedom. Nothing had changed for me yet, I was still only connected to the mecca at the level of heir, but for some reason I could feel the magic everywhere. Should that be happening before I was crowned?

As the wind brushed through my fur and my paws pounded the ground, I reveled in the fact that this was all mine now. This city, these wolves, my responsibility and my people. The very energy of the world was thrumming through me. Along with the realization that this would be my last carefree moment before the responsibilities of being queen were placed upon me.

Calista slowed as we saw a woman jogging with her gray pit-bull. The dog met my eyes briefly and then cowered, running past us as quickly as possible. I chuckled internally, and as I turned to meet up with the rest of the group, a flash of white caught my eye. It quickly disappeared, before reappearing again in the midst of some bushes. I had to blink twice, wondering if I'd just lost my mind. There was no way ... that was one animal I'd never expected to see again. Finn must have felt my shock because he let out a whine and ran to my side.

What is it? He stepped in front of me in a protective gesture.

I couldn't even fathom it. I'd seen her blood all over the library, and her body lay frozen in the palace. It wasn't possible.

I think I just saw the late queen's lynx.

What in the hell was going on in my city? A secret heir walking around with a lioness familiar, and now this? But it couldn't be Ragnar. Once a queen dies her familiar dies too. Still, something inside me pushed to check it out further. Finn and I were a little separated from the others, so when we both dashed into the bushes, following the trail of the lynx, no one noticed. My guards and Calista were going to kill me, but I had no time to call for them. If that was the queen's familiar, he could be gone in moments. Plus I had Finn, and not much could best him. He'd even had control over Larak until the snake went for the underhanded sneak attack. Should have cooked that little creep.

Is there any possible way her familiar could not have died with her? I asked Finn, our pace picking up as we dodged around trees and trash cans.

No, we are even more tied to you than you are to us. We cannot live without our heir.

That damn snake flashed across my mind again, and a shudder tore through me.

I can't live without you either. My soul and yours are equally linked.

I could feel his love and joy. We were soul bound, best friends. I wanted for nothing more than him to live forever with me.

The faint scent of the animal I was following led me into a denser part of the park, which was a relief because even disguised as dogs, if animal control got wind of us roaming around there'd be trouble. We were relatively covered by all the bushes.

Over there! Finn said with urgency, and I caught sight of another flash of white.

I was full-on sprinting now, uncaring about the people around, barely even noticing as they screamed and dashed out of the way from two huge dogs.

Finn and I were fast, I had no idea if we were actually chasing the queen's familiar – seriously, it was impossible – but whatever we were chasing seemed even faster. The edge of the park was closing in, and there was now no scent, no trail, and no sight of any white animal.

I was panting a little, Finn not at all.

Maybe I imagined it, I said.

There was a small, white creature, but I never got a good enough look to confirm it was the lynx.

I shook out my fur, pacing a little, my snout close to the ground as I continued to scent.

We know that it's most likely not, but I'm starting to wonder now if it was another familiar, like that lab/lioness that followed you.

Were there like a bunch of heirs and familiars stashed around this place? Finn didn't reply, instead he started loping away from me, heading out of the nature reserve and into the city. He was not moving fast, and there was less fierceness than usual on his doggy face, but I could sense he was following something.

Even though I knew I should get back to my guards, I took off after him, wondering what the heck he was doing. I didn't like leaving him alone in the city with so much craziness going on. He'd been followed only a few days ago.

He led me across some streets, along a small alleyway, which smelled horrific to my extra sensitive wolf nose, and then back into another section of Central Park. It was damper here, the scent of water permeating my nostrils.

There was also a weird humming of energy in the air, which felt like the mecca, but then also not like it. Finn's pace never increased, but he had begun snarling, fangs on full show. I had almost caught him now, which meant I slammed into him when he ground to a sudden halt, right before a small body of water. It was one of the lakes where you'd usually find lily pads and ducks this time of year. There was nothing across this one though, nothing to disturb the water besides a faint shine, almost like a slick of oil coating the surface.

What is it? What did you see?

Finn turned to me, and I could see he wasn't sure. Something had drawn him here though, and that made me take a second look around. I paced closer, avoiding actually touching the water, but still trying to see into the depths.

I didn't like to go into water like this when I was a wolf. Our animals couldn't really swim; our bodies were too dense and we tended to sink. Frolicking in shallows, perfectly fine. Swimming ... hell no.

The shine was iridescent, almost like a dark version of the magic-born wolves' coat, shimmering and undulating across the still water. Why was it rippling like that? There was nothing disturbing the water, and yet it was almost as if beneath the water a darkness lurked.

Suddenly, energy slapped out at me and I took a step back. Finn fell into my side as a beast shot up out of the oily water. My wolf acted on instinct, growls ripping from my chest as I fell into a pouncing stance. The thing rose higher, sending cascades of water out around it.

What the hell is that? I asked my familiar. This was no beast I had ever seen before.

Finn's voice was flat and low. *I think it's an ercho, a dark fae ... you need to run now, Ari. Run and I will hold it off.*

Like hell, I said. I would never leave Finn to fight off this ... ercho thing.

It rose to hover just above the water, staring at us with its freaky blood-red eyes. It was like a cross between a bat, vampire, and human, standing around five feet tall, with black leathery skin and large wings, which were almost translucent. I could see the veins crossing through them. The face was bat-like, with red orb-like eyes, no real nose, and two decent sized ears. Two very large and prominent vampire fangs adorned its mouth. The body was humanoid in shape, but with no discerning of male or female. The hands were clawed, feet the same, and I was pretty sure there was a tail somewhere behind it too. This was dark magic.

I was about to ask Finn what the hell this thing was exactly, and if he knew how to kill it, when it attacked. Moving swiftly it dived for us, or more correctly, for me. Ignoring Finn, the thing emitted a high-pitched screech that almost deafened my wolf. I hit the ground, shaking my head to try and clear the ringing. I felt claws grasp onto my back, and with way more strength than I'd expected, it wrenched me up and lifted me into the air.

Finn, who wasn't as affected as me by the screech, was following below. With one growl, all fangs and fury, he leaped and smashed into the side of the bat thing. He was back in his normal wolf form now, looking extra-large and ferocious. All three of us hit the ground, and Finn was back up and tearing into it with a wildness which would have scared me if I didn't love him.

My familiar was so calm most of the time, I forgot there was a deadly killing machine lurking beneath his pure white fur. The ercho was not going to take it lying down though. It fought back just as hard, and as I dived in to clamp my muzzle across one of its wings it sliced me across my flank with a row of spikes along its ribs that I hadn't even noticed. The wings must have hidden them.

I fell to the side, shaking off the pain and dragging myself up. Blood was spurting across my own white fur and onto the ground. Finn's fury was beyond words now. I could see images in his head, and they were dark. Energy poured from him as he slammed the creature to the ground with one huge paw, and then used the other to disembowel it. Its skin was hard and leathery, and despite my familiar's razor sharp claws, he barely cut through it.

The ercho turned his eyes on me one more time, before managing to shove my wolf, and then with a final screech that dropped me to my belly again, it dived into the water. The shine dispersed everywhere for one second, then suddenly the water was calm and clear. No shine, no sign that some freakin' creature had just crawled out of it.

Finn was growling low as he crossed to me and licked up the side of my flank where I was injured. Immediate relief coursed through me.

I'll heal in a moment ... just need time.

He shook his head. *There is no time. The ercho wanted you. It was going to take you into the water. I need to get you to the royal home, and then to the coronation. I will always protect you, but adding the mecca energy to yours will be another barrier against this threat.*

He knelt on his front paws, and with barely any help from me, lifted my body and let me slide down over his head and onto his huge back. He started moving, fast enough to get us out of there, but not so fast that I would slide off. My side was killing me again, but I could deal.

Finn had saved my life. I'd been completely unprepared for the speed and strength of that thing. It was nothing like any shifter I'd ever fought.

So ... that's a dark fae?

Finn growled again. I could feel the rumbling within his big body. *There are myths about the Otherworld. That there is a section reserved for a fae that is akin to the devil himself, where he lives with his creatures of great darkness ... such as the ercho.*

I had no idea what to say to that. If anyone else had just said that to me I'd have laughed my butt off, thinking they were joking. But Finn would never joke about something so serious.

How do you know all of this? I asked my familiar. Finn never usually kept things from me, but he had definitely never mentioned an ercho to me before.

Finn's chest rumbled. *Ragnar told me once and I thought it was a fable or just a spooky story. Not worth repeating, more like gossip.*

I let that sink in. The queen's lynx and Finn often went hunting together in this very park in the dead of night. He even considered Ragnar a friend, so it didn't surprise me that they would share stories during their hunting trips. What did surprise me was that Ragnar would speak about the dark fae; how did he know about them? Another Red Queen mystery, for sure.

Focusing on Finn, I nuzzled my face into him. *Thank you for always being here for me,* I said. *I love you.*

And I you.

There were shouts as my dominants came into sight. I knew Finn had been hiding us the best he could, but that was only from the humans. My guards and friends would see the truth.

Calista was the first to reach us. She was back in human form and had found clothes somewhere. "Arianna! What happened?" She turned to Ben, who was the first of the guards there. He was shirtless, which explained the clothes. "We need a healer immediately. The queen is injured."

Ben reacted in an instant, his phone already out, but before he could dial, Violet popped out of the bushes close by. She too was human and dressed in her full Renaissance garb, although I was sure it was some type of spell. "I got this, Ben. Just keep watch."

Ben looked like he wanted to protest, but clearly I was looking a little worse for wear, because he relented. He stepped back and joined the rest of the royal guard, who had formed a circle around Finn and me, hiding us from sight.

Blaine was kneeling down, his hands on my muzzle, gently stroking it.

"You're going to be fine, Princess." I would have laughed, except I kinda felt like I was dying. He didn't call me princess much anymore. That was an old nickname from when we were younger. First it had been a jerk thing because I was a queen heir, so sort of a princess, and he thought I was spoiled, but then as we became better friends it was a term of endearment. He hadn't used it for a long time and it brought me comfort now.

I found the energy to lick his hand and show him that I understood and loved him too.

Blaine remained near my head as Finn lowered himself to snuggle against my back. Together with Violet he made sure to gently hold me in place.

The magic born shot me a sad face. "Sorry, girl, this is going to hurt a bit."

She placed both hands on me, and I prepared myself as best I could. Blaine remained at my side, his huge body offering warmth and the comfort of pack. The burning in my side was intense, and as I growled and whimpered, Finn joined me in my head. My familiar's anger was still raging within him, but he managed to calm himself enough to wrap around my mind, talking endlessly, offering his support as Violet knit my muscles and bones back together. That creature had almost torn out my entire side.

When she was done, both Violet and I were huffing, almost as if we'd just run a marathon.

"Okay, you better tell me exactly what attacked you," she said, "because that was like no wound I've ever had to heal before. I'm not sure you would have been able to heal that as a wolf. It would have certainly taken you a lot longer than usual."

I was back on my paws, but was still unsteady. There was a weakness in my energy now, which I sensed was going to take time to fill, time I didn't have. Violet dragged me into a very dense set of bushes, as my front legs collapsed a little. She waited for Blaine to gather me up and silently follow her. She wanted me to change back, that much was clear. It was risky doing it here, but my people were keeping watch and I needed to be able to tell them exactly what had happened. Maybe Calista or Violet would know something; they were both smart, well read – and Calista had many years of knowledge on us.

The change back was more painful than usual, and took me longer. Blaine never left my side except to growl at Derek, who was trying to crowd in with us. He knew that Derek and I were no longer together, and that I would prefer that particular dominant not see me in this sort of vulnerable state.

For a second it had seemed as if an argument would ensure, but luckily Derek just huffed out, running his hands through his gorgeous hair, and took off.

Fifteen minutes later I was sprawled across the ground, feeling a little like I'd just been hit by a bus.

Clothes were handed to me, and with a little help I slipped on the tights and plain black shirt. No underwear, but that was fine. Just had to make it back to the royal home.

Finn and Blaine were firmly glued to my side as I emerged from the bushes, and the rest of my people circled around me again. The guards were on high alert, and I wasn't at all surprised to see more of them in the general vicinity. Ben was giving them hand signals, and I figured he was the one who had called for backup. Derek was stoic-faced, and I knew his feelings were going to cause more problems. I was loath to have to remove him from my inner dominants, but he was going to force my hand sooner or later. My own stupid fault, really, for getting romantically involved. I should have known better.

"What happened, Arianna?"

Calista looked pale. She was clutching her tablet hard enough to crack the screen. She must have made one of the guards carry it in case she ended up needing it.

"Finn and I saw something odd in the park … it kind of looked like Ragnar, the queen's lynx."

A multitude of expressions crossed the faces around me and I knew they were wondering if I'd suffered some sort of brain damage as well as blood loss.

"We followed it for a bit, just to see if we could figure out what animal it was. Only it disappeared … or was never there … I don't know. Then Finn scented an old magic and was following the trail. Led us right to a small lake off to that side."

I pointed back the way we'd come.

No one spoke as I finished the story. More than one looked confused at my mention of an ercho. That name was not familiar to most, like it hadn't been to me.

Calista was smashing her finger into her tablet, bringing up one page after another at a rapid speed. She finally said: "Looks like Finn was right. The creature you describe, which goes by many names, including ercho, Hellion, guardian of the deep, and a few others, is said to be the creation of the dark lord. Originally from the Otherworld, his master was exiled, and in his exile built a land of darkness."

I shook my head. "How is this even possible? Dark fae ..."

Calista pursed her lips, tilting her head a little. "We shouldn't jump to any conclusions yet. This is a very old story – legend, myth. It is said that the fae exiled him before the mecca was even formed on Earth."

So well before shifters and the like even existed. Calista didn't know the information Gerald had told us at the dinner that night, no one did, which was probably why she was even more skeptical than me about the possibilities of a fae attack. I was starting to worry though. Was this some sort of weird coincidence? Or the beginnings of a larger scale attack?

"I will send guards to the lake," Ben said, signaling to the shifters around us.

I nodded, not worried for their immediate safety. That thing was long gone, but maybe there was some other evidence there we had missed. "Do not go with less than a group of ten. It is strong. I would never have survived without Finn."

If my familiar had been any other wolf, they would have crowded into him and given pats and hugs. But he was not a normal wolf. He was so much more, to be respected and feared. No one touched him but me and Violet.

Calista started to usher me out of the park then. "We will continue to investigate this, Arianna, but if we don't head back you're going to be late for your own coronation."

I sucked in deeply. With all the drama I'd pretty much forgotten I was supposed to become queen of all the wolf shifters today. Who would have thought there would have been anything else that could have taken my mind off that. Guess a demon bat would do it. Just another thing to add to the list of strange goings-on in my city. The mecca energy was shifting in our world, dark forces emerging, and for once it was not anything to do with us wolves. It was so much bigger than us. Big enough to destroy everything.

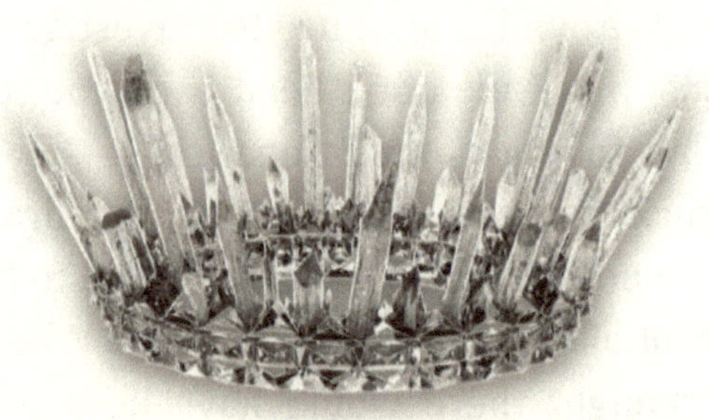

Chapter Nine

The crown of mecca.

DESPITE THE CRAZINESS of the last few hours, I was still nervous as I stood in the large hallway that led to the grand ballroom, waiting to be crowned queen. The coronation was about to commence, and I was more than dressed for the occasion. My dress was a mix of different materials, mainly silk. Hundreds of layers of tulle pushed the dress out in a bell shape, blood-red at the corset, before fading to black at the hem. New black titanium arm guards, inlaid with rubies, had been made for the occasion.

Although I wasn't one for dressing up in ball gowns, I really loved this dress. Calista had chosen well – a combination of styles which actually represented who I was as a person: modern and edgy but with tradition bleeding through. The new queen always wore a mixture of her house color and black. The black was to signify the mourning of the old queen. It was respectful and I felt pride at being able to reign and keep the red house alive.

A noise at my back had me spinning to find my advisor there. Calista wore a tailored black pantsuit with red silk blouse underneath. Her tablet was clutched tightly in her hands and her eyes were leaking tears.

"Don't cry," I told her. She'd been a mess from the first moment she saw me in my dress. Everything seemed more potent too after the park. I could have died today. Any of us could have if that creature had attacked them, but I had no doubt it had been lying in wait for me. I wasn't directly linked to the mecca yet, but I was the rightful queen, and if it had taken me out the loss would have been great – though not as devastating now that Selene was the spare heir. Still, the attack had been direct and targeted. Someone was targeting royalty, trying to wipe out the power structure here, and I intended to find out who and stop them.

Calista cleared her throat and wiped the tears. "I'm just proud of you, that's all."

My heart pinched. When my mother died five years ago, Calista had picked up the slack and attempted to fill the empty place in my heart. I reached out and squeezed her hand. No words were needed.

At that she went into business mode. "I meant to tell you this morning, but then Violet had her brilliant idea and the park thing happened, but the palace craftsman have been working all night with Sabina and Violet to fashion you a new crown and throne."

I frowned. "Oh, I had assumed I would wear the same crown as the Red Queen." I don't know why I thought it was inherited, but had figured it was simply passed to the next queen.

Calista looked aghast. "Never! Each crown and throne is magically made for the queen. It is special, a place of power for her."

Okay then. I nodded. I loved the ruby-inlaid crown the late queen wore. It was stunning. But I'm sure mine would be just as nice.

A throat cleared in the doorway and I looked up to see Derek and Torine.

"Your Majesty, the ceremony awaits," Torine said with a deep bow.

Torine ... bowing to me. Crazy.

Derek, who was looking extra refined in the black royal guard uniform, let his eyes roam over my dress. His cheeks reddened when I caught him.

"Let's go," I said, my voice lowering as nerves got me.

The large great hall would be packed with wolves from all over New York City, and the ceremony would be televised to the shifter world. I was still most nervous for the part where I linked up with the mecca and harnessed the energy to my people. The queen's death had shaken the power structure and my coronation would fix it. I knew it needed to be done, but I could trust nothing was going to go as planned with the mecca. Too much strangeness was afoot.

Before I knew it we had reached the large double doors. Two guards stood to each side. They bowed deeply before swinging the doors open, and all of a sudden hundreds of eyes were on me.

"Good luck, Your Majesty," Calista whispered, and then she was gone. So were Torine and Derek. I was just standing there with all of these people looking at me. I had always been nervous in large crowds, and hated public speaking. Becoming queen was probably not the best choice for all of that. Oh well.

A booming voice resonated around the hall: "Her Majesty, Queen of Wolf Shifters. Long may she reign!"

"Long may she reign," hundreds of voices echoed back.

Shoving my anxiety down, I held my head high as a violin began to play. Walking slowly down the red velvet aisle, I nodded and smiled to the wolves in attendance. As I got closer to the front I realized with everything that had happened I had completely forgotten about the bear king. Only when I saw two rows full of hulking figures, and caught the unfamiliar earthy scent, did I remember. The king and his royal guard were here. I scanned those two rows, prepared to meet the king's eyes and offer the first smile – make sure we started our new relationship off right.

I spotted Gerald first and gave him a smile. I was relieved by his head bow and genuine grin. I moved to the male next to him, expecting it would be the king. This male had his huge back turned, speaking to one of his guards, but I could see that his black jacket bore the royal crest, and perched in his dark hair was a golden crown with green jewels. The energy of the mecca was clearly pouring off him, strong enough that I half expected to see waves of power threading through his hair.

As I was nearing the front where Sabina and the council were waiting, the king turned from speaking to his guard and his attention zeroed in on me. The moment our eyes locked all air was knocked out of me.

No. No. No. That wasn't the king! It couldn't be.

He gave me a lopsided grin and a wink. I nearly stumbled over my dress but caught myself at the last second. That damn bear gardener wasn't a gardener at all! My jaw clenched as the realization hit me. The bear king had kissed me. Oh crap ... if anyone found out, my people would revolt. I could lose the crown, or my life. That damn bear.

Did his people have the same rule as us? Would he use this in an attempt to blackmail me into an agreement? I had a feeling our first meeting after the coronation was going to be interesting. I just had to hope he kept his big mouth shut, otherwise things were going to get very rough for me. I had reached the front now, and stood before Sabina and Violet. They both clasped a large wooden box, which pulsed with mecca energy. Shaking off my thoughts of the bear king, I forced myself to focus on the task at hand.

I turned to my people and raised my arms high. They burst into cheers and clapping. I decided to ignore the king for the rest of the ceremony and just focus. This was my day. My eyes scanned my people, and when they fell on

Selene in the front row they sharpened a bit. I was pleased to see she hadn't brought Larak. My email had been understood, loud and clear.

The side door to the hall opened and Calista walked in with a regal-looking Finn. He was dressed in his finest battle armor, the metal clinking as he walked. Pride surged within me as the crowd gasped. There was an old saying: "A queen is only as strong as her familiar." Finn made me proud, he always would. Not only was he the largest familiar on record, he was fierce, proud, and kind. He had a heart twice the size of any other, literally and figuratively. I was beyond blessed.

As he took his place beside me I found myself wondering what the king's familiar was, and why wasn't it present today? Or that day in the garden? And why the hell was I still wondering anything about that lying, kissing bastard? He had pretended he was the damn gardener. He caught me trying to break into his own house and never even said a word about being the king. And how the hell had he managed to hide his mecca energy from me? I quelled my urge to stride across the space and slam my fist into his throat.

His grin widened then as if he'd heard my thoughts. I breathed deeply, trying to convince myself war just wasn't worth it, no matter how satisfying.

"Greetings, everyone!" Torine's voice shook me from my thoughts and I stood at attention. "At the fall of one day, we have the dawn of another. Arianna of the red lineage will be stepping in as our new dawn. Long live the queen. Long may she rule."

The crowd roared their approval and I couldn't help but smile. Not only was this a truly historic moment – many shifters had never seen a coronation – the dynamism in the room was beyond anything I'd expected. I could feel the energy of my people. More than just when I was alpha of the Bronx – so much more.

Torine walked over to me, holding a worn book. The Covenants, the Bible of our people.

I placed my right hand on it and my left hand over my heart.

"Your Majesty, do you take a lifelong oath to lead our people, to protect them and keep them strong by funneling the mecca magic to them?" His voice was strong as he said the words with conviction.

"I do!" I said loud and strong. I wanted every single person here to hear my voice.

Torine nodded. "And do you swear to keep our race pure by breeding only with wolf shifters and produce an heir in the future?"

I gulped, faltering for a moment. I didn't remember that covenant. "I do!"

"And lastly do you swear to put your life before those of your people, no matter what?"

I nodded. That was an easy one. "I do."

Torine smiled. "Then please take a knee and be crowned queen of the wolf shifters."

My heart was hammering in my throat as I knelt, and Violet and Sabina moved forward; my friend lifted the lid of the box. The second the contents were visible, I gasped. A beautiful silver crown was nestled inside. It was simpler than the Red Queen's, but to me far more beautiful. Instead of rubies, the swirls and arcs of the silver were inlaid with purple mecca crystal. Most of the shifters wouldn't know what gem the purple stone was, but after the second task I would recognize mecca stone anywhere. Had any queen ever had a mecca crown? Was it Violet or Calista who had made this happen for me?

Sabina and Violet lifted the crown from its box and I wondered if it pained them to do so. Maybe that's why Torine didn't crown me – he couldn't.

The moment it touched on my head I felt a wave of dizziness before power surged through me.

"I now pronounce you queen."

Torine's voice carried, and in unison the entire crowd replied: "Long live the queen!"

I didn't think I would ever get used to that. My eyes flicked to the bear king. He had his eyes locked on me. The mirth he'd displayed earlier and during our meeting in the garden was now nowhere to be seen. His huge body was tense, and something strong was rolling across the metallic bronze of his eyes.

I was distracted by Torine crossing to my side holding a small dagger and the magical golden cup. Here came the truly scary part. I would now be linked to the mecca, to part from it only in death. I had to remind myself that I was born for this. Whatever it took to harness the mecca was flowing through my veins. I just needed to relax and let it flow.

I unhooked one of my titanium cuffs and displayed my wrist. Torine gestured to Finn. "I need him to do it first."

Finn needed no encouragement; he would always be the braver of us. He lifted one paw to Torine. The council member knelt and took a substantial blood sample from Finn before then moving to me. The blade slicing my arm barely hurt; it was when the blood dripped into the cup that I began to feel a tingle, a burning throughout my body. I hadn't been alive long enough to have ever seen a queen crowned, but I did know from rumors that linking to the mecca was tiresome and a bit painful. The attack in the park today had already left my body and energy strained, but I would not fail. I would be strong enough.

Once the cup was full and magically drained, Torine stepped aside and I was hit with a magical force so strong it knocked me backward. I crashed onto the ground panting as a visible purple haze ascended up through the stone floor I was lying upon and wrapped itself around me so tightly I couldn't breathe. Finn was panting beside me and nuzzling me with his head. I couldn't think ... couldn't communicate with him.

"Something is wrong! It's too much," Violet cried out. Her voice was muffled through the haze choking me.

My brain began to hammer with sharp pains; my eyes watered and I sensed the distress of the crowd. This wasn't normal, this was going to kill me. I was sure of it now. I felt a wetness fall from my nose and reached up to find it was blood. Barely conscious, I somehow noticed that damn bear as he took three long strides toward me. Derek got between me and the king, the tip of his sword resting against the king's neck.

Gerald stepped in beside his king. "He can help her. It's his gift," he said fiercely.

Derek seemed to consider it. That's when I whimpered like a puppy, because my insides were boiling hot. Derek took one look at me and dropped his sword. No point protecting me from the king, if the mecca was only going to kill me anyway.

The bear's handsome face swam into view. Somehow he was able to brush aside the purple haze and reach me. He gently removed my crown and almost immediately some of the pain eased. Then he placed a big meaty hand on my bare chest and the crowd gasped at the inappropriate gesture. But the second his warm skin touched mine, the burning stopped, the heat lessened, the feeling that I was near death fled. With his eyes closed he took in deep breaths, letting them out slowly. The surge of energy slowed and started to move more rhythmically, almost like the king was filtering the mecca to me, acting as a shield. Instead of pain I only felt power. The purple haze that had settled over me had initially been so thick I could barely see through it, but now it was a thin, smoky sheen, which continued lessening.

The mecca was settling into my bones, my blood, and for the first time the true strength of it crashed through my mind. In that moment I wasn't alone though, and the overwhelming power was shared between me and the bear, who still had his hands on me. It allowed me to adjust, and soon enough strength rocked my core.

After a few more deep breaths, the king opened those amber eyes and they were blazing, locked directly on me. My lips tingled as I remembered our kiss in his garden. He removed his hand and placed the crown back on my head. Then he helped me stand and gave me a slight bow.

"Your Majesty." His gruff voice tickled my ears, sending shivers down my spine.

As he walked back over to take his seat, I was sure of one thing. The bear king had just saved my life.

Violet got to me first, and she barely even flinched as her arms wrapped around me. "The mecca is unstable. I've never seen it like this before."

"We need to get her out of here," Calista said. She was steps behind the magic born.

Torine hurried across. "Yes, the queen needs to be examined, to make sure she sustained no injuries."

Everyone was talking over the top of me, like I wasn't even there.

Violet had already let me go, the energy riding me too much when combined with her own magical powers. In a way, both of us now were filled with mecca energy, and sometimes too much can be explosive, as had been demonstrated not two minutes previous.

I moved away from the group of concerned shifters fussing around me. I was queen now, and it was time for me to step up and reassure my people. The crowd was panicked, the wolves across the world probably glued to their televisions. With this in mind I took a deep breath and stepped to the edge of the stage. My dominants and guards crowded below me to stop anyone from approaching.

"Silence!" I shouted, needing them to calm so I could speak. My voice sounded the same, but mecca laced every word, and a magical silence descended. Now I was starting to understand how the Red Queen had commanded a room so easily.

"Please, I understand your concern, but there is no need." I held my hands up, palms wide as I sought to comfort my people. "The mecca was stronger than we anticipated, but now that I have bonded with it, the effects will start to filter out to the boroughs. You will feel the dissonance ease. We will once again be strong and united!"

I knew I sounded confident, that the worries and fears plaguing me were not obvious on the outside. I wanted to believe everything I'd just said, and in some ways it was the truth. I could already feel the power filtering out of me and to the rest of the alpha wolves. From them it would continue on to their shifters, until every single one of my race was touched.

Need crushed my chest, the need to prove to my people that I was strong enough, that I could be a queen they could depend on. Taking a deep breath, I felt for the Manhattan pack first, those nearest to me, then spread my energy out to those in all of New York City, and finally across the world. When I felt the mass consciousness of my people, I let the mental bells toll. The same bells the queen had sent when she died, I sent them to signify a rebirth for our people. As the bells knelled, every one of my people bent to one knee and bowed their heads. Every person but the bear king and his men.

There was definitely a change with the mecca power. Now that I was connected, I could feel it much more than before. How was I going to figure it out though? The only person I could have asked was murdered not more than a week ago.

Had the Red Queen discovered a problem? Something she shouldn't have, that led to her death? And how was I going to be able to figure it out without ending up with the same fate?

Chapter Ten

Never look a gift bear in the mouth.

THE CHAOS TOOK longer than expected to die down, but eventually order returned and the coronation continued. The council members swore their allegiance and wise counsel to me, and all except one or two showed the due amount of respect to my position. It wasn't easy for me to replace council members. They were elected based on more than the queen's approval, but I could make life very difficult for those who tried to exert their power.

The entire time I felt the eyes of my people watching each step with eager interest. But the eyes that burned through me the most was that ... that damn bear's. Who maybe wasn't so damned after all. Why had he saved me? If I had fallen during the coronation, the wolf shifters would have descended into anarchy and our boroughs would have been vulnerable to a takeover. That was what the bears had battled us for, for over three hundred years. He could have had all five boroughs, total and complete power over the mecca and vortexes, and yet he had chosen to save my life.

Maybe he wanted the life debt I now owed him. I had no idea if bears followed such practices, but wolves did. If he ever called on me for anything that was in my power to grant, I had to follow through. And I had a lot of power in my hands now.

Still, if he'd become the ruler of five boroughs, he'd have been the most powerful shifter in the entire world. He'd have had no need for me.

That bear had a game plan, and I was going to find out what it was.

"Arianna ... Your Highness..."

Calista startled me from my thoughts, and I realized that the last of the ceremonial chanting and speeches were done. "It's time to greet your people."

I plastered a smile to my face, hoping like hell it didn't look as brittle and fake as I felt at the moment. With guards around me I made my way down off the elevated floor. The shifters pressed in closer to me, all of them wanting to see their queen, for no other reason than the power now entrenched in my very skin.

I had a thought and turned to Violet. "Do I look different?" There seemed to be a lot of wide-eyed looks going on.

My best friend grinned. Some of the tension which had been lining her pale face eased. "Uh, yeah, you could say that. You always look beautiful, Arianna, but right now you're truly radiant. You literally glow with the mecca, and for once I'm not the only one who can see it."

That was interesting. I never remembered the Red Queen ever glowing, even when she connected to the power. Another mystery for me to unravel. My list was getting a little too lengthy for my liking.

When I was finally done, it was time for the dinner and ball. This was a black tie, invite only event. The alphas from across the boroughs would be present, and so would the bear king. He had the place of honor apparently. Well, the most honorable place behind me.

Calista cornered me just before I was about to enter. "Hold still, Arianna, I need to fix your hair."

My hands flew up to feel my braid crown, forgetting of course I was wearing an actual crown. I almost knocked the heavy, ornate piece off. Calista let out a little shriek and her tablet went flying as she lurched forward to save the crown. Only she couldn't get close to it. Her hand bounced off about a foot from my head.

She blinked wide eyes at me as both of us held our breath. "Why can't I touch it?" she whispered. "Violet, can you touch it still?"

She called across to the magic born, who'd been patiently waiting close to Blaine and the rest of my dominants. Violet strode to my side, her white hair fanning out around her like there was a nice breeze fan in effect. My friend paused, reaching out a tentative hand toward the crown. She managed to get a little closer than Calista, but still couldn't actually touch the piece.

I reached up and eased it free of my hair, holding it in front of me. Both girls tried to touch it again, and both of them were rebuffed. "The crown has bonded to you and the mecca," Violet said. "I warned the council that using the mecca stones could possibly create an unstable energy, but the Covenant lays out a special magical test that dictates the stones for each crown, and your results were without a doubt the mecca crystal. You are literally, more than any other queen, queen of the mecca."

Okay, so now I understood why my crown was filled with mecca stones; it had not been Violet's idea. She seemed to be almost against the idea. I wondered what this magical test entailed.

I had always loved magic. As a child I was envious of Violet for being magic born. It's something I had wanted to be.

"Quick question: why is my copy of the Covenant missing all of this information?"

I knew that damn book by heart, and yet I continued to be surprised by these new pieces of information.

Calista reached down and retrieved her precious tablet, thankful the case had saved it from smashing. "The council has the extended version of the Covenant. It's not viewed by any but them, not even the queen."

One-handed, she started to fix my hair while I let her information mull around my mind. Once she declared me ready, I had to secure the crown, as no one could help me. Except for offering some little suggestions ... like a bit to the left...

"If no one sees this extended version but the council, then how can we trust that their rules are even real? Or correct?"

Violet led the way to the double doors; my guards fanned out, preparing to enter first. "Because the council is spelled to speak truth of Covenant laws. They're the guardians. The upholders. The mecca would punish them if they abused that power. Still, with everything odd going on, it pays to be cautious. Absolute power corrupts absolutely."

Yes. Yes it did, and I was a firm believer in knowledge being power so I was going to do everything in my power to get my hands on that extended version of the Covenant.

The first two hours of the night went by in a flash. I mingled, talked politics, and even managed to finish a few of the delicious treats being served on huge silver platters. Calista cornered me soon after this, handing me a glass of champagne. I took a quick sip, needing a kick of alcohol to perk me up. As the delicious bubbles washed across my tongue, I sighed.

"Benefits of being queen, you always get the good alcohol."

My advisor tried to glare, but even as she shook her head at me, a smile managed to break free. "You've done exceptionally well tonight. I only observed four eye rolls, two times feigning of deafness, six mumbled curse words, and three deliberate elbows."

For the love of ... she was a ninja. I hadn't seen her all night until now.

"I think it was four elbows. That shifter from Queens was really handsy, and if it hadn't been an elbow to the ribs, it was going to be a foot in his ba—"

"Your Highness!" she cut me off. "Seriously, I can't take you anywhere."

I surprised her then by leaning forward and wrapping my free arm around her. It was frowned upon for the queen to touch a submissive, but I didn't care. "Thank you," I whispered. "You have been preparing me for this. You have sacrificed your own life and happiness many times for heirs. Everyone wanted you as an advisor when you finished the last heir group, and you chose me. I would not have been even remotely equipped for this role without you. I don't thank you enough."

I would have sworn she was crying. I heard a few sniffles, but when I pulled back there was no evidence, just a beaming smile and a proud expression. "It's been my honor. I love you like a daughter. You know that, and you're a true queen." She started to fidget a little bit then and I narrowed my eyes on her.

"I recognize that look, Cal. What is it? You might as well tell me now."

She swallowed. "The bear king has requested a dance. He is not taking no for an answer, and the council are hoping you'll be prepared to play nice. Especially after he helped out with ... the mecca thing."

Sucking in a deep breath, my eyes sought out the massive figure. I hadn't exactly been avoiding him ... just making sure that whenever he moved in my direction I was extremely busy and couldn't stop to chat. Okay, yeah, I was totally avoiding that big, gorgeous, distracting bear. I tried to recall his name. He'd told me when we were fifteen ... Kallen ... Kaden. It was definitely a K name, but I couldn't recall which one. Everything but the kiss had been purged from my memory. The kiss I still couldn't shake, and after that moment in the garden I knew exactly why.

Our peace talks were scheduled for later tonight, so there was really no need for me to see him at this dance. I was worried that he would start making demands, and I would have to figure out how to deal with the fallout of our kiss.

Calista still looked nervous, so without too much effort on my part I fixed a pleasant expression on my face and strode across the huge room.

Dozens of eyes followed me. I was now the most watched female in the three boroughs. I wasn't sure the whole queen thing had really sunk in yet; it would take some getting used to. One set of eyes in particular were very disconcerting. It was as if he had heard my conversation with Calista and was already waiting for me. He stood alone now, towering over everyone else in the room. I had no idea how I hadn't noticed in the garden, or even at fifteen, the commanding nature of his stance, the confidence he exuded, the power trapped beneath his corded muscles and caveman attitude.

No one in any of the world would doubt he was a king. But there was no denying the bastard had hidden it from me, and deliberately. I hadn't changed that much since fifteen, but he was almost unrecognizable.

"Your Majesty," he said, when I was a few feet from him. He did not bow, or even incline his head, which was fine by me. I sure as hell wasn't going to bow back.

"Would you like to dance, Your Highness?" I replied, drawing on every ounce of my training and etiquette. Although I did not hold out my hand as I should have, because I wanted the upper hand. He would have to come to me.

And come he did, stepping across the space between us in one giant stride and engulfing me with the same energy and heat that he had in the garden. I swallowed hard, fighting my own urge to step back. He was too much of everything, and I wasn't sure this dance was a good idea at all.

Then he held out his hand and I forgot all misgivings and fears. My instincts kicked in, and when I placed my hand into his, energy sizzled between us. Mecca danced in the space, surging through each of us and our connection to it.

He grinned, and with steel-like strength hauled me into his arms. I stiffened enough to stop our bodies from colliding, but the dance of mecca energy between us was almost enough to crumble my resolve. We started to move, both of us highly trained and able to easily follow along with the current traditional song and its intricate steps.

"Thank you, Your Highness," I said first, needing to get it out of the way. "For helping me tonight. I'm not sure what would have happened if you hadn't been there."

I knew exactly what would have happened. The mecca would have ripped me to pieces, but there was no need to give him too much ammunition. As he moved us further into the mass of shifters already dancing, he leaned down, lessening the distance between us to a slightly inappropriate level.

"Call me Kade," he said, which was a complete break of protocol. I sure as hell wasn't letting him call me Arianna. I needed whatever barriers there were between us to remain intact. "Do you know what actually happened tonight? Because I've never seen the mecca act in that way. The power ... it was far beyond anything I've felt before."

I fought for composure. This was not a male you let know your weaknesses. But the mecca affected him also, and I knew eventually we'd have to discuss the possibility that there was a problem. Not today though. I wanted to do my own investigating.

"I really have no idea. The mecca is a vast power, and it has definitely reacted to the death of the Red Queen. How were you able to filter it like that?"

He swirled me around, tightening his strong arms around me again. "I have a special affinity with the mecca. A born connection to it. It's rare in our world, almost unheard of, but it's definitely helpful as king." His voice lowered. "I'm glad it was you who earned the crown. You are worthy of the role."

Well that affinity probably explained how he'd hidden his energy that day in the garden. Something I was still annoyed about. Staring into his eyes, which somehow managed to swirl like the melted copper of their color and yet still have the depth of an aged whiskey, I found myself asking: "How is one to know they are truly worthy? Living day to day with a power beyond anything a single entity should handle, the lives of thousands in your hands. How do you do it? How do you truly become worthy?"

His eyes lightened, his fierceness relaxing slightly, and for a moment it felt like we were old friends. In fact, had I ever been so rawly honest with anyone before? Maybe Violet. But she was different. I didn't know what had come over me.

He took a second to answer, and I found myself waiting with more anticipation than was queenly for his reply. "The fact that you even stop to question your worth is part of what makes you worthy. You had honor even at fifteen. You had fire, and passion filling every facet of your being. You talked of your friends like you would die for any of them in an instant … when as an heir they should be the ones dying for you. A ruler should never ask from their people more than they are willing to sacrifice themselves." He paused. "I never wanted to be king. That was the role my brother was groomed for, but sometimes these things are not in our hands. You are queen because you are best for the job at this moment in time. It's up to you whether you build on the worth you already have."

It touched me that he remembered our long ago meeting on the Island. I was also a little taken aback by the deeper nature of our conversation. I shouldn't have been surprised, it had been exactly the same when we were fifteen – sharing of thoughts, and conversing in a way which spoke of a true connection. The dance was over now, the music taking a few beats' break. We pulled apart as the crowd clapped around us and he leaned a little closer.

"I'm sure you'll live up to the potential I saw in you at fifteen. See you later, Arianna."

I narrowed my eyes at him, hands flying to my hips. First names were not used unless permission was given. How arrogant.

I wanted to remind him of that but he was gone. Somehow, despite being a giant, he moved with the grace of an athlete and disappeared with the skill of a thief in the night.

"Well, that looked like it went well." Calista was back by my side, and I had to blink a few times to break the spell he'd left over me. "Not a single eye roll or elbow to be seen."

That was true. I'd actually enjoyed the brief chat. He was far less of a pain than I'd expected, and no mention of the kiss. As Calista led me to my next duty, I couldn't stop thinking about what he'd said. Had I made a mistake with my honesty? Would he use that against me somehow? I'd always had an issue with people telling me I was worthy; I'd been hearing it for years. It wasn't a confidence issue – I understood my worth and I had trained hard for the role – but it still bothered me. That word ... worthy. I had done nothing yet to deserve that. I was worthy because royal blood ran in my veins. Why had I made myself so vulnerable right before the peace talks?

The bear king, on the other hand ... I could see his worth in the way his people loved him, and he in return gave back just as much to them. I might not know a lot about him, but I knew that much from the rumors spread about the new beloved bear king. The fact that war did not interest him, that said a lot.

I wasn't naïve, I knew he would take our boroughs if the opportunity arose. Gerald had all but admitted they had plans for that, but he didn't attack us when we were weak. He wanted to win with honor. He didn't want war.

Damn that bear. At some point during our brief meetings over the past years he had earned my respect. I hoped I wouldn't have to try to kill him anytime soon.

Eventually it was time for me to wish my guests a good night and retire to my private study. Time to renegotiate the peace terms with ... the bear king. I needed to reinstate the protocols between us. He already had me thinking of him as Kade. Despite the friendly nature of our dance, I was on edge, knowing that if there was any moment he'd use the kiss or the fact he'd saved my life against me, it was now.

After I gave a closing speech, written by my advisor, Calista led me to the private study. Two plush chairs were situated a respectable distance from each other. A small coffee table between them held a teapot and a scroll with ink and quill – the peace accords. The same accords our ancestors had started right after the dark war. Every time a new king or queen took office, they pledged to keep these accords alive. It was also a good time to ask for more land or less strict sanctions for vortex travel. Who knew what the bear king would want.

As I took my seat Calista fussed over my dress. "Be strong but polite. Remember your lessons in negotiations."

I nodded. There was a reason I played poker so often. I'd been relaxed during the dance, but this was business. The bear king would get nothing from me today ... unless of course he asked for the life debt I owed him. Doubtful that would be what he demanded of me though.

Calista slipped out of the door and I wiped my sweating palms on the velvet chair beneath me. The door creaked open and suddenly the room was filled with his presence. I stood, as protocol dictated, and he strode across the room to stand before me. He wore no smile this time, but he had taken off his heavy embroidered jacket, wearing a simple light linen tunic that showcased his chiseled body.

"Your Highness," I said.

His expression didn't change, but his eyes darkened. "Your Highness," he repeated back to me. "I appreciate you taking the time tonight to discuss these accords. However, I need to return to my people soon. These are not safe times."

It was like the dance had not happened. The warmth and friendliness was gone, and in its place were two rulers who would fight for their boroughs and people with a ferocity that had caused wars in the past. Hopefully it wouldn't come to that.

We both sat, each of us glancing down at the peace accords.

"Are these the same peace accords from last time?" he asked in his gruff voice.

He must have met with the Red Queen when he was crowned. I nodded, prepared to fight him on every single issue outlined in them.

But then he picked up the quill, dipped it in the ink, signed his name and handed the paper to me. He didn't even read it! My mouth dropped open in shock, which elicited a smile from him.

"Did you expect me to argue every little point ... ask for more land or taxes?" He seemed pleased to have caught me off guard. I grabbed the quill from him and signed my own name before tucking the accords away.

"Yes, I did," was all I could say.

He waved a hand. "I have no need of that. But I would like one thing from you." He leaned forward into my personal space.

Here it was. He had signed to make me happy and would now ask for the favor, one I probably couldn't refuse because he'd saved my life earlier with the mecca.

I plastered my best poker face on. "Oh, and what is that?"

At this close range his scent mingled around me, and it had my wolf practically purring inside of me. *You don't like bears,* I reminded her. But damn, there was a pull in that smell. It was amazing ... like freshly chopped wood and ... roses. I swallowed hard.

"I need us to be friends," he said.

It took me a few moments to focus again, and then his words registered.

"Friends?" I repeated, perplexed.

He nodded. "Historically, the wolf queen and the bear king have barely tolerated each other. That needs to end. We have a common enemy now and we can only defeat them if we work together."

His warning of a common enemy sent ice water through my veins.

"Common enemy?" I needed to hear him say it, to confirm what Gerald had told us that day, and what I was starting to see was the truth.

He nodded. "The Tuatha de Danann."

"I just don't understand. Why now? I thought they were all long dead. What do they want?" I'd never done much study on the fae. We were taught they were dead and that was pretty much it. Why had we not learned more about them? My history classes seemed to cover every detail of the shifters, but not the fae. It was odd. I should have known what that creature in the park was. How easy it would be for an enemy to take us down when we knew nothing about them at all.

The bear king leaned even closer, until we were only inches apart. "The Tuatha de Danann hold a special interest for my family. When they ruled this world they were known as the tribe of gods. They held power beyond any understanding of humans, and when they left this world the shifters were born. We had a lot of teachings early, but the stories have vanished. Each generation knows less and less. Why is that?"

It was almost as if the fae had deliberately wiped this information from our world, which worried me.

The air pulsed between us again, and I really wished it would stop doing that. I briefly contemplated slapping him again, just to break the tension, but I sensed he wouldn't be so forgiving the second time around. Needing a distraction, I jumped up and took a few steps around the back of the chair in the pretense of searching for a book on the full-wall shelf behind me.

Sucking in deeply, I calmed myself. "Maybe we could work together. We need to be prepared." I turned back from the shelf and faced him. He had not moved, but his eyes were tracking me. Then, in the spirit of friendship and working together, I decided to ask him one of the questions plaguing my mind.

"Have you ever heard of an ercho?"

His eyes darkened but he didn't look confused. "Hellions are no more than myth. Beyond even fae and gods."

I let out a huff of air and changed my mind. Now was not the time to tell him about my attack. There was no reason to lay all my cards on the table. I was here to learn about our enemy, not really to be best friends with the king of the bears.

I changed the subject. "Do you have any knowledge of a female heir with a lioness familiar?"

His brow furrowed, and I knew he wanted to go back to the ercho thing, but I made it very clear I was done with that conversation for now. "A female heir would be a wolf," he finally said. "We keep track best we can, but there are none with lionesses listed that I know."

Before he could ask me why I was randomly throwing these questions at him, I recounted Finn's story of the woman and her familiar. He listened intently until I was done, then his huge hand came up to scratch the edge of his beard.

"Maybe we're looking at this all wrong. It doesn't have to be a wolf ... the fae have heirs too."

When he said that my mouth popped open. "So you think these fae are just running around New York City?"

He nodded, standing. "Seems like a very logical possibility. I know Gerald told you that we were attacked the same night as your queen, as all the heirs were. They were too strong to be human, and did not have shifter energy. I think the fae are definitely on the earth again, and they are coming for us."

He crossed closer to me, the chair thankfully still between us, as I leaned against the bookshelf trying to contain my shock and fear. Reaching into a side pocket of his black dress pants, he produced a small palm-size book. "Since you know very little of the fae, as my first act of friendship, let me give you this."

He extended his hand and I grabbed the book, our fingers touching, the already familiar dance of mecca between us strong. The cover was leather and had two words stamped into it. Two very important words: *Fae History.*

"Thank you..." This was not how I'd expected this night to go. But maybe something even better had actually emerged. A true friendship.

He nodded. "See, this friends thing is going to be fun."

Well, it was kind of nice to have a friend who understood the duty of a ruler, who shouldered the same burdens that I now did. Somehow I knew I could learn a lot from him. And to be a good leader, one should never stop learning.

Not to mention if the fae were gearing up for some huge attack, for whatever reason, it was good to have the bears on our side – assuming our people would ever side together. I moved away from the wall and rounded the chair to stand close by him. He held out a hand, and with barely a hesitation I took it, ignoring the familiar lurch within my stomach.

"Our people will think us weak for this alliance," I said, as we shook hands once. I went to pull away but he held on for an extra beat.

"No one questions my strength," he murmured, before finally releasing me. "But as a new queen you will have to prove your own. So we can keep this just between us for now. If you have need of me, send word with Finn. He will find my eagle and we can meet on the Island."

So his familiar was an eagle. Interesting, those were very rare.

As he moved toward the door, our meeting finished for the day, he turned back at the last moment. "Read the book. You will have questions, and for the most part I don't have any answers, but I do know some of the facts. For one, I can sense that this is going to be much bigger than either of us could guess. We have to try to be prepared for an all-out war."

And with that worrying and cryptic prediction he was gone. I stood there for many minutes, clutching the small book, wondering what drama I had just been crowned into.

Chapter Eleven

Revenge is a fickle stone to throw.

THE NEXT MORNING I asked Calista to return the king's mecca stone, the one which Selene had stolen for the Summit task. He had given me the fae history book to mark our friendship and I wanted to give a peace offering as well. I had a bunch of other things to deal with also: staffing issues, getting a wing set up for Winnie – who would be moving into the palace soon – figuring out if the fae were amassing an army to come and wipe us all out...

But my first order of business as queen was to run a full and thorough investigation into who killed our late queen. It was expected of me, and I was personally determined to find out. All the strange happenings seemed to be tied to her death and it felt important to look closer at everything to do with the Red Queen.

By midday I had already interviewed her entire royal guard and her three personal maids. They all said the same thing. The queen went into her library for tea alone, as she did most mornings, and an hour later a metallic scent alerted her guards. Blood. They had to bust the door down; it had been sealed somehow – not by any sort of magical means or otherwise that they recognized – and by the time they got inside she was already dead. No one else was in the room.

They immediately barred the door and called in Sabina. Since there was only that one guarded entry into the room, the magic born had been the first call to make sure there was nothing of a magical nature going on, which included invisibility and other weird and wonderful spells.

Sabina found nothing also apparently. I'd just finished interviewing her, and she confirmed the guards' stories, and added that she had detected nothing of magical significance.

It just didn't add up to me. The Red Queen was clearly murdered, brutally so, and yet no one had seen her assailant. But all confirmed there had been two cups of hot tea. The most logical explanation for the queen's death was that a magic born or maybe a fae had killed her. The attacks on all of us happened shortly after her death, but those assailants appeared to be human, even in death. Were they some sort of weird fae hybrid? Surely they would emit a magical essence. Humans had a barely detectable energy. The fae were supposed to have been the original creators of the mecca. They must be filled with magic.

Was there a magic-born shifter helping a fae? Violet was totally in the clear there. I trusted her above all others, which left Sabina, Jesabele, and Seamus.

All I had were more questions and no way to get answers.

Sabina could have been lying to me. That Violet – who had been hiding behind thick curtains, acting as my lie-detector – had not picked up on any lies from her, didn't mean there weren't any. Magic born were not like other shifters, and Sabina might have figured out a way to hide the information.

Could it have been her all along? Maybe she'd had a fight with the Red Queen. Maybe Selene hired her to take out the queen. But what could Selene offer her? Sabina was already the queen's magic born, the one with the most access to the mecca. There had to be more to it.

My fingernails were anxiously drumming the side of my new throne, which had been installed sometime last night. Calista hadn't been kidding when she said that each one was specially designed for the new queen. Like my crown of mecca stones, this high-backed, silver and ornate piece had scattered energy stones in a zigzag pattern up each side pillar. The tingle rushed through me, and it was almost like sitting atop pure power.

I was almost done with my interviews for today. Just one more: Bethany, the queen's advisor. The moment of the queen's death, Bethany took a leave of absence and went into mourning with her family, who lived on the lower east side. Now I had requested her presence to give a full detail of what she knew.

There was a knock on the door.

"Enter!" I called out. I had requested complete privacy, no guards or even Calista inside the chamber. I didn't want anyone afraid of telling me a secret with others present. The only exception was Violet, still hiding behind the thick velvet drapes. My guards were not happy about being excluded from the room; these were perilous times and with a queen killer on the loose, but they allowed it only if they could search and remove all weapons at the door.

Bethany approached me, her hands wringing together nervously and her mousy brown hair hanging limp. She had dark circles under her puffy eyes and I could tell she had been crying for days.

"Your Majesty." She gave a low bow and stayed down.

"You may rise, Bethany." I liked her. She had always been a strong and loyal advisor to the queen. Seeing her in this frail state pained me. I tried to soften my voice. She looked easily spooked. Fragile.

"I want you to be able to speak freely, no protocol. Just tell me what happened the night the queen died."

She nodded, chewing her lip. "I had been busy that day arranging Violet's itinerary in London and the work the queen wanted done there. The queen said goodnight to me around 7pm, as she often does, and that's the last I heard of her that night until–"

I nodded. "The queen had tea with someone early the next morning. There were two cups. Do you have any idea who it could have been?"

"No," she answered, a little too quickly.

"Lie!" Violet jumped out from behind the curtain, scaring us both. Always with the dramatic entrances.

Bethany looked like she had been slapped. Her eyes were wide and brimmed with tears.

"Please don't," she whimpered at Violet.

I stood now, approaching her. I never in a thousand years would have suspected Bethany of harming our queen. No way. She loved her.

Violet's head was cocked to the side as she stalked Bethany like prey.

"Who killed the queen?" Violet's voice carried a musical quality.

Bethany's upper lip broke out in a sweat. "I don't know."

Violet relaxed a little. "Truth."

I phrased the question differently. "Who do you think killed the queen?"

Bethany was panting now as if speaking of this caused her pain. "I can't say."

Violet's eyebrows drew together. "Truth."

What the hell was going on here?

Violet reached out to touched Bethany's arm and recoiled immediately like she'd been burned. "She's magic touched."

Bethany dropped to her knees now, sobbing.

I was at a loss.

"A very, very powerful magic born has spelled her so she can't tell us what we want to know." Violet looked at me with a gaze that sent shivers down my spine.

"Who is more powerful than you?" I asked.

Violet looked lost, shrugging her shoulders.

"Did Sabina do this?" I asked Bethany.

"No," she whimpered.

I could see the former advisor was nearing her breakdown limits, so I broke protocol and knelt next to Bethany, making her look into my eyes. "Was it a bear shifter who did this? Did the queen have a bear lover?"

Had the king been lying to me this entire time, trying to cover up an affair with the Red Queen? Implicate an ancient myth of beings who had not been seen for centuries to throw us off track – just the mere thought had fury raging through me, the need to skin him alive tingling within my fingers.

"Not a bear," Bethany scraped out.

I looked at Violet, who nodded. Truth.

Not a bear, so that meant...

"Did the queen have a lover that you suspect killed her? Someone strong and magical?" This was like pulling teeth, but clearly the *right* question had to be asked to get around the spell.

Bethany's eyes began to bulge as her skin turned purple, like she couldn't breathe.

"...yes." She barely got the word out before going cross-eyed and collapsing backward.

"No!" I leaned over her body to feel for a pulse ... nothing.

Violet was just standing there frozen.

"Do something!" I yelled at my best friend.

Violet shook her head. "I can't. The spell had a safeguard built in. Clearly her confirming that information triggered it. Instant death."

Falling back and sitting on my heels, I released my frustration by letting loose an ear-piercing howl.

Violet matched mine with her own, and my guards burst through the doors to see what was wrong. I stood, holding my head high as they surveyed Bethany's body.

The queen had a lover. I should have guessed. Now I just needed to find out who it was and how it was possible they could be powerful enough to kill her. Other than the bear king, who was powerful enough to kill the queen of the mecca? The immediate answer my brain supplied made me sick to my stomach. She wouldn't ... there was no way in shifter hell the Red Queen had a fae lover ... was there? A week ago I'd have not even given it a single consideration, but there was just too much fae activity now for us to ignore the possibility that they had been in our world, behind the scenes for far longer than I'd expected.

I met Violet's eyes. She still looked shaken. "I need you and Calista to meet me in the war room in five minutes," I said, keeping my voice low.

Violet nodded and took off to find my advisor. The best part about being queen was that I could involve the council as much or as little as I wanted, and right now I didn't want to bring this to them. But I did need to act, and fast, because I had a feeling something awful was going on. As Kade … the bear king … had told me, something huge was coming and we needed to be prepared.

My guards looked at me expectantly, standing over Bethany's body.

"She was bespelled to die upon revealing any information about the queen's killer." The guards were well trained, but still, a few mouths did drop at this news. "Give her a proper burial," I said to them. "Make sure her family is compensated. It's the least we can do."

There was no reason to treat her as a traitor. She seemed to be as much a victim in this as the late queen.

They nodded and removed her body, leaving me alone in the room once more. Not exactly how I wanted to spend my first full day as queen.

Closing my eyes I focused on my breathing, calming my mind.

Finn, meet me in the war room.

I sensed he was on the roof sunbathing in the warm summer air.

Be right there, he replied as I felt him brush my mind to pick up on my feelings. I hadn't wanted Finn present for my interrogations because he made people nervous, but now I needed him by my side if my next plan was going to work.

Five minutes later we were in the queen's war room – well, my war room now. I was still getting used to that. The room was large and circular, set up for strategy and meetings. In the center there was a 3D sculpture replica of the entire mecca, each vortex point, and every major building or entry and exit point. Calista and Violet stood on the one side of the map, I was across from them with Finn at my feet. They were all no doubt wondering why I would bring them to the war room when I had just declared peace with the bear king, but this was the best place for me to reveal all the information I'd been concealing.

Sucking in a deep breath, I started at the beginning. "So I know you've both heard bits and pieces of Gerald's information from that night he came to dinner, but there was one thing he told Torine and me in private. Something I was forbidden to reveal. He said that when they were attacked by the same spelled individuals as us, their magic born sensed an old magic; that of the Tuatha de Danann. The fae." I let that information sit for a second before I continued. "The bear king believes the fae have returned and he sent his councilman to warn us. I'm sorry

I didn't tell you both straight away, I wanted to, but Torine swore me to secrecy."

Calista's right hand was covering her mouth. Violet just stared at me, a glazed look in her eyes – her thinking face; she was mulling over my words.

I continued: "There's so much more, just last week Finn was stalked by a woman with an unknown familiar. A lioness. At first I thought she was a bear heir or maybe a long lost wolf heir. But Kade … uh, the bear king, confirmed that they only have male heirs. He suggested it could be fae. Then we had that attack in Central Park by a creature believed to be a myth, a guardian of the dark part of the Otherworld, which is ruled by the Tuatha de Danann. I have no other options but to believe that the fae have returned to our world."

Letting out an exhalation, I dropped the biggest bombshell. "And while I have no concrete evidence yet, I think the queen was killed by her secret lover whom I believe to be a fae."

Calista and Violet both gasped then, even the unflappable magic born looked shocked. Neither of them would have ever considered the possibility before this day; I knew exactly how they felt.

My advisor recovered first, and as her brow furrowed I knew her computer brain was surely trying to calculate all the possibilities.

She finally said: "You think this woman who stalked Finn was the queen's lover?"

The queen had always had male lovers, so I doubted it. "Not necessarily, but she's here for a reason, and I want to draw her out again and hopefully talk to her. If she doesn't want to talk, then we might have to lock her down long enough to force her to talk."

Violet grinned, looking like her old self again. "Wicked."

I nodded. "Wicked and possibly stupid. If the fae are strong enough to kill the late queen, then I alone may not be able to subdue her."

Violet rolled her eyes as if this was child's play. "I'll be there."

Yes. I was hoping that would be enough, but I didn't like going after an enemy I knew nothing about. But I liked an enemy running loose in my city even less. Especially if it was one who might possibly be a queen killer.

I gestured to the map. "She wouldn't be stupid enough to come to Manhattan with my royal guard crawling all over the place. When she followed Finn she stuck close to the vortex. I say we travel to Queens – I won't go near Selene's territory right now. Hopefully the woman will follow us there."

Calista put a hand up. "I just can't agree to you going out after this woman. What if she is fae? We know nothing about their strengths or weaknesses. And what if she did kill the late queen? You could be next. Violet and I can take Finn, plus a couple of the royal guards, and report back to you."

I smiled. "Nice try but no. I'm going, and no guards. She won't come out if she knows she's outnumbered. Besides, the last thing I need are rumors of fae killers running around. Torine at least was right about the chaos such rumors would cause. The best way to keep this locked down is to keep the information just between us."

Calista opened her mouth like she wanted to argue more, but just shook her head knowing there was no real argument she could give that would sway me from this. I was honor bound to three shifters, three deaths to avenge. I had to dig deeper into the queen's death. Everything linked back to her. And finding this woman felt like the right move to getting to the bottom of things. Or at least having a decent place to start.

We prepared to leave, each of us gathering weapons and stashing them around our person. Luckily the war room was set up for immediate battle. Violet dashed off to grab some of her potions and such; she had already made changes to Sabina's old quarters, and was in the midst of putting her special touch on the place. On the way she'd also drop my crown in the royal vault, as it was probably not a great idea to wander around the streets with it on. We had figured out a way for her to touch it, though only if it was enclosed in that special wooden box.

I was glad to be able to remove it for a few hours, almost felt like some of my responsibilities went with it. If only. I would still wear my braid crown, full queen makeup, and official sheath with royal emblem of my house on it. I could have changed, but that would make the guards suspicious – which would make it harder to escape from them.

When I was finally ready to go, Finn at my side and knives scattered about my person, Calista reached out and halted me.

"I still think this is a bad idea, but since your safety will be compromised until we can figure out who killed the queen, I accept this is the best lead we have right now. But I urge you to reconsider not taking guards. It's their duty to stand between you and death."

I shook my head at her. "Cal, you know that if this woman sees the full royal contingent she's just going to disappear. Otherwise, she'd have already walked to the front door and asked to speak with me. She's hanging around for some reason, following Finn, and most likely it's not going to be okay with any of us, but I need to know what she knows. No guards."

My advisor said no more, but worry was very clear across her delicate features. She gave me a moment's pause. Was I being rash going out without my guards? My own safety was one thing, but I felt confident in my mecca power and Finn. Yet I didn't want to risk the lives of my best friends, who would not let me go alone, no matter what the danger was. I knew on instinct that bringing guards was a bad idea, but ... maybe there was someone else.

I had an idea.

Can you let the king or his familiar know what we're doing, and where we'll be going. I don't know if he'll come, but in the spirit of friendship ... I feel like he should be aware. This could impact the entire mecca.

Finn nodded, before letting loose with a single howl and taking off from the room. Calista jumped, frowning after him.

"He'll meet us there," I said. "He's got a task to do first."

She gave me a look, one which said she was on to my evasive and weird behavior lately, but she didn't comment further. It was probably lucky for me that she was such a stickler for protocol. It meant she hated questioning her queen. Still, something told me it wouldn't last long. I had no idea what she'd do or say if she knew about my friendship with the bear king. Or the fact we'd kissed. Twice. As far as she knew, I had some random kiss with the king's gardener, she would die if she knew that the queen of the wolf shifters had kissed the king of the bears like he was the last male on Earth.

It was probably safer for my eardrums if she didn't know those things. Calista wasn't one for yelling, but when she did ... ouch. If Kade actually showed up in Queens today I'd have to let her in on some of it – but definitely not the kisses.

Violet was back now, cutting through the tension which hung heavy in the room. "The guards will be distracted for a few moments. Your sister has arrived and her room could possibly be the home of some weird little creatures.

I snorted, very queen-like. "You let animals go in Winnie's room? Classic. She'll be screaming the place down. No wonder the guards have been called."

My heart ached to see my little sister; it had been too long, but I would have plenty of time for her when I got back. I needed to take advantage of this situation.

"Not all of the guards left," Violet warned me, "and can I just tell you, your dominants are tough. It took at least three blasts of confusion spell for them to check out."

Calista gave a gasp, before quickly schooling her features. Attacking the royal guard was punishable by death, and what Violet had just done, even though it was not meant to harm, was enough to have her executed. Of course, the only one who could pass that final judgement was me, and since she'd been doing it for me, I would protect her.

Calista's voice was hard. "You better hope the council does not find out about this, Violet. They'll want your head."

I'd deal with the council if and when I had to. No one would take my friend's life without going through me first. Of course, Violet looked supremely unconcerned by this. If anything, amusement danced across her icy eyes. I was starting to understand it now ... now that the mecca lived within my very bones. There was very little magic born needed to worry about. But none of us were invincible, and the Red Queen had been very powerful, and that didn't help her in the end. Calista's caution was valuable here as well.

I led the way past some very dazed guards and was glad they would not remember what had happened. Calista would post to the queen's message board that I was retired to my suite for some quiet time and the guards would be none the wiser. Yes, they'd have questions, but for the most part would know better than to ask me outright. I could deal with their curiosity.

Violet cloaked all of us just before we reached the front doors. It was a lot of strain for her to hold three of us like this; she only did it when absolutely necessary. I could have helped but my training with mecca energy had not even started yet. I was basically worse than useless when it came to using the power now at my fingertips.

On the streets of Manhattan we blended in with ease. My outfit wasn't even out of place in the sea of unusual dress styles humans liked to wear. The journey to the vortex was short, the humans around us thinning out the closer we got. The energy here was strong, and my body reacted immediately.

"No wonder humans can't come any closer to this building," Violet said as we arrived at the rundown-looking warehouse that hid the magical disc. "Even for us it's a lot to step into all of that power."

It was true, humans were repelled about fifty feet in all directions from this space. It was for their own protection, the mecca was a deadly force. There were only two perimeter guards on this particular vortex, and we slipped past them using Violet's cloaking power.

Inside, the energy almost dropped me to my knees and I had to take several deep breaths to calm the haywire mecca shooting around my body. Violet and Calista were behind me, almost as if they were taking shelter from the energy.

"Let's do this," I said once I had gained full composure.

Hopefully when we got answers about the queen's death and possible fae attack, we'd also figure out why the mecca had gone haywire.

We crossed the space quickly, not wanting to remain in this energy longer than necessary. Violet would be able to travel the vortex no problem, but Calista needed my help. I could see her pinched expression and knew she wouldn't be able to remain here too long without getting ill. Drawback of not being an alpha.

Slipping her hand in mine, we stepped up to the vortex and I connected with the mecca, channeling that energy to the Queens borough. The familiar tingle began at my feet and then spread throughout my body. I heard Calista take in a deep breath and then we were sucked through. The journey was short and only a tad turbulent. Then, just as we were being pushed out into the Queens vortex, I heard a voice from deep within the mecca, my name whispered with the force of a thousand winds, chiming across time and space and wrapping around me with an uneasy note.

"Arianna..."

The faint distorted whisper sounded familiar. For a split second I thought it was my mother's voice. But ... it wasn't quite right. It was not my mother ... someone else my wolf recognized. I fought to stay inside the energy, but this was a one-way ticket and the train had reached the station.

I stumbled off the disc, Calista still clutched close to me.

"Your Grace!" Two guards appeared before me and took to their knees.

Violet appeared right after, looking calm and unruffled. I needed to ask her if she'd heard anything during her journey across, but now was definitely not the time.

Behind the kneeling guards were two more, swords drawn, but not in any sort of threatening gesture yet. More of an alert wariness. I gestured for the two on the ground to rise and one of them spoke as he stood.

"We didn't receive word that you were traveling to our borough today. We're not prepared and..." He trailed off and then the four of them parted, allowing me the briefest glimpse of the wall beyond. Propped against it was the bear king, one leg crossed over the other, broad shoulders filling out a simple button-up shirt and a huge eagle perched on his shoulder. Finn was standing off to his side.

"The king said he's here at your invitation?" the lead guard finished. I could tell he was not happy, that he felt he had failed me somehow, even though none of this was his fault at all.

Sucking in deeply, I plastered my queenly face on and worked to calm him. "Your diligence in this matter is much appreciated. I have some business in Queens today, in regards to the Red Queen's death, and some of the finer details of the peace accords. This is why the king is present."

The four guards relaxed a bit, but then one of them looked behind me.

"You're alone? Where are the royal guard?" They closed in on me, all of them again on high alert.

I gave them a playful smile. "I'm well protected. Violet will get you up to speed on what's going on."

I met Violet's eyes and she winked, gesturing for the guards to follow her into a corner of the building. Calista stood firm at my side, gazing at the king in curiosity.

"Thank you for coming." I nodded to Kade ... the king. Dammit. I was just going to have to accept the fact that protocol was always going to be a bit off between us. I knew he'd call me Arianna, and I could not seem to break the habit of referring to him as Kade.

His eagle was gigantic, peering at me with wise beady eyes. As we stepped closer to him, I noticed a hulking figure outside the window. Gerald.

Kade straightened and again had my attention. "Finn didn't say much. Just told Nix here that you were going to capture a fae and might need help. That was enough to get me to cancel all plans for the day."

"When you say it like that it does sound a bit crazy."

Calista cleared her throat and I scolded myself for not acting more professionally.

"King Kade, this is Calista, my royal advisor."

The king stepped forward, his hand extended first, which was unusual. Calista barely hesitated before placing her much smaller hand into his. He bowed deeply, touching her hand to his forehead. "We are well met," he said formally.

That must be some respectful custom of his people, because royalty bowed to no one in mine. Calista seemed taken aback, so she simply smiled and curtsied.

Now that he was close to me, the outdoorsy scent of him wrapped around me. And again my wolf rolled over like she was a pup having her first run. There'd always been a fiery attraction between us, even at fifteen. I was woman enough to admit that – I'd never have kissed a bear otherwise. But I still needed to be cautious around this man. When he'd kissed me in the garden, during the Summit, he'd known I was an heir and that it could get us both killed or exiled from our people, and yet he'd still done it. He was either completely reckless or he wanted something more from me. Only time would tell which one it was.

His eyes met mine and I swallowed.

Violet stepped in beside me. "Ready?"

I turned around to see all four guards playing poker on the ground, looking confusedly at their cards.

"Ready," I said.

Kade opened the door for all of us as we piled out of the building and into a deserted side alley. He took one look at his eagle and then nodded. Nix pushed off of his leather shoulder guard and her wings opened, taking flight.

She was beautiful. Violet, Calista, and I all gave an audible gasp at the sheer size of her wingspan. It must had been ten feet wide; she was nearly touching the walls of the alley as she flew higher and higher to the top of the city. Wow, a familiar with size to rival Finn. Luckily her bonded shifter was a giant. No one else would have been able to support the massive familiar on their shoulder. Finn, in his dog form, started barking and running in circles looking up at her.

"Finn! No time for playing," I playfully scolded, and the king laughed, deep and husky, and ... focus.

Gerald, who'd clearly been the lookout, crossed over to stand with our group. He gave me a deep bow. "Your Majesty. Thank you for the invitation into your territory."

Always the diplomat. Though I liked that the bears' lead war councilman had acknowledged that I had invited them into my territory. I smiled genuinely, unable to resist. Some people just gave off a first impression that stuck with you. I was comfortable around Gerald after his honesty at our first meeting and the respect he'd shown me.

I quickly introduced him to everyone and noticed his eyes lingered on Calista just a little longer than was necessary.

"Now, the woman we're looking for has a lioness familiar disguised as a golden lab. I have some suspicions that she is either directly involved, or may know who was, with our late queen's murder, so I want to find her and question her."

Gerald tightened his grip on his hip where I assumed he had a weapon stashed. "How about Lady Calista and I walk ten paces behind you and the king. Violet can be across the street with Finn, giving us a wider vantage point. If she sees anything, she can communicate to you through Finn."

Kade put his hands up. "Gerald, this isn't our mission. Let's see what the queen wants to do."

I smiled. "No, no, that's a good plan. Thank you." It kept everyone safe but didn't have us clustered together to scare her off.

Gerald gave me a slight bow. "Sorry, I'm used to being in charge of these things."

No doubt two heads of the royal races had never gone on a mission together. I waved him off. "It's quite alright. Let's move out."

The king stepped in beside me as Violet hooked Finn up to his leash and Calista stood awkwardly next to the hulking mass of muscle that made up Gerald. The moment we stepped out of the alleyway, Violet took off across the street with Finn, and Kade and I took a left, walking at a leisurely pace.

"I've never been to Queens," he said, and it dawned on me that he had probably only ever been to Manhattan, and then only on official business.

"I've never been to Staten Island or Brooklyn."

He slanted an amused glance in my direction. This was such an insane conversation. I wasn't sure a bear king and wolf queen had ever had a conversation like ours. Or a friendship. "Well, you should come by sometime for a tour. Coney Island is a blast."

"So I've heard," was all I said. I couldn't really just "come by for a tour," it would need to be official business. People would talk.

The king gave me a side look. "Do you still draw?"

"Huh?" Then it dawned on me. When I was fifteen I had been into manga art. I tried desperately to draw like the illustrators did but I was awful. When he had met me at the Island I'd had a sketchbook with me.

I laughed. "No, that was a phase. Never stuck."

I searched my mind for a memory of what he told me he used to like to do back then. I'd spent so much time trying to repress that day. Then I recalled a fact that had intrigued me at the time.

"Do you still play that drum?"

His whole face lit up, and for a second I had to remind myself to breathe – and that he was a bear. "The *tabla*. Yes, I do."

Golden retriever, three o'clock, Finn reported.

I darted my eyes around until I spotted it. "Three o'clock," I said to Kade.

The dog was alone, which was suspicious, as most dogs in the city were walked by owners, and strays were picked up by animal control. The dog was sitting at the entrance to Astoria Park across the street. Astoria Park was huge, like roughly sixty acres huge. They had a skate park, public pool, running track and more. It would be hard to find anyone in there unless they wanted to be found. When we were within five feet of the golden lab she turned and began to walk away, peering over her shoulder to make sure we were following.

The king and I shared a look. That wasn't a normal dog. We followed her past the dozens of people playing sports or lounging on blankets reading in the afternoon light, until finally she crested the hill and began leading us to the water. Near the bridge. I looked behind me and was happy to see Calista and Gerald not far away. They were chatting and Calista looked slightly uncomfortable; this was probably her first conversation with a bear shifter. Focusing toward the bridge again, there was now a tall, lanky woman waiting just at the water's edge, her blue gauzy dress billowing in the wind, as was her long black, silky hair. The dog trotted to her side.

Her expression was unreadable. As we neared, Kade seemed to take point, orienting himself so that he was slightly in front of me. I wasn't sure if this was a bear custom, or just a Kade thing, but it was time for him to learn that wolves did not shelter their females. We were not defenseless.

In a smooth, quick movement I stepped around him and made my approach to the female.

"Who are you and why have you been following my ... dog?"

I decided it best not to use the word familiar until she admitted that she was a magical being.

She made a fist with her left hand and held it lightly to her chest, bowing her head. "Your Majesty, I meant no disrespect, but I saw no other way to get your attention."

Your Majesty ... she knew of our world but wasn't a wolf. I could tell that immediately. She also didn't scent as bear, or magic born. Plus, magic born were lacking in skin and hair pigmentation and she was clearly filled with color. Her skin pink with the flush of vitality, hair rich and vibrant, depthless almost, despite the black coloring.

There was an odd energy about her, and yet I didn't feel a threat. I decided to cut straight to the point.

"You still didn't tell me who you are." I narrowed my eyes at her. Violet had taken a walk down the sandy beach and now stood about twenty feet to my right, watching, waiting. Calista and Gerald were behind us and well within earshot.

She sighed, as if this conversation was already paining her.

Buckle up, lady, I'm only just getting started.

"I am what you suspect and I don't have much time here."

Her dog whined and she silenced it with a look.

Kade cut in: "You're a fae?"

I'd been avoiding saying that directly. Probably because once it was confirmed I'd not be able to lie to myself any longer about the possibility of their return.

She nodded. "I am. And my world is..." Her voice faltered and I noticed her appearance change. Her ears grew to pointy tips and her nose slightly more upturned. Her eyes went from an uninteresting dull blue to this wash of greens and blues that would have made the ocean jealous. Through these colors were sparkling streams of light, unnaturally illuminating her eyes. The humanness she'd been exuding was gone, and in its place was a being of such ethereal beauty that I almost couldn't look directly at her.

"I'm not very powerful and I cannot hold an illusion for long. I was sent here to warn you. There is a problem with the *Livestia* ... the mecca. It is the magical force upon which both of our worlds are built and sustained and it is weakening on our side. Our world is dying and the dark queen blames you. You and your kind. There is talk of war, of the fae returning to the world of humans."

My chest tightened as the truth of her words hit me. "I don't understand. The mecca is the energy of Earth, and it's mine, the same way it was the Red Queen's before me, and so on. The fae left this world centuries ago."

Her blue billowy dress began to shimmer and I saw it flashing from the dress into black leather pants, a silver metal corset and sword, then back to the dress.

"The mecca isn't yours, it's all of ours. We share it," she said with just the slightest bite to her tone.

I didn't like that one bit. Sharing anything with the fae seemed dangerous.

Kade's features were dark now. A feralness moved within his gaze and I was actually a little taken aback by the scary he was exuding. "Who sent you here? If the fae are planning on destroying us, why warn us? You are fae, so you must want your mecca energy back too." Those low, husky tones had bumps sprouting across my skin, the hair on my neck standing as it did when I was in my wolf form.

She turned her eerie, but stunning eyes on him. "Not all fae are your enemy. Some think there should be another way. We are warring within our own world too, which might be the only thing to buy you some time. You need to figure out what is going on with the mecca. Fix it before the fae decide to leave the Otherworld. We have power beyond your ken and you would not survive a full attack."

More of her battle gear appeared and she glanced down at her figure. "I must go. Revealing my kind to humans is not advisable for many reasons."

She began to back up into the water. "How can we find you again if we have more questions?" I asked her when she was knee deep in the water. Fixing the mecca sounded like a great plan, except I had no idea how to do that.

Her expression turned sorrowful, and I suddenly felt like crying. "We don't know what happened to affect the mecca. We don't know why fae attacked your people. We don't even know how the Red Queen died, but we do know that much of this is tied to the dark fae, the ones on the other side of our war. We want to work together with you, but now is not the time. You do need to look into your queen though. Figure out how she died. This is information we all need, because rumor is she was working with the dark fae. I'll find you again if we have any more news. Prepare your people for war. We're doing all we can to stop it, but if we fail then there are none other to stand before the dark ones."

By now she was chest deep in the water, and her words had morphed into a musical language I had never heard but somehow understood. Suddenly she fell backward into the water, along with her familiar, and she was gone. A sizzle and a popping noise let me know that she had somehow just traveled in the water like we traveled the vortex.

The Red Queen had been working with the dark fae?

I turned to the king, my mouth open in shock.

"I need a drink," he said.

"Make that two."

She'd said war was coming from the dark fae. Clearly I was either going to be the queen who saved us all, or the queen who led the shifters to their final destruction.

Chapter Twelve

The dead tell tall tales.

WE WERE SILENT on the way back to the vortex. I don't think any of us knew what to say. One thing was for sure, the fae had given me a lot to think about, and as a newly crowned queen I did not need any more on my plate.

Kade was the first to break the silence. "It worries me that she didn't know who killed the Red Queen. She confirms that it may be linked to the dark fae in origin, but somehow knows nothing else."

I faced him fully. "She was clearly here to make first contact with us. What is the opposite of the dark fae? Do you know?" I was hoping there were some light happy fae who didn't like killing.

He nodded. "The light, of course. But from my readings light and dark don't necessarily mean good and evil. Nothing is that clear cut in the Otherworld. Both sides have different motives, but both are capable of mass destruction."

Great.

"We need to examine the bodies of the ones who attacked us the night of the queen's death," I said, thoughts rushing through my head. "They're the only evidence we have of the fae. That light fae wants us to figure out why our queen was killed and all the heirs attacked. This is the only place I can think of to start."

Violet spoke up then: "I examined the body, and I went to the vortex to check the attack site. I dug deeply, and, well, I used magic not known to most, and that body was still human. But ... I can't shake the feeling that we are missing something. We have to suspect they are fae, after seeing her use a human illusion, but I can't prove it."

"Our magic born says the same," said Gerald. "Human. Nothing to dispute it."

I had a thought. "Should we bring the bodies to the same place and have both of our magic born examine them together? I'd like to be there too. Now that I've joined with the mecca, maybe I will see more than a normal shifter."

Kade agreed. "That's a good idea. All of us together may be able to confirm it was truly fae that attacked us that day."

Calista looked extremely uncomfortable but said nothing.

I remembered then that I hadn't mentioned the weird thing which had happened in the vortex. I slowed my steps. We were a few hundred yards from the vortex now and I wanted to talk about it outside of the direct power source. Everyone paused around me, facing my direction.

"When we traveled here via the disc, did any of you hear whispered words? Your name being called?"

Eyes narrowed, and heads shook to tell me that I was the only one on that particularly crazy ride.

"I swear I heard my name from within the mecca, and it sounded familiar. At first I thought it was my late mother, but ... it wasn't. I'm sure of that now. Is the mecca a living entity, one with a consciousness? I thought it was just power, pure power, which could be good or bad, depending on who wielded it."

Kade was tense, and then in a flash he thrust his arm to the side, and all of us jumped as a huge screech signaled the return of his familiar. Nix landed on him and folded those massive wings back in. "The mecca is unstable," the king finally said. "It was not this way when I received the crown. It has happened recently, and it's rapidly growing worse. If that fae is to be believed, it's due to the balance being thrown off."

I nodded. "Yes, if what she says is true, the mecca sustains two worlds, Earth and the Otherworld, which is the mirror of ours. What happens if too much energy is funneled to Earth? She said her world would die, but what about ours? The mecca is not going to be able to be controlled."

Kade stared off thoughtfully, his lips creased, dimple just visible through his dark facial hair. "There is a good chance this could destroy both of our worlds. We must make this our top priority. I think your idea is a good one, Arianna. We should examine both bodies together and see if any clues are there. Can you meet me tomorrow night at my palace in Staten Island?"

I was glad that he'd agreed to my plan. I definitely felt there was a huge piece of evidence we were missing with these dead. A part of me was also intrigued to see his palace. I had only heard rumors of its opulence.

Calista cleared her throat. "Will her royal guard be welcome to attend as well?"

A flash of something dark crossed the king's face. His next words were low, and almost without inflection. "We're allies, and I will do everything in my power to prevent harm befalling her in my territory. However, should you feel the need to bring her royal guards, then I will not object. I want the queen to feel safe in my home." He said those last words directly to me, wisps of emotion bleeding into them.

I wasn't sure if I should be upset by Calista's insinuation or not. Maybe I was too trusting of Kade. Despite our newly formed friendship and his promises, he was still the king of people who had tried many times over the centuries to take our boroughs and kill our people. As queen, I needed to be responsible for my safety, which Calista was very aware of. This was the reason she was my advisor. She had a level head and didn't make decisions based on emotions or gut feelings.

I nodded. "We'll be there. Thank you for your assistance and hospitality in this matter."

When in doubt, fall back on protocol.

I wouldn't bring my entire royal guard, but it wouldn't hurt to bring my strongest five. Calista and Violet walked Finn inside while I lingered behind with the king. Gerald kept his distance, still looking out for any trouble.

We were semi-alone now, and I struggled with my next words, wanting to remain formal, but somehow they still came out with a strong emotional resonance. "Thank you for being here today."

Kade's eyes darkened as he stared at me. "You can always call on me, Ari. Always." And the air charged with electricity. I wasn't sure if it was the use of my shortened name, which only close friends and family used, or the way our energies mingled together, but a potent and tangible bond was forming between us, and I didn't like it one bit. It could only end in disaster. His expression lightened then as he took a step back. "That's what friends are for, right?"

Just like that the barriers were back between us, and I was relieved they were. Definitely relieved. I cleared my throat. "Well, I'll see you tomorrow." Turning on my heels I walked as fast as I could away from that damn bear.

The next day I was distracted through my morning queenly duties. My body hummed with anticipation of our task this evening. I would be seeing the bears' territory. The royal home. My curiosity couldn't be abated.

We had come back yesterday to a confused royal guard, but no one had asked questions. I had ordered the frozen body of our human intruder to be transferred to Staten Island ahead of our arrival today. Now I was preparing myself for one final task before I could leave.

The queen's body was to be brought down to the basement for my viewing. It was time for me to have her cremated. This was a step in our death ceremony and I could not delay it any longer. Her ashes would be kept in the royal castle, and Violet informed me they could be used for powerful spell craft.

I had been avoiding seeing her actual body – I'd only been at liberty to see it once I became queen, but still, I should have checked it out a few days ago – because the blood-strewn library scene had been bad enough without a body. But I couldn't delay any longer, the council was demanding we initiate the death ceremony, so it was time I checked her body, made sure there was no evidence missed, and then let her rest with the gods.

Calista knocked on my open door then. Behind her was a four-foot-tall dominant.

"Winnie!" I shouted, opening my arms. She was fast asleep when I had finished with my royal duties last night.

"Sissy!" Winnie shrieked, and leaped into my open arms. Her red fox familiar, Rhett, nuzzled up to Finn. She pulled back then, eyes wide. "Did you hear there was a lizard infestation in my new room!"

My mouth dropped open in playful pretend shock. "I did! How awful."

Winnie nodded. "It was. Rhett was chasing them all over the place and made a mess of my new pink rug."

I smiled, smoothing her hair. "Are they all gone now?"

She nodded, but then chewed her lip lowering her voice to a whisper. "Well, all except Prince Castle."

I widened my eyes, playing into her game. "Oh, you must tell me ... who is Prince Castle?"

Winnie smiled with her gorgeous innocence. "He's one of the lizards. Rhett tried to bite him and kinked his tail. I need to nurse him back to health now."

I nodded. "We must get Prince Castle a proper cage."

Her wide blue eyes lit up and she nodded. I pulled her in for another hug and relished the smell of her strawberry shampoo. "I love you, Winnie."

"Love you too, Sissy."

She was my reason for nearly everything I did. If the mecca was threatened, if the fae were going to wage war on Earth, I would give it my all to protect the people I loved.

"Your Grace," Calista said formally. "Everything is in place, as per your previous instruction."

Yes, I needed to see the queen's body now. I bade Winnie farewell, leaving her in the capable hands of her attendants, and followed Calista to the basement, down to the room where I had fought for my life and almost killed Selene, the place where I had held a dying Finn in my arms. I shuddered at the memory.

Just as I was stepping inside, Violet appeared out of thin air, as she often did, and followed us through. She also wanted one last look at the body. Gazing at the back of the room, I saw the white marble casket with the golden royal emblem on the side. Why had I insisted on seeing her dead body? Because I was queen, I had fae popping up, and her lynx possibly in Central Park. I half expected to open that coffin and her body not even be there.

Violet stayed close, but in her usual manner did not brush against me. My heart ached when I thought about how she had to hold herself from close contact with others. It must be hard being bombarded with all of people's energy and emotions. I wondered if one day she'd find someone to allow her the freedom to touch and be touched.

"I have searched the body already, Ari. Not ten minutes ago. She's most definitely dead."

Violet was trying to reassure me, but I knew that her being down here for one more look before we cremated her said a lot. With the fae involved, who knew what was true anymore.

"I know she's dead, but the council and our people are crying for her to be sent back to the gods. We have to cremate her now. We can't wait any longer."

Some of her ashes would be spread within the mecca, the rest kept for some powerful spell work. The perfect circle of life. The queen gave back to that which sustained her people. It would be my fate one day, and I was honored to be able to play that role.

Calista stood to the side. She wasn't keen on viewing the body.

Slowly I reached out and cracked the lid. The marble was cold; they had been keeping her in the walk-in freezer until a queen was crowned and she called an end to the investigation. I wasn't a stranger to death, but I was nervous to see her like this. She'd been queen for my entire life, held in such high esteem. Lifting the lid fully, I peered down. There she was. Her skin had taken on a bluish, translucent hue. They had tried to do her makeup and hair, to cover up the deep slashes which must have marred much of her skin, and make her presentable, but she definitely still looked dead.

For some reason that actually lifted a weight from my shoulders. I don't know what I was thinking coming down here like this, what I expected to find, but this closed the chapter for me. My queen was dead, her lynx was dead – I'd seen some other animal and mistaken it for her familiar – and I was the new queen now. Time to continue with chasing after her killer and let her rest in peace.

"I will avenge thee," I said, restating my promise to her, to myself.

Violet stepped nearer. The whiteness of her skin seemed even more pronounced than usual. Whenever she drew on the mecca, her mass of white hair would swirl, almost as if a breeze ruffled it. I wondered if mine did that now too.

She held both hands out, running them just above the queen, not touching but close enough it was hard to tell. She murmured in a rhythmic, chanting style, and continued her glide up and down.

"Her body is pretty much fully drained of blood," Violet said, her voice trilling with energy. "Catastrophic loss like this would have resulted in death in seconds. Her injuries were beyond any shifter or mecca healing."

We already knew this, but it was good to have it confirmed by someone I trusted.

"I sense no trace magic on her, but there is a faintly odd scent I'm detecting."

Scent! Crap, we had overlooked our most important investigative ability. I knew the guards had scented as a wolf; they'd reported nothing but blood and the leaking mecca energy, but I hadn't done it. It was my duty to confirm there was nothing more.

In seconds I had my clothes off and was calling on the beast inside of me, letting the change wash over me. Shifting was always painful, as your body slowly morphed. This was the first time I'd shifted since joining with the mecca energy and I probably should have worried that something was going to go wrong, but thankfully I ended up as my normal white wolf with a red slant of color across my nose.

In this form the world was a different place. My senses were enhanced, especially my smell, and that was what I would focus on. The first and most overwhelming scent was that of decay. Despite the fact she'd been kept in the cold, her body was already starting the process of returning to the earth. Cataloging each scent, I shifted those connected with death to the side, and focused elsewhere.

The blood was familiar. She had been cleaned, but there was no way to remove it all. I knew the scent of the Red Queen's blood and it was everywhere. But then as I got close to her right hand, another smell jumped out at me. Not shifter. The scent of bear and wolf carried quite an animalistic tone. This was lighter. Almost floral.

Was this fae? The woman in the lake had not had a smell to me, but then I had not gotten very close to her and was in human form at the time of our meeting. Violet and I continued to circle the queen, each of us doing our best to sniff out every last iota of information, but I found nothing more. Just that small floral spatter of blood, which I had now committed to memory in case it ever appeared again.

Violet, too, stepped away, and appeared to be done. I shifted back to human and stepped into my clothes. Then with one last deep breath I walked back to the casket and gently shut the lid.

"Do you think it's okay to allow the cremation now?" I asked Violet.

The magic born nodded. "Yes, there's no more information I can gather from the body. It's time."

My shoes clicked against the hard tile floors as I walked over to the attendants. "You may cremate her now. May her soul rest in peace with the gods."

They bowed deeply. "As you wish, Your Majesty."

"Make sure all the ashes are returned to me for the mecca ceremony."

They nodded quickly and then got to work.

Calista and Violet stepped in line beside me and we walked out of that awful room, heading toward the queen's personal library. I had not been in there since it was sealed. Now it was time to see if there were any new details to learn.

"Has the human body arrived at Staten Island?" I asked Calista. I needed everything to be ready so I could get all of this investigation wrapped up today.

She tapped away on her tablet. "Yes, the king's men have confirmed the arrival."

Calista gave me a side look, a look that said she wanted to say more.

I stopped and faced her. "What?"

Her lips were pinched, eyes serious. "Are you sure this close friendship with the king is a good idea? Even though it appears all of this is fae related ... he's still a bear."

"Calista, I know it's your job to look out for me, but the king isn't going to hurt me." The truth of this rang in my voice.

Calista's professional manner faltered. "I know he saved you at the coronation, but how can you be so sure he doesn't intend to harm you? How can you be so casual in front of our sworn enemy? He knows an awful lot about the fae. How? What if he's the ally of the dark Tuatha de Danann and all of this is some elaborate ploy?"

I shook my head. She was raising suspicions I didn't want to acknowledge. I needed his friendship. I couldn't face the fae on my own.

"His people died too. He gave us the history book that his family have been ferreting information into for years."

She shook her head. "We know nothing about him. We know nothing of his family."

This was true, but I intended to find out more when I got the chance. I decided to share with Calista one of the real reasons I trusted the king.

"I have known him for a long time. We were friends. We met on the Island when I was fifteen, and then again during the Summit."

It was time she knew everything. My words hung in the air like a wet blanket, but as realization crossed Calista's face she nodded. "That's why he looks at you that way." She inched closer to me, locking eyes with me like one of my dominants would. "Be very, *very* careful there, My Lady. Matters of the heart have cost even the greatest of leaders their lives."

I stood taller, jutting my chin out. "I'm fully in control of this situation, and am only doing what's best for my people. If the fae are coming, we need the bears as allies."

She nodded, but the look in her eyes said she didn't believe me. I wasn't sure I believed myself but now wasn't the time to deal with it.

I had one final task to do before it was time to set out for Staten Island. Violet, who'd been silent during our argument, met my eyes. She inclined her head slightly and I knew I had her support.

"I'll meet you both back at your quarters," Calista said, parting ways with us at the main stairs. "I have no desire to see the blood again."

Couldn't blame her. I had no desire in that direction either. But this was what a queen had to do. My guards, who were always trailing me, stayed several paces back as Violet and I crossed the many halls and floors to reach the mammoth library. The huge doors were closed, a magical seal along with reinforced bars, marked the very locked nature of them. Violet stepped forward first, taking a few minutes to unravel Sabina's spelling. Then it was Blaine's turn. He used his shifter strength to remove the bars.

Then it was my turn to step inside and find out everything I could. Luckily I had my best friend by my side. The moment I stepped in the room I was hit with the memory of seeing this scene the first night of the Summit: the two tea cups, the horrific splatters of blood.

"Talk to me, tell me your secrets," I said to the room. Violet began to disrobe; this time we'd both be wolves. I was hoping we would find more than a floral scent to give us a lead.

I never tired of seeing Violet's shimmering pearl-colored fur. Her wolf was breathtaking; all of the magic born were, like mysterious figures out of a fantasy painting. It took me even longer than usual to shift; this was my second shift in such a small period of time. I would need to consume massive amounts of calories when we were done here or risk being fatigued on Staten Island.

Once I was wolf again, I let my nose skim the ground and started scenting the corner of the room where the most blood was. *Death ... the queen ...* it was all I smelled. Next I went over to the chairs. Sniffing the one on the left I smelled the queen instantly. Moving to the one on the right, my wolf froze. It was that floral scent again. I remembered now the first time I viewed this scene thinking that the queen had been in her garden. But maybe it was nothing to do with flowers at all.

Violet... In this form an alpha could speak into any of their packs' minds. As queen I could speak to all wolf shifters in any form.

She trotted over and smelled the chair. I could see her wolf mulling over that floral scent. Then she leaped up onto the chair and smelled the two tea cups, and met my eyes.

If this floral scent is fae, then we have our killer.

I agreed. Someone got into this room undetected. They were someone my queen trusted enough to be without guards and serve tea to. And they were powerful enough to kill her. I had a lot of questions for that water fae the next time we saw her. And this time if she didn't answer them, I wasn't letting her go.

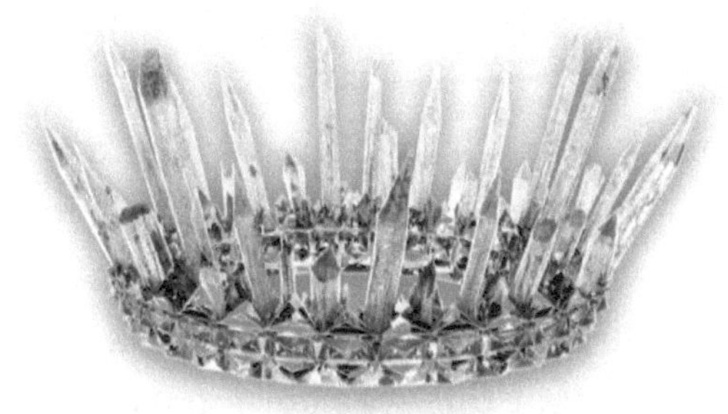

Chapter Thirteen

A bear's den is no place for a wolf.

THAT NIGHT, JUST as the sun was setting, I gathered Monica, Derek, Blaine, Victor, and Ben and prepared them for the task at hand. I was reasonably energized, having consumed two queens' worth of food in my last meal, but still the worry of what we were slowly unraveling was constantly beating at me. If a single dark fae, a member of the Tuatha de Danann, had managed to kill our queen of the mecca and then escape, leaving nothing behind but a dash of floral scent, we were in a world of trouble.

As soon as my dominants were geared up and ready to go, I gave them a quick rundown. "This is a joint meeting whereby we are guests of the bear king. We'll be comparing the bodies of our intruders in a better effort to find the queen's killer."

They nodded. No one questioned me. Part of me wanted to ask Calista to stay behind. After her stern words I didn't want her watching my every move in front of the king, but a wiser part of me knew that this was her job as my advisor. She needed to be strong where I was weak, and I would be lying if I didn't admit the king had become a weakness of mine.

Violet had left earlier, right after we examined the library, and would be waiting there for us. I'd protested this, worried for her safety. But she simply laughed at me before taking off. She wanted extra time to get started on the examinations of the bodies, and also, to Calista's delight, have an early insight into the safety of the territory for me.

Sending my dominants out to wait, I finished getting ready and was pleased that Finn arrived just as I needed him. I wouldn't dream about going into the king's territory without my familiar. I zipped up my knee-high leather boots, sliding in an ornate silver dagger, which had been my mother's. I wore skinny jeans and a silk top, casual but still professional. I wanted to be comfortable in case I had to run or fight my way out of there. After the ercho attack I knew we weren't safe anywhere anymore.

We traveled with ease from the Manhattan vortex to the Staten Island one. I hadn't ever been here before but I recognized the different energy signatures. The second we arrived I stepped off the disc, crossing to where my guards stood. They had come through the vortex first to ascertain it was a safe environment before I made the journey. Just beyond the dimly lit building were distinct and giant outlines of two bear shifters, Kade and Gerald, already waiting for us, with no other guards.

This allowed me and my people to relax a little. He was outnumbered. Of course we were in bear territory, but that show of trust went a long way.

Kade surveyed our group. "Welcome," he said.

His familiar was gone and he had cleaned up. His dark mass of wild waves looked styled; his beard was trimmed and neat against his rugged features. He wore a black button-down shirt over dark-wash jeans and a heavy sword hung from a sheath in his belt. Shifters tended to prefer swords over most weapons. Guns were rarely used; bullets didn't do much damage to a fast regenerating shifter ... but cut their head off with a sword ... worked every time.

"Violet and our magic born have already found some interesting anomalies with the bodies," he told me as we walked outside.

I nodded, but my guard was up. I was walking the streets of Staten Island with the king of the bear shifters. Not a comfortable place for me, even if he was a friend. Two blacked-out Range Rovers waited on the curb for us, engines running and drivers at the wheel.

"My drivers will take us to my home." He gestured for me to get in the back seat, but Ben stepped forward.

"With all due respect, Your Majesty, I will be driving the queen. I have memorized the route." Ben's tone was respectful but his words implied he didn't trust Kade's driver.

Kade's jaw clenched the slightest bit. "Of course."

The king asked his driver to get out and let Ben take the wheel. Then he sat shotgun while I sat in back between Blaine and Monica with Finn in the back cargo hold. Calista went in the other car with the rest of my guard and Gerald.

That was so like Ben to memorize where the king lived and have three exit points. He was a damn good dominant. We drove in silence as I admired the view. Staten Island was so different than Manhattan. There was more space, people seemed more relaxed here. There were so many trees and actual houses. We began driving toward the water, and pretty soon we had pulled up to a beautiful tree-lined street with large mansions perched on manicured lawns. I don't know why I'd assumed he would live in a tall high-rise estate like I did.

Ben pulled up to a large wrought iron gate where two men stood out front. Both of them were huge, burly, and very bear-like. Each wore an identical expression, fierce and filled with mistrust. Kade rolled down the window. The guards stood even more to attention, both of them giving a genial head nod to their king.

They stared for a moment at Ben, probably wondering how the heck he was allowed to be driving the king, before opening the gate. My light-haired guard met their gaze, no flinching as Kade's men stepped back. We continued our journey, and I found myself leaning forward to take in the sight. His home was breathtaking, one of those old brick mansions; lanterns lit our way up the long driveway. It was massive yet quaint, and the two rocking chairs on the front porch set quite the romantic scene.

Ben pulled right up to the door and we all got out. The other car stopped next to ours and Derek was at my side in an instant. He'd clearly been annoyed to not be in the front car with me. I could feel the simmering energy coming off him. Calista found her way to my other side as Kade strode up the large steps to the double doors. Finn remained close to my side.

"Welcome to my home," he said. The doors were flung open, and I could see no staff or attendants in sight. I got the feeling Kade preferred privacy, which is maybe why he had chosen to live in this style of mansion rather than a compound. Although, this estate did actually look pretty huge. I tentatively stepped in, ignoring Derek's arm trying to hold me back. If the king wanted to kill me he would have tried by now. He'd had plenty of chances.

The entrance of the home was as breathtaking as the outside. A wide tiled foyer led to two huge marble staircases leading to the upper floor of the home. The rest I could see was ornate but still correct to the time period. Care had been taken to preserve the touches of this house which had stood for many, many years: detailed cornices and moldings, paneled walls and high ceilings. I immediately wanted to kick the king out and buy this place for myself. Of course no wolf queen could own property in a bear borough, but a girl could dream. His estate reminded me of the Island, close to the water with large sprawling homes. I decided right then that I loved Staten Island.

Calista interrupted my drooling over a home which would never be mine. "We need to hurry and view the bodies. The council do not know of this visit, and should word get back to them before Arianna has returned to explain, they may think of this as an act of war. We do not want them to do that."

The council were pains, like a thorn partially embedded in my side. Sometimes they were simply annoying, but other times their actions dug deep and made it hard to breathe. I hadn't seen them too much since my crowning; it had only been a couple of days, but the official summons were starting to arrive. The first had been the cremation of the queen, the rest would come in due time, when they started flexing their muscle, their control.

They didn't care that I was investigating the Red Queen's death. Now they had a new queen to control, they promptly forgot they were supposed to care and mourn and avenge her.

They didn't care or probably even believe Gerald's warning of the fae, and so far I'd shared none of my discoveries. That would change after tonight. We needed to prepare, and unfortunately I needed their help.

One conversation I was not looking forward to having.

Gerald, who was standing close to us, had his phone out and was typing away. He lifted his head briefly to say: "Violet and Nikoli, our magic born, are outside in one of the outbuildings. Follow us."

The entire group left, my dominants fanning around me, a slight wolfiness to their features. They would be connecting to their beasts inside, making sure their senses were as strong as possible to detect any sort of threat. I was blessed to have such strong and loyal friends; it was nice to know they had cared about me in my old life, before becoming queen. They had proven their loyalty to me many times over and I felt secure in my inner circle.

Despite the darkness, each path through the opulent garden was well lit with lanterns. Kade strode along to my right, not close enough to touch, but I could still feel the energy he carried around within him. I enjoyed the way he brushed his hands along the plants as he walked, and I was starting to understand why I had found him shirtless and acting as gardener on the Island's bear territory. He loved his plants, and since this looked like a prize-winning abundance of flowers, bushes, trees, and shrubbery, I was guessing they loved him right back.

I'd never had much time or room for plants, having lived in concrete jungles for most of my life, but I couldn't deny the true joy I felt being outdoors like this. I wanted to drop to my knees and dig in the dirt, to watch seeds bloom and blossom before my very eyes. It was almost like magic the way a tiny seed could grow into something so spectacular.

A surge of mecca energy beneath my skin had me wanting to reach forward. I paused beside a massive old tree, one of those that stretch high into the sky, with gnarled roots which twisted and turned, covering the ground beneath my feet. I knew the others were confused behind me, wondering what I was doing. I wasn't even sure myself, but for some reason I had to touch this tree. I needed to rest my hands on it and let the mecca flow from me.

As both palms pressed against the roughened bark, I felt a tight knot inside of me calm. It had been sitting in my chest probably since the death of the queen. A sense of peace and tranquility flowed from me.

Then the tree responded. And I don't mean that in the philosophical sense of it felt happy or something. No, it actually responded to me with words.

Princess of the fair. It has been many years.

I was frozen, trying to figure out if I'd just lost my mind, or whether it was possible that a tree was talking to me.

Can you hear me? I asked, hesitant.

A heavy object landed on my feet and I realized that Finn was protecting me. The huge wolf was staring at the tree, same as I was, determined to shield me, and I loved him for it.

Yes, we hear many things. We have been standing since the dawn of both worlds.

Finn, who could apparently hear our conversation too, spoke then: *Wise and ancient treeling, you have blessed us with your presence here on Earth. How long have you been gone from the Otherworld?*

The Otherworld ... this was a fae tree? They could talk to trees? That was so unfair. We needed to be able to do that too, it was so amazing, a sense of something bigger than the simple life I lived, that felt like eternity and I was no more than a blip.

"Arianna, is everything okay?"

Calista had obviously decided I'd spent enough time acting like a weirdo tree hugger, but she had no idea. I wasn't sure I could ever tear my hands away from this magical presence. I wanted to bask in the warmth forever.

"Just give me a minute," I murmured to her, and she gave me a respectful head bow before taking a step back.

The tree took a long time to answer Finn, which might have been it thinking through its answer or ... the fact that a being like this had no need for rushed or hurried conversation.

I was brought across half a millennia ago, by the people of the summer lands. I once grew in their royal garden. It was to be a peace offering, but things did not go as planned. There was war. Battle. I was left to die on the side of a river. But then I was saved. Planted within this ground of mecca, and here I have stayed.

What war was he talking of? Actually, what peace was he talking about? Was this another piece of fae/shifter/human history that had been lost or forgotten? I needed to finish Kade's book. I hadn't had time to get all the way through. Who knows what important information might be in there.

I darted my eyes toward Kade. The king stood closer to me than the others. His coppery eyes were unreadable, hard and flat. Our gazes remained locked for many moments and I wondered if he knew. Did he know that his garden held a tree from the lands of the Otherworld?

I knew we needed to go, there was much to do, so with great reluctance I breathed deeply and said, *Thank you for letting me speak with you, to feel the great power of nature and the worlds ... I have no words. Would you mind if I visited with you again someday?*

A rustling of leaves and a breeze swept through us. *It would be my honor, fair one. I bid you well. Death is not always the end. Sometimes it is simply a step into the next world. You would be wise to remember that. And when in doubt, look to the dark queen. She knows all.*

I pulled my hands back, my body almost crying at the loss of its presence. What did it mean about death? Was it talking about my death, or someone else's? Could it be referring to the Red Queen? That was the most pressing death on my mind right now. And who was the dark queen?

What is a treeling? I asked Finn, as we moved out of the magical tree's presence.

On the Otherworld, nature is much more alive than on Earth. A race of ancient fae were so enamored with their tree homes that when they died their souls became one with them. After time, this spread to the rest of the forest, and soon the woods were alive. Their trees and plants now have real sentience ... a soul. But I have never heard of any person being able to speak with them in the manner you just did. I don't know if it's because of the change in the mecca, if this particular tree is special from so many years on Earth, or if it is you, Ari.

A few throats cleared, and I swiveled to face my very confused people. "Apologies," I said, turning my eyes to each of them before finally landing on the king. "Did you know this was a tree from the Otherworld?"

He nodded, and I grew silent waiting for him to explain. "One of my ancestors saved it from being swept into a lake. The story is that this tree was shining with light, and that each leaf was so perfect that he could not leave it behind. It was planted in our royal estate, and here it has stayed since then." He crowded into me, dwarfing my form. "What happened? Did you feel an energy from it?"

I wasn't sure if I should tell him or not. This felt huge, and I sensed it was tied to these changes in the mecca. If more of the mecca was coming to the earth side, were we starting to get spillover into our nature? Or land?

Kade hadn't removed his eyes from me, and I knew he would not budge until I gave some explanation. "I will tell you later," I murmured very softly. This wasn't a conversation I wanted to have in front of everyone. I felt like it should be shared between just the king and I.

Violet was there then; she must have sensed me. Beside her was a tall and handsome bear magic born. With their matching pale hair, ice blue eyes, and fair skin, they looked like they could be brother and sister. But Nikoli was big and burly where my friend was delicate and less imposing.

"Arianna, you have to see this!" she told me, tugging at my arm.

Whoa, for her to touch me like this, she must have found something big.

I followed her and Nikoli into a side building that was set up as part garden shed and part indoor seating area. The floors were brick and the walls were made of glass. It was like some sort of gazebo or greenhouse, but it was huge, at least forty feet wide by sixty feet long.

Turning the corner I was assaulted with two dead bodies. I halted. Even though I was prepared to see them, you were never really prepared for so much death in such a short time span.

"What do you notice?"

The majority of our people had hung back, and now it was just the king, Nikoli, Violet, and me.

The first body I stopped by was a woman, beautiful, young, and thin. She looked like a model. Even in death her hair was shiny and splayed out perfectly, her lips the barest tint of red, her alabaster cheeks slightly rosy. I knew exactly what had caught Violet's eye. I might not have noticed so quickly if I hadn't examined the queen only hours before this. Her complexion looked nothing like the bluish sickly hue of the Red Queen. I turned to the other one, a male … he looked the same, like they were sleeping.

"They don't look dead."

"Exactly!" Violet jumped up. "I didn't notice this the first time I checked out the body, as it had been preserved and was only a few days dead, but now both of them have been without any cold or magic for a while now, and still no decomposition."

She was right. They didn't even smell. In fact…

"They have no scent," Kade said from close behind me. "They did have a scent when we killed them. They smelled human. But whatever caused that has faded away."

"Apparently only some of the illusion holds in death," Nikoli said. "Although I believe more of it will fade in time. If it was me I would have focused the strongest of magic on appearance and less on scent." I turned to find him staring between Violet and the dead bodies. His features were hard to read, but whatever he was thinking it was intense.

"You're confirming these are fae?"

He nodded in a gesture of respect, and then shrugged. "I have never encountered a fae before, but based on the information we now have … well, it makes sense."

Kade's strong voice bounced from the walls: "Why can't you break the illusion? I want to look upon those who dared attack us in our territories."

Not to mention we could very well be on the edge of war, and if we were to take this to our people we needed evidence of the fae.

Nikoli looked like he wanted to please his king but was at a loss. "We tried everything."

Violet was staring off to the side, thinking.

"Not everything." She had that hyped look she got when she was about to suggest something insane.

"Vi..." I trailed off, using my queen voice. It was necessary, my best friend had no self-preservation instincts. Our whole lives she'd thought herself invincible. And yes, she hadn't killed herself in a reckless move yet, but there was still time. And I needed her.

"Let's take them to the vortex," Violet said, and before anyone could protest Nikoli was nodding.

Time to assess the risks. "You want to toss a dead body into the vortex and see what happens? The mecca has been unstable lately ... this could cause us a lot of problems."

If these were fae, what would happen? Clearly there was still some magical illusion holding up.

Maybe this would break it, or maybe it would wreak havoc.

"We have no choice, we should take this risk. I'll keep the mecca from getting too unstable," Kade said, clearly deciding for all of us. As if that settled it, Violet snapped her fingers and the male body began to hover a few feet off the ground.

"Leave the other body here. I have a plan B," Violet murmured to Nikoli. He nodded and they made their way out the door, walking along with the floating body like it was no big deal. As Kade turned to follow, my hand snaked out and grabbed his wrist.

"The king and I need a moment alone," I said to Calista and my guard. They all looked ruffled, Derek especially. He eyed my hand on the king's wrist like I was touching a crocodile. I dropped it.

"Come on." Calista recovered first, before shooing everyone out.

Once we were alone – well, alone except for the creepy dead/undead body – Kade turned to me and arched one well-shaped eyebrow.

I took a deep breath. "I need you to tell me about your gift with the mecca."

We were about to experiment with an unstable energy here and I wanted to know that he could handle it. I was also thinking of Calista's queries from before; I needed to know more about him. We had time for this one question.

He exhaled deeply and ran a strong hand through his thick hair. "I've always had an affinity for the mecca, even as a child."

"Affinity?" I said, hoping for more explanation than that. Affinity could mean a million things. All heirs had an affinity for it, so he must be talking about something more.

He met my eyes. "I can see it."

What. The. Heck?

"Like the magic born can? Like you can literally see it?" Magic borns had the ability to actually trace the lines of power that crisscrossed beneath the boroughs.

He shrugged. "More than the magic born. I can not only see the energy lines, I can touch them. I can even control ... or guide ... the energy, to a certain extent. When you were crowned it looked like the mecca was eating you alive, like it was going to take every last breath from your soul, and well, instinct urged me forward. Even if it killed me too, I had to try to save you."

I stepped forward without realizing it. The way he spoke, so gentle and poetic, it made me want to be closer to him.

"Thank you for what you did," I said with sincerity. "You didn't have to save me. You risked your own life. It is why I trust you, and respect you even more."

He gave me a crooked smile. "I figured if a woman could kiss me like that and then slap me in the same moment, she was worth saving."

This time I returned the smile, but before I could respond there was a rap at the glass window. Derek, looking stone-faced, indicated it was time for us to join the rest of the group.

I stepped back from the king and put the queenly mask back on, before leveling a look on Derek. We were going to be having a chat very soon. I was queen now, he did not get to command me in any manner. No past familiarity or trust between us could trump my new position.

"Your boyfriend?" Kade asked, sounding casual, but a flicker of shadow stirred in the copper depths of his eyes.

"Ex," I said. Then before I could say or do anything more to jeopardize my crown, I stormed out of that glass house like my life depended on it. Which maybe it did.

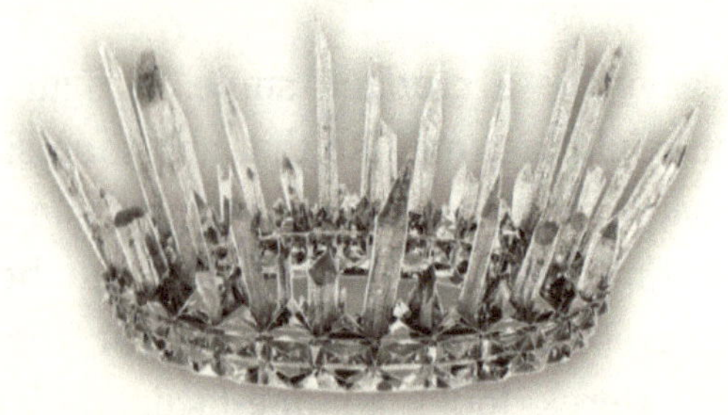

Chapter Fourteen

Fee Fi Fo Fae.

MY GUARDS WERE stationed at the perimeter of the Staten Island vortex. Calista was waiting in the car. If the mecca exploded I wanted her far away from it. Gerald, Kade, Violet, Nikoli, and I were all situated around the body, only a few feet from the vortex disc.

Finn was stationed behind me. I didn't worry much about him, he had no problem when we traveled via the vortex.

Violet turned to Nikoli then. "Throw him in, friend."

The bear magic born grinned, his teeth as white as his skin, before snapping his fingers and levitating the body. The strong mecca energy around him increased, and the stirring inside of me responded. The king stepped forward then, planting himself firmly in front of the disc, clearly using his big body to shield us all.

Nikoli flicked his hand and sent the body up over the king's head and toward the vortex disc. I could feel the mecca pulsing as if it were alive, conscious, and somehow expecting this.

I crept closer to get a better vantage point.

"Here goes nothing," Nikoli mumbled, and he released his hold on the body.

A loud bang echoed the moment the body dropped onto the disc. Kade flinched but remained steady in his position. A shockwave blasted out and the windowpanes behind me shook with the force.

Even though moving forward was more difficult, I managed to cross through the mecca energy and stand beside Kade. Both of us had our eyes locked on the disc.

The theories were correct. The dead "human" body was not human anymore. Sprawled across the vortex disc was a dead fae. His face was scrunched in a frozen sneer; his ears were jagged and pointy. With the release of the magic illusion, a scent appeared. Distinct. Floral. Similar to the one I had smelled on the Red Queen and in her library. But it was not exactly the same. Kade knelt down, grabbing the male fae by the ankle, and yanked him out. *Good idea.* Who knew what keeping him too long on the vortex would do. What we might have already done. Had we alerted the Otherworld to their death? To our knowledge of them?

Violet was grinning. "It worked!"

The king turned and met my eyes. "Seems our visitor in the park was correct. We have a new enemy and it is most definitely the fae."

I nodded. The female fae's message definitely held more strength now. The dark fae had tried to take us out. We didn't know why, but we knew who. Which was a step in the right direction.

This was also a step toward my vengeance. I had no doubt these two fae were nothing more than help. Someone much more powerful was orchestrating this entire thing, and that was the fae I needed to find.

"My king!" a shout came from outside, distracting us all. Kade quickly made his way out and I was right behind him. One of his guards was holding a cell phone.

"The other body ... it's gone," he said.

Kade frowned. "What do you mean gone?"

The guard shook his head, that slightly worried expression never leaving his face. "Brett said he was making his rounds around the greenhouse and one minute it was there and the next it was gone."

Violet had followed us outside; her hair was doing the windblown thing that happened when she was drawing on mecca power. "If the two bodies were linked somehow, then when this illusion broke, the female's may have also. But the body shouldn't have disappeared."

I started making my way toward the SUVs. "Come, let's go check it out. I want to sniff out the area."

Derek jumped into action from his place on the curb and stepped in front of me. "Your Grace, this could be a trap." His voice was low, but not low enough for shifter hearing. Everyone around us would have heard him.

I met his eyes and gritted my teeth. "I just found out that the fae killed our late queen! That they killed Damien and Marco. The fae are alive and they have declared war on us already. And I intend to find out why. Now ... move!"

I put the power of mecca into the command, and almost as if he couldn't control it, he stepped off the curb, head bowed. I shouldn't have been so hard on him, but part of me felt he wasn't just protecting me because I was his queen. None of the other guards were acting like Derek. He was taking this personally and I couldn't afford that in a guard.

Piling into the two cars, we sped off, making our way back to the king's house. I was on edge, needing to get there so I could see the scene myself. A dead body doesn't just get up and walk away.

Of course we knew next to nothing about the fae. Maybe their bodies disappeared after a certain amount of time, but then the other body would have disappeared too and it was still safely stowed in the trunk. No, this was something else. The tires spun briefly on the gravel as we came to an abrupt halt in front of the king's house.

Kade stepped out and opened my door, letting Monica out as well. A thought came to me. "You think maybe this is a prank?"

One of his guards could be playing a joke. Mine had certainly pranked me many times over the years. The body might be hidden somewhere in the backyard.

The king shook his head. "My guards would never play a prank on me while the queen of the wolf shifters was visiting my home for the first time. They would have to find new jobs if they did."

His tone was fierce and I knew then he was genuinely worried about the missing body.

"You don't think ... someone stole it, do you? That there are fae here right now?" I was hoping he'd tell me I was crazy, that there was no possible way.

I inhaled deeply but could only smell the king and the fresh water that backed onto his house. Nothing floral. Or even foreign. But we already knew they were masters at disguise. So that meant nothing.

Kade looked like he was starting to partially shift. His body expanded, features broadening out, and his voice was extra deep as he spoke. "I don't know what we are going to find, but if you want to go back to Manhattan I will call you with a full report when I find out what's going on."

I gave him the look, the look every woman gives a man when they want to tell him to shut the hell up, and amusement crossed his bear-like features.

"After you, My Lady?" He waved me forward. He'd probably stay in this partial shift stage until we knew there was no danger to us, because in this form going full bear would be a lot quicker for him. Not to mention his heightened senses. Only the most powerful of shifters could do it, and I wasn't at all surprised that he had the ability. Personally, I preferred to be in one or the other state, not between, but the king didn't look like he was uncomfortable.

Kneeling down, I pulled my mother's sharp dagger from my boot. Finn was in his largest of forms, teeth bared, his energy thrumming with unease. I would have loved to have had my sword or spear, but this would have to do. Surely the king's guard and my own could handle any body snatchers. My guards sped up ahead of me and fanned out inside of the house.

As Kade and I entered, his lead guard met us.

"Your Highness, we've done a sweep of the area and there's nothing. None of our securities have been broken, and no intruders are around. But a few of the boys shifted to bear form and smelled an odd scent."

I stepped forward. "Was it floral?"

His guard looked at me directly. "Yes. It was."

Okay. Two scenarios. One: the body we dropped on the mecca was linked to the other body here, and when we tore the illusion apart this body also lost its illusion and released its natural scent. Of course that still didn't explain where the body went, which led to scenario two: there was a fae here – a body-snatching, probably dark fae, who was powerful enough to hold illusion over magic-born shifters, and might have killed my queen.

I turned to Calista, who was at my back. "Give me your sword."

Without question she unsheathed her blade and handed it to me. "Wait for me in the car," I said finally, and my advisor paused before giving me one last head bow.

"Be careful, Arianna. You are our queen, you are our power."

I sucked in a ragged breath, watching as she walked out of the house and hopped back into the SUV. Focusing my thoughts, I stepped up to the main group. The king was already moving, his clothing starting to tear at the seams, and I knew he was going to fully shift.

"Call in reinforcements," he said to his guard, his voice guttural. I waited for the final pull of shifter energy, but he continued to maintain this half beast thing he was working. How damned powerful was this shifter? No wolf could do what he was, hovering on the edge of a shift and not following through. It took massive control.

We made our way outside as a group, my senses immediately alert. I would have shifted to wolf myself, but I needed to have my human brain for a while. The wolf could be a little too instinctual. Plus, the ability to pull mecca was stronger in my human form.

I scented the air, having committed that floral scent from the queen and her library to memory. If that fae was here now, he would meet his death.

We fanned out. The king had five of his men stationed around us; more were spanning out across his land. My five guards remained close. Plus we had two magic born and two high royals.

Surely this was enough to kill a dark fae, should there be one here.

A loud shriek came from the sky and we all froze. I had forgotten about the king's familiar. She must have been staking out the sky, reporting back to Kade.

The bear king furrowed his brow. "Nix tells me there's suspicious activity at the water's edge."

Kade's guards went first and we followed. As I neared, I could see a swirling in the water while the rest remained calm. As we stood there staring at it, a horrible feeling crept into my gut. At the same time a floral scent washed over me. It was a fae, not the one who had killed the queen, but one who had a strong scent and energy. Was this the leader, the one who spelled and controlled the fae who had killed my guards? I hoped so. Tonight I would take some of my vengeance.

Finn's howl tore through the night and I spun around holding my sword in front of me like a shield.

Standing in the middle of the king's garden, somehow behind us all, was a tall figure. Even in the dim light his face seemed to be lit up, almost as if he had miniscule lights dotted across his skin. I clenched my hand tighter around the hilt of my sword and stared for many long moments.

He was not like the female fae we had seen in the park that day. She had been a beauty, her perfection obvious. He was ... not that. He had black hair slicked back from his face and hanging halfway down his back; despite the dotted illumination on his face, much of it was still shadowed, almost distorted, making him resemble an animal more than a human, with a pointy chin, high cheekbones, and large eyes that looked to be a swirling multitude of colors. I knew he would stand well above my five feet ten in height, but not quite as tall as Kade. He wore no expression, but the glowing was eerie, and I found my heart rate increasing just by being in his presence.

He lifted his hands, and we all focused on the two discs within them. They glowed green, and even from this distance I could tell they were razor sharp. He moved then, so fast there was no time to cry out, no time to warn anyone. His weapons sailed through the air and beheaded two of the king's guards, the ones who had stepped closest to him.

"Restrictum!" Violet shouted, thrusting her hands out, sending a shockwave of purple magic at the dark figure.

He slid back a few feet, his heels digging into the dirt, but otherwise remained unaffected. Then he smiled, which was about ten times scarier than his neutral expression from before. He made an O with his mouth and blew in Violet's direction. A gust of wind, with the force of a mini tornado, slammed into my best friend, picking her up and tossing her out into the water.

"No! Stay back!" I shouted, my focus torn between Violet and my guards. Derek and Monica had just run at the fae with their swords raised but they slowed at my shout.

Beside me the king's body was vibrating; he'd lost the final control he held over his half form and was going to shift. It would leave him vulnerable for a few minutes. Our remaining guard closed in around Kade and me. I pushed my way back, trying to see the lake, ready to rescue Violet if she needed it, but then I saw her climbing from the water.

"Run, Ari! I'll handle this bastard," she cried out. Her eyes were glowing, and even though she had fallen into the water, she wasn't wet. She scared the crap out of me when she got like this.

"Vi, he threw a tornado at you," I yelled as she dashed closer.

She shook her head, white hair flying around her in a breeze of magical energy. "Yeah, I was trying to capture him so we could question him, but now I'm just going to make his blood boil until his brain liquefies."

She blasted past me and I actually felt heat coming off her body.

I turned around, prepared to follow her, but the guards stepped in front of me. Breathing deeply I fought against my instincts and let my logical side have a little free rein. I knew I couldn't just run into this. I was the queen, I controlled the mecca. The wolves would be weakened to devastating levels if I died, and if I died here in the king's territory, we would have more than one war to worry about.

Calmer, I took stock of the scene. The fae was calling back his discs; Derek and Monica hovered close, swords out. The king's remaining guards and the rest of mine were positioned around me and Kade in a half-moon shaped protective shield. In bear form, Kade was massive, standing probably ten feet tall and weighing a least a thousand pounds. He was crouched over as the last of his body reformed, clothes gone and dark fur covering him all over. I wouldn't be able to see his full bear until he stood up, but I could already tell he was going to be one scary, massive beast. Would it be enough against the fae though?

I heard my best friend shout, and I turned back in concern. The guards tightened even closer around me, and I couldn't halt my annoyance at being protected when I should be out there. I caught sight of Violet. One second she was charging at the fae and the next she disappeared, reappearing in front of him, before thrusting her arms out. He slid backward under the assault of her magic. A burst of energy joined Violet's attack then. Nikoli. The bear's magic born had crept in from the side, and now the two of them were hitting the fae with everything they had.

Derek and Monica stepped in to attack now, probably hoping to either severely injure him or at least distract him long enough for the magic born to do their thing. The fae remained unconcerned. His glow was increasing, and I had the very scary realization that he had barely even started with his power.

I didn't see the green spinning disc until it was too late.

"Derek!" I shouted, just as the disc cut through his neck.

I cried out again, almost falling to my knees as grief and pain slammed into me. I could see the movement of a bear in the corner of my eye, but I couldn't focus on anything but my loss, the pain tearing at my insides, threatening to rip me in two. My breathing was so ragged I felt like I wasn't getting any real oxygen, which had me lightheaded.

This couldn't be happening. I couldn't let this happen to any more of my people. Screw being queen if I couldn't actually use my power. A true queen does not cower on the back line and let others die for them.

Straightening, I moved forward but my guard tightened, closing me in.

"Move!" I said, the force of the mecca behind the word. I had embraced the power and was letting it flow through my body and out of my hands. All five guards were thrown back with the force of it. I didn't even have time to process that before I was running toward the fae.

He was stuck in a magical standoff with Violet and Nikoli. He would blast two spells at the magic born and they would block, throwing energy back at him. Monica was kneeling over Derek's headless body, trying to contain her shock. As I strode across the lawn, trying to take everything in to figure out the best way to help, a streak of black caught my eye. It was a huge, menacing black bear. King Kade. He had taken a leaf from Nikoli's book and was coming in for the sneak attack, somehow having made his way unseen around the back of the fae.

His eagle shrieked from the sky and I caught sight of Finn off to the left by the greenhouse. *You okay?* I checked in with him. It was odd that the familiars had not attacked the fae; they must have been doing something else important.

The fae is trying to open the portal in the lake again. We're keeping it closed. I'm not sure what is attempting to come through, but it has the distinct energy of the ercho.

Thank you! At least we knew we only had this one to deal with today and that an entire army wasn't about to march through.

Just then the fae slammed his hands together in a huge clap and every standing guard dropped to the ground. At first I couldn't tell if they were unconscious or dead, until I saw them still breathing. Thank the gods.

His spell had given me an instant splitting headache but nothing more. Nikoli, Violet, myself, and the bear king were the only ones left upright. This bastard needed to die. Now.

As if the fae sensed the bear king sneaking up on him, he twisted in a half turn.

In two quick motions, I pulled my wrist back and let loose the dagger I had been holding. I instilled mecca energy into that movement, hoping it would guide its course and land true.

The fae flashed forward, closer to me. He deflected the dagger easily, and then with a wave of his hand sent Violet sliding ten feet to the right, her feet digging six inches into the dirt as if she were resisting with such force that it had literally grounded her like a tree. Nikoli went to help free her, as she couldn't seem to get out on her own. Then, the fae began stalking toward me.

"Your reign is done, child. It's time for the Tuatha de Danann to return and claim all of the powers of Earth." His lips never moved and yet the words played out in my head. "Your queen hid truth from us. She betrayed the dark ones. Now we shall extract our price from those who still walk on Earth."

I had no time to worry. Something in Kade's book had said that the fae couldn't outright lie, but that didn't mean that what this dark one said was the full truth either. Truth can be twisted. I knew that better than most.

Retrieving Calista's sword from my belt, I held it before me and fell into a fighting stance. I called the mecca to me. I was the queen of mecca and had more power at my disposal than anyone standing in this garden, even Kade. I might be untrained in the use of its power, but it was still there, thrumming through me, waiting for me to command it.

Just as the bear king leaped up into the air, Violet and Nikoli both shot out their energy and I let out a war cry, thrusting my hands out as well. I imagined the mecca as a living thing, a physical force which had no match, a power I both respected and feared. As I called it through me, memories of my coronation were still strong in my psyche, but I would not let that fear control me. I would control it.

At first my burst of mecca went wild, saturating the ground and the air. With a shout I focused further, praying to whomever was listening that I could figure this out.

Arianna.

I heard the voice again, and this time the energy shot straight and true, knocking the fae backward and into the bear king's open jaws. Just like with the fae body we had thrown into the vortex, my strong shot of mecca shattered whatever shield this dark fae might have had, and he was not prepared for the strength of Kade, who was a giant even among the massive bears. The king sank his huge jaws into the fae's ribcage and bit down so hard I heard the bones crunch.

Violet appeared at my side looking feral. A wave of dizziness washed over me but I managed to remain standing. I had channeled a lot of mecca tonight, and it was taking its toll on my body. Violet stalked toward the fae with her arms raised and I followed close by, swaying once or twice.

Up close I could see the fae was sweating with pain but hadn't yet cried out. Even with his body stuck in a bear's mouth, he only grimaced. Those lights that had seemed to be embedded in his skin looked dull, his dark aura dimmed.

"Boil," Violet said, flinging her magic at him, and that's when he cried out with a whine-like curse. His skin dripped sweat as the bear king held him in place.

Calling forth the mecca once more, my body aching slightly as it funneled more of the power, I directed it through the sword in my hands and gasped in awe as the blade lit up with a purple hue.

"I avenge thee," I murmured for Derek, my guards Damian and Marco, and the Red Queen, before stepping forward and swinging the sword down and across his neck, taking his head right off.

It was a clean and quick death. Not a death he deserved, but I had no time for torture.

The king let his body go, which was lucky because the moment his head was severed, Violet's spell took full effect and his body melted like it was doused in acid, eating a hole into the green lawn.

I dropped the sword then, clutching at the sudden strike of pain to my head. Another wave of dizziness hit me. Violet was trying to talk to me but it sounded garbled. The mecca was still thrumming through my veins and I couldn't stop it. The bear king began to shift, but before he made the full transition to human my vision blurred. I tried to take a step forward, and the last thing I remembered was being caught by a strong embrace.

Eventually, as my shifter healing kicked in, some of my awareness returned. Hovering on the brink of waking, I let my senses soar out, an instinctive thing to determine if I was safe or not. A soft surface was beneath me; there was warmth above. A familiar rich scent surrounded me and I knew I was in Kade's home.

Safe.

I opened my eyes, taking a few seconds to let my body adjust. I scanned around the room to see that I was alone. Despite my forced rest, I was still weary, my body hurting from an overload of mecca, and the realization that a war was coming. If we'd had that much trouble killing one fae, how would we handle an entire army of them? We weren't prepared. We needed to get prepared. Which meant I needed to tell the council and our people. Today. It was time for them to know.

I rubbed at the ache in my chest, everything inside of me clenching in pain at the loss of Derek. He had been an old friend of mine and a brief lover. We'd been through a lot together, and even though I had decided he wasn't a fit for a mate at this time, who knew what the future might have brought. Now that was all gone for him. He would join our ancestors in the sky, in the great realm of spirit, but he was not earthbound with me anymore. I needed to organize a ceremonial death for him. He was a warrior and should be sent off as such.

Having rested long enough, I let the soft throw which had been draped over me slide from my body. Another quick glance around the massive room and I had absolutely no doubt. I was in the king's personal bedroom. Well, suite was more like it. The bed I rested upon was huge, fitting for the male it belonged to: strong frame, dark wood, cream and tan bedding, and the scent of Kade everywhere. There was a lounge area, an office of sorts, and a huge cinema-style entertainment zone.

My wolf wanted to curl up and snuggle back into the softness and sleep again. But we had things to do, responsibilities to our people. We could no longer indulge in fantasies of some world where maybe I could act on the attraction I had for Kade.

"You're awake."

I sucked in deeply as his growly voice washed over me. I hadn't the strength to stop myself from turning to him, and I had to clench my jaw to prevent my mouth from dropping open.

He was standing in the entrance to his bedroom, shirtless and dirty, dressed in what looked like the exact same pants he had been wearing when he kissed me in his garden. Clearly he had been taking out his frustration on his plants. And ... he actually looked calm. His garden must do that for him.

"You shouldn't have brought me to your personal bedroom," I said, the reprimand given without thought. "How will this look to our councils, to our people?"

I straightened, and there was a heaviness in his step as he closed the distance between us. "The king rules supreme here. My council is appointed by me, and they do as I say."

I needed to take a leaf out of his ruling book. Our council had been acting independently of the queen for too long.

"And my people trust my actions. The fact that I trust you enough to let you into the inner chambers of my life tells them that they too can trust this new queen of the wolves. The previous Red Queen was never invited to this estate. We met only on neutral grounds, or in officiated circumstances. She I did not trust. Besides, I couldn't convince my bear to place you anywhere other than my own bed."

I tried to ignore his final statement, despite the fact my stomach was filled with butterflies and my wolf was jumping around like a pup inside. Instead I forced myself to focus on the Red Queen. Kade had not trusted her, and apparently neither had the dark fae. What had she been up to? What had she hidden from the fae?

I wasn't sure anyone else had heard the dark fae's words; Kade in bear form might not have even been processing words. I would have to speak to him about it later, once I'd done more investigating into it myself.

"So where do we go from here?" I asked, reluctantly pulling myself from the most comfortable bed I'd ever lay upon. "What is the next step to ensure the fae do not destroy us all?"

He was close to me now, and I found myself trapped in the force of his energy. "First thing to do is warn our people. Next thing is for you to learn to control the mecca. It almost killed you today. You expelled too much of your own energy, and then burned out on all the power. You have to learn, and fast. I'm the best one to teach you, and considering it is in all of our peoples' best interest that you master your power, we need to start straight away."

Great. That was going to be a pleasant conversation with the council. Old prejudiced bastards.

"You're right," I said with reluctance. "I'll not be a weak queen. No more shall die on the front line while I am relegated to the back."

Kade was blocking out everything else in the room. He was close enough now that if I reached out I would be touching him. When we were alone together like this, it was hard for me to remember that he was forbidden to me. I couldn't stop myself from placing my flat palms against his warm chest. His skin was so many shades darker than mine, the contrast startling between the two of us.

Kade closed his eyes, just briefly, long lashes hiding the swirling depths.

"You need to go, Ari. Go now before I put you right back into that bed."

Something hot expanded within me, starting in my gut and trickling across my limbs, leaving me aching. I forced myself to focus, closing my eyes, wrenching myself from the bear king and storming out of the room. It secretly annoyed me that he was the strong one this time. I should be able to control my body, my hormones, but when it came to Kade I was weak. I couldn't be weak like that any longer.

I was almost out of the room when he called out to me: "First lesson will start in three days, Arianna. I'll send word to Finn via Nix with a location."

The way my full name rolled off his tongue was really hot … damn him. I spun back to see him again. He was wearing his confident, kingly expression. But I could see beneath that to the rigidness of his stance and the dark shadows on his ruggedly handsome features, both of which revealed his own loss of control when it came to our attraction.

For some reason that made me happy. I gave him a single head nod and then I was gone, out the door and out of the king's home. I knew my people would be waiting for me downstairs. Then it was time for me to convince the council that war was coming, and that the bear king might be our best chance for survival.

Torine's face held almost no expression, but I could feel the simmering of anger within. I had just told them everything. Well, almost everything. They knew of the fae, the warnings, the threats and deaths. I left out my budding desire for the bear king. That was not of any importance, and would only muddle the very real threats out there.

The body of the dead fae that we threw onto the vortex lay on the ground between us, and I knew without it no one would have believed a word I said.

"And there is one more thing..." I held my head high. Kade's words about how he ran his council, gave me confidence in dealing with mine. "The bear king will be training me on how to control the mecca."

The words barely left my lips before half the council stood up in anger. "Absolutely not!"

"The bear is the enemy."

"You would disgrace us as wolves."

Their angry words washed over me, and I knew I needed to pull them into line now.

I set my face in its hard, queen wolf expression. "I am your queen and I do not ask permission. I am merely informing you of my plans. King Kade has an affinity for handling the mecca, which you all saw at my coronation. The mecca has been unstable ever since the Red Queen's death, and if you want to survive the upcoming fae war you will do as I say and not conspire against me!"

My anger got away from me and I took a calming breath. Every single council member looked aghast, slack-jawed and silent.

There was nothing more to say. "You're dismissed," I said with a wave of my hand.

After a few more moments of shocked silence, the council stood and gathered their things. They gave me a slight head bow before leaving. Torine approached me and bowed deeply.

"Let it be known that I strongly advise against trusting the bears. A fae war is all they would need to take over all five boroughs of the mecca and completely wipe out our entire race."

Torine hadn't been there. He didn't see that one fae toss around ten guards, two magic born, and two royals like it was child's play. "Advice noted," I said, my tone leaving no room for rebuke. Torine's jaw clenched a little before he left.

Now was the time when loyalty would come into question. I would have to only trust my most inner circle of friends and confidants. I might not be the most popular queen among the council, but I would not let my legacy be tarnished because I did not properly prepare us for the upcoming war with the fae.

There was a knock at the door.

"Come in!" My voice carried across the great meeting room hall.

Calista entered clutching her tablet in her arms. She didn't speak until she was close to me, and even then she whispered: "Just thought you should know that the rumor mill has started. Already the wolves speak that you're having an affair with the bear king and that he has sided with the fae to bring down the wolves."

I groaned, putting my head in my hands. I was going to be accused of having an affair and not even get the perks?

"Do we know who started the rumor?" Wolves loved to gossip. Rumors spread like wildfire, and if I could cut that person out right now it would send a lesson to the others.

Calista's face went deadly, and I almost took a step back. "Can't prove it yet, but I'm working on it. All evidence points to Selene."

I whispered out a barrage of curses. The one person I couldn't cut out so easily was another heir, and not just any heir. She was the spare if anything happened to me.

"Your advice?" I asked, because I was at a loss.

Calista chewed the inside of her cheek. "You won't like it."

I sat up a little straighter. Hire an assassin to kill Selene? Cut off her royal funds? I waited with bated breath. It must be good if Calista looked so nervous.

"What is it?"

Calista's next breath was loud and labored. "Take a mate."

She cringed back a little, and I knew my previous arguments on this had been loud and defiant. She expected a retaliation. I paused, assessing her words. Certainly taking a wolf mate would shut everyone up, but ... I wasn't prepared to do that just yet. My heart couldn't do that yet.

I might be queen of the wolf shifters, and I would sacrifice a lot for my people – everything really – but unless it was life and death I would not sacrifice my heart.

A queen with no heart would lead only in darkness. I would be the one to lead with light. I would trust my heart on this, and I would move forward with our plan. The next time the fae came for us, I'd be strong.

I'd be a true queen of the mecca.

Coming March 2017 – Book 2

Arianna might have won the Summit and taken the crown of wolf shifters, but there is no time for her to settle into the royal life. Something is off with the mecca and if she doesn't fix it the fae might just make another earth side appearance.

Now she must work with the king of the bears to save both of their people. Which is easier said than done when he tempts her in every way and a relationship between them is forbidden.

One slip up could cost her everything and in the NYC mecca someone is always watching.

Acknowledgements from Leia: This book started as all of our books starts together. I email Jaymin with an idea and she took it and ran and I ran with her. We are so so proud of this book. Arianna is so different than our other characters and this story is so developed, we really poured our heart and soul into it and we hope you love it. Thank you to Lee and Patti for your eagle eyed editing. Thank you to the Enforcers for being down to read all books Jaymin and Leia. A huge thank you to my husband and kids for dealing with me running off and writing in the closet because this story just poured out of us. Jaymin, I never imagined a world in which I would write books with another person so seamlessly that it sounds like my own inner voice at times. Thanks for being my author twin. <3 To all our readers, we do this for you! Much love.

Acknowledgements from Jaymin: We're back!! Leia and I have so much fun writing together, that there is no way we could stop after Hive trilogy. This new series is one we both love, a lot. And we hope you all do too.

My biggest thanks is to my family. Thank you so much for all your support and love. I couldn't do what I do without you, and I never forget that. I love you more than words.

To my bestie Leia Stone. I love you, girl! Authoring would be a much lonelier place without such a wonderful friend to share it with. <3 BAFFs always. Big thanks also to my great friend Donna Augustine for keeping me sane, and offering countless advice on cover and many other things.

Next thanks is for my betas, who have shown so much love and enthusiasm for Queen Heir. You guys rock!! Couldn't do this without you.

Thanks as always to my release teams, the Nerd Herd, and Enforcers group. All of you are amazing, and I am so grateful to have found so many friends to share these worlds with.

Thank you to Lee for your wonderful and detailed editing. And to Tamara, our cover artist. You're awesome! We love every single thing you do for us, you bring our worlds to life.

To our fans. We love you. All of our books are for you. xxx.

Books from Leia Stone

Matefinder Trilogy (Optioned for film)
Matefinder: Book 1
Devi: Book 2
Balance: Book 3

Matefinder Next Generation
Keeper: Book 1

Hive Trilogy
Ash: Book 1
Anarchy: Book 2
Annihilate: Book 3

Stay in touch with Leia:
www.facebook.com/leia.stone/
Mailing list: http://goo.gl/0EX98P

Books from Jaymin Eve

A Walker Saga - YA Paranormal Romance series (complete)
First World - #1
Spurn - #2
Crais - #3
Regali - #4
Nephilius - #5
Dronish - #6

Earth - #7

<u>Supernatural Prison Trilogy - NA Urban Fantasy
series (complete)</u>
Dragon Marked - #1
Dragon Mystics - #2
Dragon Mated - #3

<u>Supernatural Prison Stories</u>
Broken Compass - #1

<u>Sinclair Stories</u>
Songbird - Standalone Contemporary Romance

<u>Hive Trilogy (complete)</u>
Ash - #1
Anarchy - #2
Annihilate: #3

<u>NYC Mecca Series</u>
Queen Heir
Queen Alpha (released early 2017)

Stay in touch with Jaymin:
www.facebook.com/JayminEve.Author
Website: www.jaymineve.com
jaymineve@gmail.com